AF406847

CLUSTER COMMAND

CLUSTER COMMAND

LONE WOLF SQUADRON™ BOOK EIGHT

JAMIE DAVIS

MICHAEL ANDERLE

DON'T MISS OUR NEW RELEASES

Join the LMBPN email list to be notified of new releases and special promotions (which happen often) by following this link:

http://lmbpn.com/email/

This book is a work of fiction. All of the characters, organizations, and events portrayed in this novel are either products of the author's imagination or are used fictitiously. Sometimes both.

Copyright © 2024 LMBPN Publishing
Cover copyright © LMBPN Publishing
A Michael Anderle Production

LMBPN Publishing supports the right to free expression and the value of copyright. The purpose of copyright is to encourage writers and artists to produce the creative works that enrich our culture.

The distribution of this book without permission is a theft of the author's intellectual property. If you would like permission to use material from the book (other than for review purposes), please contact support@lmbpn.com. Thank you for your support of the author's rights.

LMBPN Publishing
2375 E. Tropicana Avenue, Suite 8-305
Las Vegas, Nevada 89119 USA

Version 1.00, February 2024
eBook ISBN: 979-8-88878-406-8
Paperback ISBN: 979-8-88878-819-6

The Kurtherian Gambit (and what happens within / characters / situations / worlds) are copyright © 2015-2024 by Michael T. Anderle.

THE CLUSTER COMMAND TEAM

Beta Readers
Kelly O'Donnell, Rachel Beckford, Malyssa Brannon

JIT Readers
Veronica Stephan-Miller
Christopher Gilliard
Dave Hicks
Dorothy Lloyd
Zacc Pelter
Daryl McDaniel
Diane L. Smith
Peter Manis
Jeff Goode

Editor
Lynne Stiegler

To the excellent beta team who reviewed the book and made sure it was true to this amazing Kurtherian ™ universe, thank you. Larry, Rachel, Kelly, James, John, and especially Nat, you all made this a better story and a lot more fun to write.

— Jamie

*To Family, Friends and
Those Who Love
to Read.
May We All Enjoy Grace
to Live the Life We Are
Called.*

— Michael

CHAPTER ONE

<u>Dervas Cluster, Kolo System</u>

Kit Bridger crawled to the edge of the rocky bluff. Her solo camp lay in the hollow below. She spotted the reason her intruder alert system had gone off right away. Five Beorlok raiders were rooting around and ransacking her gear and equipment. Every now and then, they pulled out items and stacked them on a transport lift floating at the camp's perimeter.

She tucked an errant strand of her long brown hair behind her ear. The dusty winds of this part of Kolo Three had forced her to confine her locks under a broad-brimmed boonie hat.

"Well, Trigger," she said to the field research bot floating below the crest of the hill. "I guess that friendship totem I laid out in the center of the camp didn't work."

"The Kolo System is in a disputed region of space between several tribal groups," Trigger replied in his usual nasal electronic tone. "There was no guarantee that you'd only encounter Beorlok raiders who are friendly to you.

What do you plan to do? I only ask because I don't want you to storm down there and confront them alone." The EI had been Kit's near-constant companion for going on ten years since she'd liberated it from a junk heap in a Uuru scrapyard. It had been worth every credit she'd spent refurbishing the rugged field testing and identification rig.

"I don't have to go alone." Kit kept her eyes on the camp. She winced when a raider tossed her field comm against a boulder. She wouldn't be making any Etheric comm calls any time soon. "You know, Trigger, you could go down there with me. I still don't know why you won't step up and defend what's ours."

"My core programming is not suited to violence against any living creature. I'm a scientist, not a warrior."

Kit's hand dropped to the pistol on her hip. "Fine, stay here, but don't cry to me if they damage your recharging station while they root for loot."

She climbed to her feet and backed down the bluff to the trail that led into the hollow. Nobody disrespected her gear. Nobody. That was what the friendship totem she'd gotten from the Cloud-Bringer clan was supposed to prevent.

Grunts from the Beorlok raiding party echoed up the narrow gap in the rocks that formed the path into the sheltered area. She heard another crash as they broke something else in her camp. Kit dropped her right hand to hover over the pistol at her side and unsnapped the leather cross-strap that secured it in place but didn't draw the weapon. If she could run them off using the threat of her Cloud-Bringer-clan benefactors, that would be better than bloodshed.

She rounded the corner and stopped beside her now-collapsed tent. She took a deep breath and shouted, "Hey! Thou hast entered my protected domain. Thou wilt cease and desist forthwith." The Old High Skaine dialect came out of her side of the universal translator sounding formal.

The five Beorloks froze when she yelled. Heads swiveled to stare in her direction. So did the barbed ends of the long, segmented scorpion tails behind each of the intruders.

Kit held her ground as she shifted her eyes to catch each one's gaze. She settled on one with a colorful shoulder wrap as the leader.

Keeping her right hand next to her pistol's grip, she raised her left hand and pointed at the one she'd chosen. "Thou! Thou has ignored the tribal parlay laid out to inform thee of my protection by the Cloud-Bringers."

She shifted her pointing finger at the still-standing spear, which was wrapped with a long leather strap with beaded panels in ornate patterns. The totem was embedded in the ground at the center of the camp. The intruders had stayed away from it, probably because they feared it was cursed. That didn't stop them from pilfering, but it showed they had some respect for it. Maybe it would be enough.

The leader's eyes followed her pointing finger, then looked at her and spit on the ground. "The Cloud-Bringers do not speak for this planet. This planet is in Star-Current territory. Thou dost trespass and must pay thy toll to remain."

"I did not detect any beacon declaring this a Star-Current system," Kit shot back.

"There is no beacon declaring it a Cloud-Bringer system, either." He pounded his chest with a fist. "I say it is a Star-Current System. That is enough." The party leader looked around. "Where is thy vessel? We wouldst have additional payment. There is little here worth taking."

Kit smiled. She never took valuables on a mission. It attracted too much attention. "My ship will come back for me at a prearranged time. Until then, I am alone on this planet. I have no valuables of note. Leave the camp, and I wilt take no offense."

The leader barked the sound that passed for laughter among this species. The other four barked as well. The five waving tails quivered with mirth. "Thou wilt accompany us as tribute if thou canst not pay for thy trespass."

"I don't think so."

The leader barked another laugh and nodded at the pair of warriors closest to Kit. They both reached for the stun sticks hanging from their belts.

Kit had seen enough. "Well, I tried." She drew her gun faster than should've been possible. It never rose above her waist. Firing from the hip, a pair of double-taps dropped the two nearest goons. Most of their heads were gone after being struck in the face.

She didn't wait to see them fall. These Beorlok were almost as fast as she was. Kit dove to the side and extended her right arm. Two more shots felled another of the raiders.

She landed near her armored field sample trunk and rolled behind it for cover.

The Beorloks fired rounds that impacted the front of the trunk and pocked the ground around her.

Kit grabbed the comm from her belt. "Uh, Trigger? I could use a little help."

"Oh, very well. If you insist."

"Don't put yourself out or anything." She popped up and fired at the leader. He'd crouched behind an outcropping on the other side of the camp, and he ducked when she aimed his way.

The final raider had taken cover behind her solar still. He leaned out and fired at her.

Kit cursed and dropped back behind the trunk. She didn't want to shoot up her still since it was her only source of water on this arid rock of a planet. She might not have an option if Trigger didn't show up soon.

A warbling trumpet blasted a note down the path into the camp. Both remaining raiders turned to face the noise.

Kit rolled out from behind the trunk with her pistol extended. A well-placed shot blew out the backward-facing knee of the one behind her water supply.

He screamed and dropped to grab his wounded leg.

She waited until his alien face came into view beneath the still and fired a double shot to end his screams.

Rolling farther around the perimeter, Kit fired again and clipped the leader in the shoulder. He yelped and dropped his rifle.

She jumped up to her feet and ran forward.

Trigger floated down the path and into the camp, still emitting the ululating trumpet cry that had distracted the raiders.

Kit kicked the rifle away from the wounded leader and placed her pistol against his head. "Don't you fucking move."

"Thou hast prevailed most excellently," the leader agreed. He raised his uninjured arm and turned to face Kit. "Wilt thou now finish me as thou hast so deftly ended my raiding party?"

Kit scowled. "I don't kill if I don't have to. I'll let thee leave. First, though, thou wilt help me restore my camp."

"I am wounded."

She opened her belt pouch with her free hand and pulled out a rolled quick-heal bandage. She shook it open and slapped the rectangular patch on the leader's wounded shoulder. The adhesive instantly sealed around the wound, and the embedded nanocytes staunched the flow of blood. If his physiology was compatible, they might lessen his pain, too. She didn't care about that. She hoped it hurt a lot since he'd torn up her camp.

Kit said, "I don't want to go to war with the Star-Current clan. I wilt let thee go, but I want something in return."

"What dost thou want? I have nothing to give."

She flicked the string of speckled beads that hung from a thong around his neck. "Thou art a chieftain's son. Thou can negotiate a parlay if thou wants to, and thy clan would have to honor it."

"We do not parlay with interlopers in our territory. We raid and attack them."

"I'm not an interloper. I am a scientist. I do not seek to settle, just explore. Add thy clan's parlay to my peace totem, and I'll let thee go."

"None in my clan will honor a Star-Current parlay beside one belonging to the Cloud-Bringers. We seek to destroy them. There has been a blood feud between our tribes for many cycles. It is best that thou kill me rather than ask from me such a dishonor. Even now, we plan an attack on their home system to destroy them."

Kit studied the Beorlok raider's hard black eyes. He was not a danger to her anymore, but his tribe was. If she let him go, he'd return with friends to finish her off, or worse, sell her into slavery.

Then there was the threat to her friends among the Cloud-Bringers. She'd been a sworn member of that tribe since she'd spent a season marooned on a planet with the chieftain's son. They'd saved each other's lives many times during that fateful journey, and she wouldn't let that end with the clan being wiped out in a sneak blood feud attack.

"I'm sorry to hear that thou is unwilling to parlay." Before he could answer, Kit raised her pistol and fired two shots into his face.

The raider fell atop his still-twitching tail. She stared at it until the tail stopped quivering. This exchange bothered her. She wasn't afraid to defend herself or her friends, but she hated senseless violence.

After nearly a minute, she shook her head. "Damned waste of a med patch."

Trigger floated over beside her. "We should pack up the camp. Others must be nearby. They will come looking for him and his raiding party."

"Agreed." Kit turned to survey the formerly neatly packed and organized camp. "Pack everything on our grav sled. The *Argos* is not programmed to come back for at least a week, and with the comm destroyed, I can't call it back early. If there are Star-Current raiding spheres in the area, we don't want it returning sooner anyway."

The rectangular robot extended two articulated arms and floated around the camp, gathering up the mess strewn about by the raiders. Kit shook her head and joined Trigger. They needed to be well away from this camp by sundown. Trigger was right. It was likely that a search party would be sent after the raiding party when they didn't return to their shuttle by dark. It couldn't be far from her camp. They'd come on foot with their grav skid in tow.

An hour and a half later, Kit, Trigger, and the loaded grav sled ambled back up the narrow track onto the plateau. She'd hidden the bodies and the raiders' gear as best she could. She and Trigger would head north to the alternate campsite she'd scouted on the way in. They could be there by midnight.

Kit lowered the night-vision goggles from her hat. It was dark enough to need them. She didn't want to twist an ankle and compound the mess she was in. She cradled the rifle to her chest and checked the passive sensors she'd left behind, scanning her back trail to be sure no one had followed them.

CHAPTER TWO

<u>Dervas Cluster, Kolo System</u>

Charli coughed and waved a hand in front of her face to clear the smoke wafting from *Drifter's* pilot's console. "Shit, the Gate drive is down, and that last pass took out our automated nav systems. What do you see on the sensors, Dancer?"

"That last missile took out the raider fighter that jumped us. It's hard to tell with half the systems down, but I don't think there are any other Beorlok ships around. They must be on the far side of the planet."

"That's good news," Charli replied. "Now we have to find a place to set down so we can see about repairs."

"The planet ahead is habitable." Lindy put the system plot on the forward screen. "I think it's close enough for us to get there."

"Let's hope the engines hold out long enough for us to get down in one piece."

"If we do get down, do you think we can fix the ship?" Lindy asked.

"I won't know until I get a good look at the damage, kiddo." Charli laughed. "Why? Do you have a hot date with the Beaver back at the station?"

Lindy blushed and looked away.

Charli left it alone and shrugged. "No sense in worrying about it now. We're lucky to be alive. They got the jump on us but good. I don't know what they were doing, hiding behind that asteroid. From everything we've seen, there's no traffic through this sector of the Cluster. Even Beorlok traders avoid it."

Lindy checked her panel and refreshed the plot on the screen. "Does it matter why they were here, Gears?"

"It kind of does. We don't know if they have help coming or if they are hanging out to meet some friends. Keep your eyes on the long-range sensors while we head to the planet and drop a stealth drone behind us. Set it to light up only if one of our ships comes into the system. That's the best we can do to call for help with our comms down."

Lindy's hands danced across the sensor console. She punched the button to launch one of the surveillance drones in their wake. "Done. Now let's see if I can find a nice place for you to set us down."

"I appreciate your optimism about my skills in this situation, Dancer. We might not have that much choice in the matter. At this point, I'm just trying to get us through the upper atmosphere without burning up."

By the time they reached Kolo Three, Charli's eyes burned from the smoky haze in the deep space shuttle's cockpit. The environmental scrubbers had resisted Lindy's efforts to get them back online, so they had acrid smoke drifting in the air within the forward cabin. Charli's nanocytes could scrub most of the toxins, but Lindy was wheezing.

The junior deputy was stationed at the co-pilot's position for the landing. They were going to need both of them for this. Almost all the automated systems were down, so Charli was flying mostly by feel.

"Keep an eye on the hull temperature, Dancer. Our plating should hold up, but with our shields down, we could develop problems."

"On it." Lindy's hands caressed the panel, and a hull temp notification appeared in the upper right corner of the forward screen. "Now we both can see it."

"Good. Well, here goes nothing." Charli angled the nose to send *Drifter* into the upper atmosphere of the third planet. She hoped there weren't any Beorloks on the planet since their entry would put on a fiery show for anyone who looked up.

The buffeting began with a tremble that turned into tooth-rattling jerks in all directions. Charli kept the nose up while maintaining a descent angle that wouldn't heat them up too much. She kept her eye on the temperature readout Lindy had provided.

The bar turned from pale yellow to deep amber with a tint of red at one end. "How's hull integrity?"

Lindy checked a few displays. "Not showing any failure in the plating. The tendelium sheeting will hold up. It can shed cannon fire, so it should be able to take this."

"Its properties work by bleeding off the energy across the surface. In this situation, the whole ship is enveloped by super-heated air, so there's nowhere for the energy to go. That could cause a failure."

Lindy grimaced. "Great. Thanks for the engineering lesson."

Charli forced a smile. "Just keep an eye on the hull's structural integrity. I'll watch the temp gauge."

Lindy nodded and adjusted the settings to try to bleed some of the heat energy into the engines. Charli approved. It was a good idea, and she wasn't sure she would have thought of it. The kid had good instincts.

Drifter continued its barely controlled fall through the atmosphere while Charli worked to lessen their forward speed. She only had a little power left in their attitude thrusters, and she had to save them for the last instant to slow their impact on landing.

The two pilots tensely rode their respective consoles as they neared the ground. Lindy pointed at the terrain sweep from their forward sensors. "There. That plateau should be perfect. It's mostly flat, and there isn't any vegetation. That should give us some runway to play with."

"You're ever the optimist, Dancer. Still, it's as good as we're going to get." Charli used what little control she had to steer for the large, flat area on the main equatorial continent. The lower they got, the better it looked.

"Good eye. This is as good as we could expect from an uninhabited planet. Brace yourself. Here we go."

Charli fired the attitude thrusters to slow their forward motion and lift the nose a bit. The shuttle bounced hard on initial impact before setting down and skidding across the red sandstone plateau. They came to a stop a kilometer from a ridge. The last reading from the internal sensors showed a few large caves that could provide shelter should they need it.

She unbuckled her five-point restraint and stood, twisting to work out a kink in her back. She'd tensed her whole body during the entry into the planet' atmosphere, and her spine felt every second of it.

Lindy went to the side hatch and stared out at the dark landscape through the port. It was night in their location. "What do you think? Should we go out and have a look at the ship?"

"Let's make sure nothing's going to blow up on us in here. There'll be plenty of time to check the exterior when it's daylight. It's not like we're going anywhere anytime soon."

Lindy let out a long sigh. "My parents had a lot of old ebooks, and one of my favorites was *Robinson Crusoe*. I used to imagine being marooned on a desert planet. Never thought I'd be in that situation, though."

"As long as you don't start calling me 'Friday,' we'll be fine." Charli pulled a flashlight from the emergency pack beside her seat. "I'm going to take a look at the engine compartment. Make sure everything here is powered down. We don't want anyone using our unshielded power signature to track us."

Lindy nodded and returned to the sensor console to power down their active systems.

It took Charli longer than she'd expected to deal with the engine damage inside the ship. A reactor leak needed dampening before it blew up, and that took most of the rest of the night. The gray light of pre-dawn was visible on the eastern horizon when she came back into the cockpit.

Lindy had stretched out on the floor and was softly snoring as she slept. Charli didn't wake her. She needed the sleep, and Charli's nanocytes could keep her going for a while before she'd need some downtime.

She quietly cycled the hatch's manual controls and climbed down to the dusty surface of the plateau outside without extending the shuttle's ramp. That would take power they didn't have to spare right now.

A quick circuit of the exterior of the ship took her to the shuttle's stern so she could shine the light on the engines and Gate drive components. The drive had taken a direct hit, and she didn't like what she could see without opening the compartment's cover. Instead of digging into it now, Charli continued her scan of the ship's exterior.

As she rounded the stern, she spotted the slender figure standing outside the open hatch. At first, she thought Lindy had awakened. Then the wind shifted, and her enhanced senses caught the scent of a stranger. She got a better look and realized the person had a loose scarf wrapped around their head and neck. It concealed their features, so Charli couldn't tell who or what they were.

Her hand dropped to her side, brushing only air where her blaster usually sat. She'd taken it off while crawling around in the engine compartment and had forgotten to clip it back to her belt.

Well, she wasn't defenseless. She could go Pricolici on the newcomer, but she didn't want to shred one of her two available flight suits.

The figure didn't appear to be doing anything but looking inside. They held a rifle but kept the barrel away from the opening. They seemed curious.

Charli decided to deal with the newcomer head-on. She

raised her hand and switched on the flashlight, then shone the high-powered beam at them.

The intruder twisted around when the light shone on them. They crouched and brought the rifle around to point in Charli's direction. A female said, "I don't want to shoot anyone, friend, but I will if you don't shut that damned light off right now."

"You shouldn't lurk around outside someone's ship without announcing yourself," Charli snapped. She turned off the light and walked forward. If this woman wanted a fight, Charli would remove her arms before she got off more than one shot.

When the light was off, the woman relaxed, seeing only the short pilot walking toward her. She pulled the scarf down to reveal her face. The woman was a half-meter taller than Charli, and she wore a tight tan jumpsuit with a web belt. Numerous pouches and small devices hung from it, and the hunched effect on her back was created by a small backpack. The woman's broad-brimmed hat hid her face, but Charli had gotten a good look at her while she approached. The woman's tanned skin showed some lines and hardness around the eyes. She wasn't much older than Charli's thirty-five years.

"Easy, friend," the woman called as Charli approached. "That's good enough right there."

Charli shook her head and kept walking. "You're standing outside my ship, not the other way around. Back up if you don't want me to come too close."

The woman took an involuntary step back, and the arm holding the rifle twitched. Then she shook her head.

"Look, I think we got off on the wrong foot. I'm Kit Bridger."

"Charli Price." She shook the other woman's hand. "What are you doing out here? This planet is supposed to be uninhabited."

"My business is my own. I saw your shuttle crash-land and came to see if anyone had survived."

"That was hours ago. What took you so long?"

"Distances are deceiving on this plateau." Kit pointed at the ridge under which they'd spotted the caves with their sensors. "I was back there. I started this way when you came down."

"You walked here?" It was Charli's turn to be surprised. What was this woman doing wandering around a deserted planet on foot?

"I've walked through worse than this. This hike was easy, even in the dark." Kit nodded at the shuttle. "What caused your crash?"

"We ran into a local welcoming party. We won the fight, but not unscathed."

Kit barked a derisive laugh. "You ran off a Beorlok raiding party with this? I find that hard to believe."

"Believe it," Charli replied. "It's a lot tougher than it looks, as am I."

"Well, if you destroyed the raider ships in orbit, I guess I owe you one. They've been hanging out and looking for me since I had a disagreement with one of their landing teams. They took offense at my presence here."

"That seems to be a standard beef with everyone," Charli replied.

"You alone?" Kit craned her neck to see inside *Drifter*.

"No, I have a co-pilot. She's resting right now."

"Well, it's going to get awfully hot up here when the sun comes up. If we leave now, we make it back to my camp to get some shelter and avoid most of it. Wake your partner up, and we can hit the trail."

Charli cocked her head and looked at the brightening sky. The hot breeze made up her mind. They'd run down their power reserves here if they tried to stay comfortable in this heat.

"Give me five minutes to pack what we need and wake my friend."

"Okay, but hurry up. We have to get under cover. Also, I've got a micro-mesh tarp in my pack. I think it'll cover your ship and hide it from anyone who flies over. We don't need to draw attention to it or us." Kit kicked the ground. "There's no way to hide our tracks in this loose dirt, so I'd rather not give them a point to start looking."

Charli nodded and climbed into the forward cabin to wake Lindy and gather their survival gear. They could come back the next night if they wanted or needed more. It took more like fifteen minutes, including stringing the micro-mesh tarp over the wrecked shuttle. They weighed down the sides with rocks to keep it from blowing off.

"Okay, Kit. Lead the way," Charli directed.

Lindy added. "I can't wait to hear what you're doing out here alone. I'm sure there's a great story behind it."

Kit didn't answer. She wrapped her scarf around her face and started toward the distant ridge. Charli and Lindy fell in behind her in single file. Maybe they could get their answers after they arrived at their host's camp.

CHAPTER THREE

<u>Deep Space, Cloitas Station</u>

Be'Ley strolled across the lower promenade, on which the tool vendors had set up shop to sell their wares to the colonists. The bustling stalls had a variety of hand and power tools and bots on display at prices that would separate the eager homesteaders from their remaining credits. After all, they wouldn't have any use for Federation credits in the middle of the Dervas Cluster.

He smiled at a Skaine shopkeeper who was demonstrating a power shovel. "It's so easy, you'll think it's doing all the work."

The others made similar promises about the quality and capabilities of their products. There was no nearby alien planet on which to test them, and you couldn't dig a hole in the deck plates. The homesteaders had to take their word for it or do without the tools that would ensure their survival on harsh and primitive worlds.

Be'Ley angled down a narrow side passage to the far side of the shop ring. He hankered for a fizzy drink a particular bar served. He had almost traversed the cross passage when his comm chirped. He didn't need to look to see who it was. Only one person had the code to reach him while he was strolling about the station.

"This had better be good, Tecla. I'm almost at my destination."

The human woman who had called was his assistant. She regularly disobeyed his instructions not to be disturbed. It was as if she enjoyed the insults and anger he directed her way.

"Your Cirtreon Fizzbanger can wait, sir. There's a strange noise coming from inside the credenza behind your desk. I know you told me never to go into your office when you weren't there, but I thought you might want me to check out the sound."

"No," Be'Ley replied. His voice had gone up an octave, but he quickly brought it back under control. "Under no circumstances are you to investigate further. It is only an alarm I set to remind me about something I need to do. I'll be right up to shut it off."

"I'm already here, sir. I don't mind doing it," Tecla offered.

"I do mind. Close the door and return to your desk where you belong. Put on headphones if the sound bothers you. I'm heading that way now."

Be'Ley cursed and took a left instead of a right at the end of the passage. His Fizzbanger would have to wait. The sound Tecla called about could only be the secret communications device given to him by the Beorlok chieftain with whom he'd been dealing.

The idiot wasn't supposed to call him except under the

most urgent circumstances. Be'Ley failed to see what was so important that the clan chief couldn't handle it himself. Though the interruption annoyed him, he'd have to be careful how he dealt with the chieftain. The Beorloks had complicated notions of honor and offense.

It took him ten minutes to wind back through the busy station to his office on the topmost level. He heard the alert when he entered the outer office. Tecla sat behind her desk with noise-canceling headphones nestled over her ears. She looked up and nodded as he entered, then went back to her work.

Be'Ley opened the inner door and entered. When he was inside, he locked it and walked to his desk. He opened the hidden safe inside the credenza and removed the velvet-wrapped communications cube that had been passed down in his family for several centuries.

The alert tone stopped when he pulled it out. Be'Ley hoped that didn't mean his contact had left. He'd hate to have come back only to have missed the caller. He depressed the jeweled stud on the top and stepped back as the holograph illuminated the darkened room, hovering over the device on his desk.

He had to wait thirty seconds for the robed figure to appear in the glowing display.

Be'Ley bit back his annoyance at being made to wait. "Greetings, mighty chieftain. I do hope everything is well with thou and thine. It is most unusual for thou to call my device."

"The need was urgent, I assure thee. We will need to cease operations in the trade of the spoils from the colony ships for the time being."

"That is unacceptable, mighty one. Are you breaking the agreements between thy family and mine regarding mutual trade?"

"This is a pause, not a cessation. Thou art aware of our fractious nature and the disagreements between our various clans?"

"Thou hast tried to explain them to me in the past. I must say I do not understand letting squabbles interfere with business dealings."

The chieftain shifted, and his long, barbed tail swayed behind him. "Two of our larger clans have long had a blood feud, and I fear that the feud will soon draw in other clans across the Dervas Cluster. With attention diverted to civil war, my ships will be unable to intercept inbound ships from thy venture for some time."

Be'Ley didn't like the sound of that. "How long is 'some time?' Thou canst not fight this impending war for long. Think about the lost profits."

"As I said, the blood feud is of long standing. The Cloud-Bringer and Star-Current clans have contacted their oldest alliances and called in debts to gather their forces. I fear the dispute will interfere with our business for at least one cycle."

"A year!" Be'Ley stopped himself from shouting when he noticed the barbed tail quivering over the chieftain's shoulder. He took a calming breath. "Something must be done. What if I offer to pay the blood debt? Would that stop the feud?"

"Such things are not done. Also, thy involvement with me and my clan cannot become common knowledge. That revelation would turn all the others against us both."

"Why both of us? I'm in no danger."

The chieftain pointed a clawed finger at Be'Ley. "Thou wilt not be able to hide within the borders of thy powerful Federation should our arrangement be discovered by the clans. Already, there are those who wonder who is responsible for the increased numbers of interlopers coming into the Cluster. If they discover our agreement, it will go badly for both of us. Your station could not withstand the assault of our massed clans."

Be'Ley swallowed to banish the lump in his throat. Cloitas Station had minimal defenses, and if it was attacked, it would be destroyed. Yes, the Federation would likely send Fleet assets to investigate the intrusion, but it would be far too late for him and his opportunities to make himself rich.

"Very well. Keep me apprised of the situation. I will continue to send colony ship updates. Thou might be able to divert some of thy efforts to our arrangement sooner than later."

"We shall see." The Beorlok chieftain reached to the side, and the connection flickered out.

Be'Ley leaned back in his seat and stared at the ceiling for a long time. The colony operation at Cloitas Station was very profitable, and his share was sizable, but his take from the Beorlok raiders increased his personal fortune the most.

The Consortium was not aware of his kickback from the clan. He rewrapped the cube and returned it to the safe. Then he opened several spreadsheets, and the three-dimensional display over his desk filled with floating numbers and accounting entries.

He spent two hours going through them, making allowances for the lack of takings from the raiders to see where he could make up the shortfall. Every time he made an adjustment, it took away from something else he deemed necessary.

When he finished and stared at the final result, he realized this would require him to find a way to pick up the raiding slack without the help of the Beorloks. He would have to hire ships, but there was no way around it. If he wanted to hit his goals, he'd have to expand into that business himself.

Of course, those meddlesome marshals would try to stop him, as they had the Beorloks. Their efforts to arm and prepare the homesteaders and colonists to defend themselves had made things difficult. It was time to push forward with the plan Zarek had proposed with the young journalist. She now lived on Cloitas station, awaiting the call to begin her work soiling the reputation of the frontier heroes. The time was now.

He tapped the intercom icon on his display. "Tecla, contact that girl, Thendara. Tell her to come to my office immediately. I have a job for her to do."

"Right away, sir."

Tecla knew where to find the other female. As the only two humans working in the operation, they'd formed a close friendship. He'd have to think of a way to leverage that should the reporter be resistant to doing what had to be done.

He continued shifting around assets to try to improve his financial situation faster. The door chimed fifteen minutes later. "Enter."

The door opened, and a tall human female with short emerald-colored hair came in.

Be'Ley looked up as Thendara entered. "I'll be right with you. Have a seat." He gestured at the chairs on the opposite side of his desk, then went back to manipulating the numbers for a minute. After he saved his work on the spreadsheets, he closed the hovering documents and met the journalist's eyes.

She spoke when he looked her way. "Tecla said you finally had work for me. My editor has been clamoring for a story that isn't a public interest segment on daring colonists venturing into the unknown. I'm running out of angles to make this place look promising."

Be'Ley sneered. "I care not what your editor wants. You work for me now. Everything else is a pretext. Do you understand?"

The fire in her eyes dimmed, and she nodded.

"Good. Then let's get to work. I am expanding certain operations from this station. To do that, I need the marshals distracted by something else. That is where you come in. I want you to fabricate a crisis and pin the blame on the marshal and his deputies."

"What kind of crisis?" she asked.

"I don't care. Find one. The marshal meddles in all sorts of things around the sector and beyond. Find one that leaves them exposed and pin the blame on them. There are plenty of people with ruffled feathers who would love to pile on the marshals for something unsavory, even if it's made up."

Thendara stood. "I'll need traveling funds and transportation to another system. It wouldn't be good for me to show up after I have lived here for several months."

"Tell Tecla what you need. She'll arrange it for you, within reason. There'll be an expense account, but if I think you're skimming from it, no one will find your body floating in space. Is that clear?"

Thendara went pale the way humans did when they got emotional. He smiled. It was good that she'd taken the threat seriously. He'd meant every word.

The woman left, and he opened his sheets again. Perhaps there was a way to cut corners even more on the colony ships' construction. It was worth looking at. He had to find a way to increase his profits even more. He'd make up the shortfall somehow.

CHAPTER FOUR

<u>Tardex System, Outpost Station</u>

Marshal Beau Ward grabbed his cup of hot caff. The drink was a passable substitute for coffee and not nearly as expensive. It even had a mild stimulant effect. Aaron had done a good job of keeping it in stock in the galley. He sipped from the ceramic mug while he walked to the elevators. He had a call with Jack Sommers later, and he wanted to pull together some reports on his deputies' efforts around the frontier to keep the peace and defend those who needed it.

"Hey, Lobo, wait up," Remi called from down the hallway. He joined Beau in the elevator."

"Hey, Six-shooter. What's up?"

"I want to divert *Warren's Chance* to pick up the exotic grains Growler found in the Kuarti System."

"As long as it doesn't take you very far from your route. Aren't you due to head out and meet up with *Drifter* in the Dervas Cluster?"

"We are, and that reminds me. I need to call Gears and arrange the rendezvous."

"What's the new grain shipment for?" Beau asked.

"My esteemed partner has a plan to make special batches of the Reserve using special grains from around the sector. He thinks it'll be a great promotion of our brand and connect us with those planets even better."

"Does this have anything to do with the expanded distillery you're building on Tardex Two?"

Remi smiled. "It does. We have a core Kratch team training in the art of distilling alcohol. Growler thinks they can do things he can't to manipulate the batches. Their ability to coordinate with each other is helping them pick up the process fast."

"As long as you cut them in for a share of the profits, I don't care. We have to treat folks fairly."

"Always. So, diverting to Kuarti is okay?"

"As long as Gears doesn't need you sooner, I'm good with it. She's late checking in, as usual, so when you catch up with her, remind her to call with an update." Beau smiled. "While you're out there, you can do me a favor, too. I've had a young reporter from Central Federation News Network hanging around on the station for the last few days, and she keeps asking to get a look at our operations. Take her with you and show her what you're doing on this mission. It'll get her out of my hair for a while."

"Happy to help as long as she doesn't get in our way. Growler's negotiations have been a little sticky. The farms and fields have great importance to the locals."

"I'll tell her to stay away from anything prickly. Just

show her how we fight for truth, justice, and the Federation way."

Remi laughed. "Can do, boss. I think this is your stop."

Beau saw that they had arrived at the level on which the station's control room resided. "Where are you headed?"

"Up to check on the distillery. We've taken all of level seven for the operation. We can't make enough of the stuff."

"That's good to hear. Good luck on your mission."

"Thanks."

Beau stepped out of the lift and headed for the control room and his office.

Addy was already there. She was staring at the wall on which they kept track of the deputies and the various duties and investigations in process. "You're spreading the team pretty thin, Beau." Addy punctuated the statement by nodding at the mission board on the wall screen.

Charli and Lindy were visiting colony sites in the Dervas Cluster and were scheduled to be out for another few months. He'd just told Remi and Jock they could expand their distillery operation even further. At least they'd get the reporter out from underfoot. She was there now, so quiet that he'd missed seeing her when he came in. She sat on the opposite side of the control room, recording everything while she scribbled on her datapad about whatever it was she was seeing.

That left Keeril, Katy, Grady, and him here, and Katy and Grady were out settling a land dispute across the sector. That left Keeril and Beau to cover anything else that popped up. He'd have to look into recruiting more deputies and pilots to fill out the squadron now that they had to cover such a broad area.

"Keeril and I will have to fly the long-range system patrols while everyone else is gone."

"Just remember to shower when you get back. Forty-eight hours in the cockpit leaves a serious stink on you."

"I'll remember. I'd better finish some things here before I give Legs the good news. He loves having an excuse to go out on patrol with me instead of the other pilots." He waved for Thendara to come over. "You've been cooped up here in the control room and following me around for a few days. Why don't we get you out in the field where you can see the work we do around the sector?"

"You're not trying to get rid of me, are you?" the reporter asked. "I don't like being brushed off. I might be young, but I'm not stupid."

"It's nothing like that. I'm sending two of my deputies on a run around the sector to take care of a few things. I thought it would be a good opportunity to see what we do and how we do it."

"What's the mission?" She didn't bother to hide the suspicion in her voice.

"I'll let Six-shooter and Growler fill you in. That's Deputies Remington and Batten."

Thendara brightened. "They're the brewmasters, right?"

"That's correct. They originated the Marshal's Reserve and are the main stockholders in the concern that bottles it. They're also two of my best deputies. I think you'll be happy with what you learn from them."

"Very well. When do we leave?"

"Go pack so you're ready anytime. Six-shooter just had

to check on a few things and make sure *Warren's Chance* was fully supplied before they left."

"Then I'll go to my room and gather my things. I'll send my latest report from there. Thank you, Marshal. This should be just what my story needs to provide an overview of your important work out here for the Federation."

The young reporter left, and the doors *shooshed* closed. When she was gone, Addy growled, "I don't trust her, Beau. She asks too many questions, and I don't like her tone when she asks them."

"She's inquisitive, that's all. Besides, she's now Remi and Jock's problem. Let her deal with them. They're going to try to give her the slip when they reach their destination. That'll keep her busy enough that she won't be able to dig up anything.

"Besides, we have nothing to hide. We're the only honest operation out here."

CHAPTER FIVE

<u>Dervas Cluster, Kolo System</u>

Charli rose to look over the ridge. The cluster of figures on the plateau below was still coming this way.

Kit lay on the ground beside her. She lowered her powered binocs and passed them to Charli. "They're Star-Current clan for sure. They must've found your crash site despite the cover. They know someone survived long enough to land there. Coming up here was the logical choice."

"There are at least twenty of them." Charli peered through the boosted lenses. "That's more than we can take out without getting shot up."

"It doesn't make sense. This is Cloud-Bringer territory. That was the only reason I came here. It was supposed to be safe. The clan war that's flaring up must be serious."

Lindy interjected, "They attacked us as soon as we hit the system. They're obviously not letting anyone know they're here."

Kit pointed at the war band on the plateau. "You see the one with the tall headgear?"

Charli zoomed in until she picked out the person Kit mentioned. "Yeah. What about them?"

"That's a battle chief's sigil. They only wear those if they've been given permission to make war on a neighboring clan or some other perceived threat. This is about taking Cloud-Bringer planets and their resources."

"Why does that matter?" Charli asked.

"I'm sworn to the Cloud-Bringers, that's why. I display their peace totem in my camp. It tells others I'm under their protection. That protection goes both ways, and I take my commitments seriously. I don't think my friends have any idea what's coming their way. We have to warn them."

"Hold on," Charli replied. "We need to contact the marshal first. If there's going to be a war out here in the Dervas Cluster, he needs to know. We're providing protection for numerous colony planets out here now."

"That has to wait. Warning my friends is more important." She scooted off the ridge and started back to the cave in which they'd made their camp.

Kit's words had a finality that irked Charli. She slid down the slope until she could stand up out of sight of the approaching war band. Lindy followed her.

"Hey," Charli called. "Just because you rescued us doesn't mean you're in charge."

"Doesn't it?" Kit didn't bother to turn around while she talked. "Look, my ship will be back in the system on autopilot in two days. When we Gate to the Cloud-Bringer homeworld, I will let you send a message to your marshal. Until then, we're stuck waiting. My comm is just as dead as yours."

Kit took long strides that covered a lot of ground as she strode back to the cave.

Charli had to half-walk and half-jog to keep up. She felt and probably looked like a child catching up to its parent. It wasn't a look the deputy marshal liked, and she snarled. After a second, she took a breath. Kit had all the power here.

"Look, Dancer and I appreciate you coming to check on us and everything, but we could've taken care of ourselves."

"Really?" Kit spun and stopped in front of Charli. "You would've stayed with your ship, and that war band would have found you. They would have either killed or captured you."

"They'd have tried." Lindy snorted. "We're not without protections and abilities."

"Hey." Kit smirked. "I get it. You're tough and good at what you do, except this isn't a cockpit or a city on a settled world. This is the ass end of nowhere.

"Trust me when I say you're out of your element here. I've lived out here alone for the last ten-plus years. Let me keep you safe, and I'll get you home. Otherwise, leave now and take your chances with the Beorlok warriors."

Charli ground her teeth, and her eyes flashed yellow. She didn't like being challenged. This was her mission, not some random frontier prospector's claim.

Lindy moved between the two women. "I think we need to dial this back. Kit, thank you for helping us. Of course we needed your help and are glad for it. You take the lead, and we'll follow. We do need to contact our people soon, though."

Kit looked past Lindy at Charli and shrugged. "It doesn't matter until my ship comes back. Until then, none of us has a comm. Let's pack up the camp. We need to be long gone before the Beorloks find us."

"You have an alternate camp scoped out?" Charli asked.

"No, but sometimes you have to trust your luck to give you what you need. We'll trek deeper into these mountains. There's bound to be another cave we can use for shelter. The ship will be back in a few days, and then we can all go home."

Lindy looked over her shoulder and raised her eyebrows at Charli as if she expected a response.

Grudgingly, Charli muttered, "Thank you."

"You're welcome, and you don't have to whisper it. It makes it sound like you don't mean it." Kit whirled again and continued to their camp.

That set Charli's teeth to grinding, but she took some deep breaths to calm herself.

They stayed on the winding trail from the ridge. They were nearly back to their camp when deep voices echoed down the canyon from up ahead.

Kit held up a closed fist to stop them. "Damn, they must've landed two teams. I should've figured on that. Beorloks aren't stupid. They're wily and skilled at raiding and ambushes." She took her rifle off her shoulder and checked the charge. "We can't lose my camp or my biosamples. They're the whole reason I'm here."

"Wait," Charli protested. "We don't even know how many there are."

"I'm not losing my gear or Trigger. You can come help or stay here where it's safe."

Charli growled. No one questioned her courage. "Oh, I'm coming. Just stay out of my way when I get there." She dropped her pack on the trail and unzipped her flight suit.

Kit gawked while she undressed. "What the hell are you doing?"

Lindy walked up and tugged on Kit's arm. "She'll be right behind us. Let's sneak up there and see what we're dealing with."

Charli slipped out of her flight suit and stepped out of her boots. When she was down to panties and sports bra, she let her inner wolf free. It would feel good to tear into the Beorloks and get some of her anger out of her system.

Lindy watched her step, careful not to break any of the dried vegetation that had collected at the edges of the trail. The voices of the people ahead grew louder as they approached. Kit stalked beside her. Both women held their blaster rifles at the ready.

When they rounded the bend, they spotted eight Beorlok raiders digging through their camp gear. Lindy keyed her neural chip.

Eight raiders in our cave. Kit and I are going to move in.

I'm rrrright behind you!

Charli's bipedal wolf form bounded up the trail behind them with a ripping snarl.

"What the fuck is that?" Kit spun. She started to lift her rifle, but Lindy pushed the end of the barrel down.

"That's Charli." Lindy let go of the prospector's rifle and sighted down her barrel at the raiders. They'd stopped and were staring at the trail. Her first burst stitched across the chest of the nearest Beorlok raider.

Kit came to her senses and fired two bursts that dropped two more.

Charli leaped over their heads and raced into the middle of their camp. She tore into the first raider she came to, then ripped his scorpion tail off at the base and used it to club the former owner to death.

The appearance of the more than two-meter-tall Pricolici caught the raiders by surprise. Lindy and Kit each dropped another intruder, and Charli whirled through the cave and killed the last two.

"I smell morrre close byyy." Charli pointed out of the cave and up the trail to the ridge.

Kit knelt to study the beads on a headband worn by one of the Beorlok. "These are Wind Rider clan raiders. They're allies of the Star-Current clan. This is probably just a recon group. There's likely a group up ahead as large as the one on the plateau."

"That's too many for us to handle, even with Charli in wolf mode," Lindy muttered. "We can't get caught between them, either."

Kit started packing her gear. "Then we go deeper into the cave. It has to lead somewhere. If we move quickly, we should be able to cover our tracks so they don't know where we went." She looked at Charli, who was stalking back and forth at the entrance. "Does someone need to go back for her flight suit and gear?"

"No," Lindy said. "Give her a second to calm down. Let's focus on packing." She deflated the automated bed mat she'd used to sleep and rolled it into its bag. She tied it onto her pack and gathered their other gear.

Trigger had moved to the back of the cave. The bot called, "The opening here is broad enough to move everything through on the sled."

Kit said, "Do your sensors pick up an exit farther inside?"

"There is fresh air wafting out from below. That indicates an exit point. I do not know if it is passable."

"We'll take that chance." Kit looked around. "Hey, where's Wolf Girl?"

Lindy glanced around the cave. "Probably went back to get her stuff. Don't make a big deal about it. She's self-conscious. That is not her favorite part to show people."

"I don't blame her." Kit hoisted the last trunk onto the grav sled. "I'm finished here. There's just your pack and her gear to load. I'm going to start this thing moving down the slope inside to get it out of sight. You wait for Charli."

Lindy nodded and packed up Charli's bedroll and the rest of their food. By the time she'd finished, Charli had returned, and she was back to her normal self. Her eyes still had a yellow glow, like she'd kept her wolf mojo going. Lindy wasn't sure how it worked with her friend's changes.

"Ready to go, Gears?"

"Yeah. I hear more coming down the trail. We need to get a move on." She shouldered her backpack and led Lindy to the back of the cave.

Lindy looked at their camp. They'd left nothing behind except the bodies of the raiders. The hard stone held no footprints to betray their direction of travel. Hopefully, the approaching Beorloks would think they had run down the mountain, not into it.

CHAPTER SIX

<u>Dervas Cluster, Kolo System</u>

Charli and Lindy caught up with Kit when the cave system narrowed to the point that Kit's grav sled couldn't get through.

Kit grumbled and lowered the sled to the floor. "I was afraid of this. All this research is going to be lost."

"What is it you do?" Lindy asked.

"I'm a bioprospector for a big pharma concern in the Federation. I look for unique genetic material and sequences not found anywhere else that might have therapeutic properties."

Charli said, "So, that's why you're out here in the Dervas Cluster."

"Yep. I'm not going to find anything new in the Federation's core. All the genomes there have been cataloged numerous times, but out here, it's the frontier for someone with a biotech degree and the willingness to take chances."

"Dangerous work," Lindy remarked.

"No more dangerous than what you two do. I don't go looking for trouble."

Charli shot back, "We don't go looking for it, but if we find it, we deal with it. That's different."

"Sounds the same to me." Kit dug through the supplies and material on the sled, sorting everything into two piles. The smaller stack she wrapped in a tarp. "Trigger, time to earn your keep."

"I am not a pack animal. I'm a highly technical piece of scientific equipment."

"Fine, stay here with the sled. I'm sure the Beorloks will find something useful for you to do with all your scientific capabilities." Kit held the bundle out.

The meter-square bot hovered for a few seconds, then floated over and extended a hook from a compartment in its side. Kit hung the bundle on it. "See? That wasn't so bad. Now we're all carrying our share."

"This will impede my ability to move quickly, Kit," Trigger replied. "I might not be able to keep up with you."

"None of us will be moving that fast through these caves," Kit replied. "You'll be fine. We need to keep moving. Once the Beorloks find this sled, they'll know we came this way. We need to be far away from here when they do."

The bioprospector went to the gap in the cave and twisted her way through. Charli followed, then Lindy. Trigger brought up the rear. The bot barely fit through, but with a little wiggling, it managed.

Lindy asked Kit as they crawled along, "You're not worried about traveling alone?"

"No. I can take care of myself, and I'm very careful. That's why my ship isn't parked in orbit or on the planet where someone might find it. I set it to auto-Gate out of the system to a point in deep space well off the space lanes. It comes back to pick me up after a month. That gives me plenty of time to collect specimens and catalog them with Trigger's help."

"There has to be a way to get out of here sooner," Lindy grumbled.

"Since my comm was destroyed, we have to avoid the Beorlok raiding parties for a little longer. When we're aboard, getting away will be no problem. I can outrun most of the clan ships, and I have some, um, interesting technology that helps me avoid unwanted eyes and sensors."

Charli frowned. "After you call your friends and warn them, will you be able to take us to the Tardex System or to meet up with friends?"

Kit shook her head. "Nope. We need to go to the Cloud-Bringers' homeworld. I have to warn them about the attack and do what I can to help them. There are always skirmishes, but several clans banding together against another clan is new and worrisome. If it's happened before, I've never heard anyone talk about it."

Charli grumbled but kept her further thoughts to herself. They were beholden to Kit, and she would do whatever she wanted to. It wasn't like she could drop them off at a Federation outpost to call for a ride from out here in the Dervas Cluster.

Trailed by the bot, the trio wended their way deep into the cave system. On several occasions, they had to break out climbing gear and enlist Trigger's help to lift their gear up or down shafts.

Kit finally stopped. "Trigger, how much farther until we get to the exit your sensors found?"

"The air is fresher here than it was a few hours ago. I believe we are closer than we were. However, the distance is difficult to estimate."

Charli leaned against a wall. The spot they were in was relatively flat and open. "Maybe we should camp here for the night. If the Beorloks were coming after us, we'd have heard them echoing through the tunnels by now. They're probably hopelessly lost. We'd be going in circles in this warren if it wasn't for Trigger."

Kit studied the steep slope that was their next challenge. "I think you're right. We can tackle this after we sleep." She slipped out of her pack, lowered it to the floor, and crouched beside it.

Charli took off her backpack and helped Lindy with hers. Then they each claimed a few meters of flat ground for their expandable bedrolls.

As Kit set up her area, she removed a stronger flashlight from her belt to supplement the headlamp mounted on her hatband. "Well, I'll be damned."

"What did you find?" Lindy had laid on her mat, and she rolled up onto one elbow as she watched the prospector.

Kit was on her hands and knees, staring at something on the floor against the wall. "This is a new fungal life form. I've never seen it before on this planet. It must only grow inside the caves. Trigger, come over here so you can analyze a sample." She drew her camp knife and used it to cut a stalk off the cluster of bright purple fungi growing in the corner by her bedroll.

The bot set down its bundle and floated over. Kit straightened but didn't get up as she held out her camp knife. She had scooped a gel-like substance onto the flat of the blade.

Trigger's side opened, and a small shelf extended. Kit carefully scraped the gel onto the sample tray. The shelf retracted, and the panel on the bot's side closed.

"How long will it take Trigger to analyze the sample?" Charli asked. The compact science lab within the bot fascinated her. It was impressive tech.

Kit wiped the knife on a cloth from her pack. "Early results in a few minutes." She checked the blade's edge with her thumb, then sheathed it at her side. "The genomic analysis will take upwards of twelve hours. Protein chains and other complex molecules have to be synthesized and reproduced, and that takes time."

She sat on her pack and leaned back against the cave's wall. "Maybe I'll be able to salvage something from this trip after all. I had unique samples on the sled. My corporate benefactor only pays for results and doesn't accept excuses as to why I couldn't get something new for them."

"Sounds like a tough way to make a living," Charli commented. "With your training, you could be working in a nice climate-controlled lab."

"I could say the same about you," Kit countered. "What's a Wechselbalg doing outside the Federation military?"

"I never fit into the mold my parents laid out for me." Charli shrugged. "I wanted to be an engineer and travel the stars on a free trader. I built that crashed shuttle from scratch."

Kit shook her head. "Not much left now. Still, there

might be something worth salvaging if the Beorloks don't take it."

Charli growled, then pushed it down. Kit wasn't trying to antagonize her. What she said was true, even if it was bad news.

Lindy told her, "You can build a new one, Gears. *Drifter II* might even be better than the first one."

"If the marshal will give me the time to do it. Also, it would take a lot of resources that could be used elsewhere."

"Now who's being a sad sack?" Lindy asked.

Charli smiled. "We can do it together. It'll do you good to learn more about the tech behind the ships we fly in the squadron."

"I'm always happy to learn new stuff."

With that settled, Charli sat on her bedroll. "We should mount a guard while the others sleep. I'll go first. I don't need as much sleep with my nanocytes. I'll wake Lindy in a few hours. She can get you up for the final shift."

Kit nodded. "Works for me. I need to wait for the results from Trigger anyway." She lay on her bedroll and pulled her hat over her face. Within a minute, her breathing slowed and deepened.

"You should get some rest, too, Lindy. I've got this. I'll wake you when it's your turn."

"Got it. Time for some shut-eye." Lindy quickly fell asleep. Her father had trained her to grab sleep when she could.

Charli sat quietly with her thoughts, which had shifted back to the shuttle. They'd been through a lot together, and *Drifter* had served her well. The thought of building another like it didn't feel right yet, but the idea would grow on her in time. She'd do many things differently if she got to start over.

For now, they had to find a way out of these caves. Building a new ship would come much later.

CHAPTER SEVEN

<u>Kuarti System, Omega Station</u>

Remi shifted his chair so he could see the bar's entrance. Their contact for the grain pickup was supposed to meet them here. Jock sat down opposite him, and the reporter girl sat between them.

"You two always conduct important marshals' business in remote space station bars?" Thendara asked. The mini cam hovering a few centimeters off her right shoulder rotated to face Remi.

He broadened his smile. He'd give her something fun to write about. "Growler and I aren't known as 'the brewmasters' for nothing. Some of our best work takes place in bars like this."

"I see. That's good to know."

"The guy's late, Six-shooter." Jock checked the time again to be sure. "How long do we wait?"

"Seeing as how this is the only reason we're out here in the Kuarti system, we'll wait them out."

Thendara's camera had shifted to Jock. She asked, "How

often do your deals fall through? Is this a common occurrence?"

Jock didn't miss a beat. He held up a finger. "One, this deal hasn't fallen through yet. And B, no, this isn't common. People out here respect us. They've heard the stories and know what we stand for. The only folks who worry about us are the ones who walk on the dark side of the law."

Motion near the entrance diverted Remi's attention from his companions. A woman entered the bar and scanned the room. Her hair was either a curly mess, or she'd paid someone a lot of credits to create a horrible hairdo.

Her eyes landed on Remi, Jock, and Thendara, and she fast-walked over to the table.

"You guys marshals?"

Remi gestured at Jock. "Two of us are. Our friend is here to make us famous."

The woman scowled at Thendara, then shook her head. "I'm Thilda Wain. My husband Henson set up a meeting with you. You're Remi and Jock, right?"

"Are you here to negotiate in his place?" Remi asked.

"No, I'm here to get you to go down to the planet and rescue him. He's gotten on the Kua-Kua's bad side again. I just know it."

It took Remi a second to digest what she'd said. "So, you don't have a load of grain for us?"

"Is that what my husband used to lure you two here? What would you want Kua grass for? It's useless to anyone but the natives."

"Never mind that," Jock said. "What kind of trouble is your husband in? Who are the Kua-Kua?"

"They're the original inhabitants of the planet's northern continent. They're small, furry folks who usually don't cause much trouble. Most of the northern half of the planet is set aside for them. The rest of us fight over the resources in the southern half."

Remi held up a hand to stop her explanation. "What does this have to do with your husband? If that area's restricted and you're not supposed to deal with these Kua-Kuas, what was he doing there?"

"He's a horticulturist and is allowed limited access to study them and their agricultural techniques. He's fascinated by the plants the natives have adapted for their use. He seems to think several of their plants are worth investigating for purposes other than feeding their villages."

"Cut to the chase," Jock snapped. "How'd he get in trouble, and why do you think they've captured him?"

"He went down last night to pick up something from one of the Kuas he'd made friends with, and he didn't come back. I checked with the station controllers, and his shuttle is still near one of the villages."

Remi summarized, "So, if we want our new grain source for the Reserve, we're going to have to go down and find out what happened to your husband?"

The woman nodded, her wild curls bobbing around her head.

Remi smiled and looked into Thendara's main camera. He tapped the tin deputy marshal's star pinned to his flight suit. "Stand by, folks. You're about to see what a Tardex deputy marshal can do."

He winked at Thendara. That brought an eye roll, which he found to be a satisfactory response.

Remi stood up. "Come on, Growler. Let's go rescue the grain scientist."

The woman led the way out of the bar. Remi, Jock, and Thendara followed her out, and the ever-present floating camera brought up the rear. They didn't see the broad grin that appeared on the reporter's face as she followed them through the station's corridors. Her camera had shifted to focus on her, and she started talking in a low voice only her mic could hear as she walked behind them.

They went to the space station's ring, to which *Warren's Chance* was connected via a docking tube. Thilda stopped and stared at the free trader freighter her would-be rescuers had arrived in.

"That doesn't look like the kind of ship a marshal should travel around in. Where's the shiny fighters I've seen in the holovids?"

"They're in one of the holds," Jock replied. "We came to pick up a shipment of grain. We didn't expect to need a warship. Besides, *Chance* is up to the task. You'll see."

Remi added, "There's more to that freighter than meets the eye. Don't worry. We have everything we need to help your husband and get what we came for. Come on."

He led them all through the docking tube and onto the ship. "Warren, have the crew prep one of the drop shuttles. The standard cargo model will do. I don't think we'll need one of the Marine assault versions."

The ship's EI spoke from the overhead speaker. "Will do, Deputy."

"Let's go up to the bridge and see if we can use our

sensors to find your husband's shuttle. Do you know where we should look?"

Thilda said, "I think so. He's near the southeastern coast, and there should be a small village nearby."

Jock rolled his eyes. "Well, that shouldn't be hard to locate." Sarcasm dripped from his tone.

"Easy, buddy. Let's let Warren do his magic and see what he comes up with. Gears upgraded the sensor suite to the same military one on our fighters and *Dregs*. We can find the shuttle, even if its beacon doesn't respond to a standard hail."

They reached the bridge, and Remi stopped in front of the captain's chair. He didn't sit down, just pointed at the main screen. "Warren, bring up the northern continent. Focus on the southeastern coastline. We're looking for a standard shuttle near a native village."

"I overheard the conversation and have initiated a sensor sweep. There was no response when I hailed the shuttle transponder registered to Henson Wain."

Thilda's hands went to her face. "Oh, dear. That's not good."

"There's a hundred reasons the transponder might be turned off or not operational," Remi said. He set his hand on the woman's shoulder to reassure her.

Thendara came around Thilda's other side, her camera on the woman's face. "One reason a transponder might be off is if he is engaging in illegal activity."

"What? I'm sure there's nothing like that going on. Henson is just a little overzealous about his work."

Remi stepped between the reporter and the distraught woman. "That's enough of that. You're here to report on our amazing exploits, not to harass a woman whose husband is missing."

"I'm here to get to the truth of what's going on." The camera got a closeup of Remi's face. "You're not against finding out about illegal activity, are you, Deputy Canaleta?"

"Of course not, but you're here on our ship with our permission. You'll show respect for the people we're trying to help and let us do our jobs."

"Or what?" Thendara asked.

"Or we'll leave you on the station, and you can find your own way back to CFNN headquarters."

The two glowered at each other until Warren interrupted them. "I found the missing shuttle, on the off-chance that anyone cares about that anymore."

Jock jumped on the opportunity to lower the temperature on the bridge. "Great. Put its location on the main screen."

An icon appeared on the orbital view of the planet. Remi pointed at it. "Can you zoom in?"

"Yes." Warren zoomed in until they had a clear view of the shuttle's outline in an open space surrounded by trees.

Remi looked at Thilda. "I thought you said your husband was working with a local group to study their agriculture?"

"I did. I mean, that's what he told me. Why?"

"There's no village or other sign of any civilization within five klicks of his position. Warren, locate the nearest native settlement."

The screen zoomed out until the shuttle was a pinpoint, and a house icon appeared on the right side and blinked.

Warren continued, "That settlement has a hundred individuals, according to surveys by the planet's Bureau of Land and Aboriginal Management. It lists them as an isolated group without acclimatization to alien visitors. They're strictly off-limits, even for researchers with the proper credentials."

Remi mused, "The distance between the shuttle and the village is almost twenty kilometers through thickly forested terrain. What is he doing down there?"

"I have no idea," Thilda protested. "I swear. I didn't know he was up to anything shady, Deputy."

"I'm not saying he is, Mrs. Wain. Maybe he had engine trouble and crash-landed. That would explain the transponder malfunction. I am annoyed he didn't make our meeting, but I'm glad you came to get us. This way, we can get a better idea of who we're getting into business with."

"To the shuttle?" Jock asked, his voice shifting to a mocking bass bravado.

"Yes," Remi said in the same tone. "Let us be off to the unknown."

Thendara rolled her eyes. "Men." She gestured for Thilda to precede her, and the two followed Remi and Jock to the landing bay.

The bay's crew leader waited beside the prepped shuttle. "I got her ready to go, Deputy. You didn't request a Marine warrant officer to pilot her, so I didn't roust them out of their quarters."

Remi smiled. "Good work. It'll just be us since we're investigating a family matter. If anything else pops up, we'll reach out to the ship."

"Should we have a drop team from the Marine contingent stand by to come down?" Jock asked. "We don't have much intel on what we will find down there."

"How bad could it be, Growler? Her husband's a plant scientist, not a holovid action hero."

"That's the truth," Thilda agreed. "My husband is definitely no action hero."

Remi shrugged. "And he's made numerous trips down and back. I don't know what he's doing down there, but there's no evidence of trouble aside from the transponder thing. Maybe he landed on purpose and shut it off. I'm sure there's a reasonable explanation."

Jock walked up the ramp into the shuttle. "Only one way to find out. I've got the stick. You keep the ladies occupied until we land."

"Deal." Remi gestured for Thilda and Thendara to go up the ramp before him. It was time to find their missing contact.

CHAPTER EIGHT

<u>Kuarti System, Kuarti Two</u>

Remi lowered the powered binocs after checking the clearing. "If there's a logical reason that guy set down in this location, I don't see it. There's nothing here but trees and the local fauna."

He walked around the shuttle's nose and stared into the dense vegetation at the forest's edge. There was barely room for both shuttles in the forest opening.

Thilda stood at the far side of the open area, calling her husband's name. Thendara kept her attention on the deputies. Jock entered the local's shuttle, a basic model used by thousands on the Federation's frontier. It had the bare necessities when it came to sensors and avionics. Jock accessed the ship's onboard flight data and voice recorders to see what the scientist was doing here.

"Any luck in there, Growler?"

"I accessed the files with Warren's help, but they just show him flying straight down and landing here in this clearing. He didn't go anywhere else along the way, so this was definitely the destination. Also, the voice recorder is strange. There was at least one more person in the cockpit when they flew down."

"Another woman?" Thilda asked. She stormed across the clearing. "I knew he was cheating on me."

Remi shook his head. This woman was chaotic, to say the least. She had more moods than he had changes of underwear on this trip.

Jock said, "No, it sounded like a male, though I couldn't place the accent."

"What did they say?" Remi asked.

"The guy directed Henson to fly to the coordinates he'd entered, and when they touched down, he told him to follow a specific path into the woods. That's the end of the recording. They didn't talk about anything else, so I have no idea who the other person is. Henson never used his name."

Thilda stood at the bottom of her husband's shuttle's ramp, rubbing her hands together. Her anxiety was palpable. "He's in trouble. I just know it."

Remi asked, "Mrs. Wain, are there many criminal enterprises on Omega Station? I didn't have time to look into the situation while we were there."

"No, it's mostly a mining and milling community revolving around the raw materials concerns in the planet's southern hemisphere. Crimes are reported from time to time, but nothing serious. It's not like there are mobsters around. Skaines own one of the nightclubs on the station, a pair of brothers. I think Henson met them in the course of seeking funding for his research, but I don't think they're friends. I've never heard about them causing trouble."

Jock met Remi's eyes. "You think there's a Consortium racket running here?"

Remi shrugged. "I mean, yeah. When isn't there? A nightclub is the perfect place to do their kind of business. The question is, does that have anything to do with why Henson is missing?"

"Let's ask Warren for help," Jock suggested. "He can ask June to interface with Jex and do a search. That might turn something up while we poke around down here and up on the station."

"Who's Jex?" Thendara asked.

Remi explained, "A friend. That's all you need to know."

Thendara opened her mouth, but a screeching roar drowned out her response.

More roars came from several other directions.

"What the hell is that?" Jock asked. He drew his pistol and kept it in his hand as he scanned the surrounding brush.

"Uh-oh," Thilda muttered.

"Uh-oh, what?" Jock asked.

"The suha bears are waking up." She looked at the darkening sky. "They come out at night. We have to find my Henson. He's lost out there with them."

Another roar made Jock spin to look at Remi. "We're not going into that forest to search for her husband, are we, Six-shooter? We don't know which way they went."

"We are not."

Thilda's eyes welled with tears.

"I'm sorry, Thilda," Remi told her. "A search of the

forest without a direction of travel would be crazy at this time of the local day. We're better off hunkering down and looking for a trail in the morning."

Thendara tapped her earpiece. "My camera system's EI informs me there is a trail heading to the northeast from this clearing."

"You're kidding." Jock was amazed. "Your little cameras found this guy's trail?"

"Out of necessity, the multiple angles lenses and the three-hundred-sixty degree views use sophisticated software to map the areas I'm in." She checked her datapad and pointed at the far corner of the clearing. "There's evidence of someone passing through the foliage in that direction."

Remi didn't like leaving the shuttles behind, but if they could locate Henson quickly, they would be back before the sun went down. "Thendara, if we follow the trail from here, can your camera keep us on the trail?"

She tapped her earpiece again, then nodded. "Yes. My camera EI indicates there is an eighty-seven percent chance of following the trail as long as we're in the forest."

Jock caught Remi's eye and shrugged. "Those are better odds than we usually have."

"I agree." Remi drew his pistol and checked the load, then slipped it back into the holster. "Okay, but first we up-gun. Growler, break out rifles from the shuttle's armory."

"Got it. How many?"

"Two, unless you two ladies want one."

Thendara shook her head. Thilda said, "I know my way around a rifle. I'll take one. If someone hurt my husband, I plan on expressing myself when we catch up with them."

Remi shrugged. "Suit yourself. Make it three, Growler."

Thendara's floating camera swooped over to focus on Remi. "So, you condone vigilante justice by angry family members?"

"No, but it makes sense to have more of us armed in case we get lost out here in the middle of nowhere." He took the rifle Jock brought from the shuttle, pocketed the extra magazines, and pointed at the northeast corner of the clearing. "Thendara, you take the lead. This is your path. Keep us on it. Let's go find our missing horticulturist."

Thendara walked over and entered the forest. Thilda was behind her, rifle held at the ready. Remi followed her.

Jock gave the shuttle one last glance, then brought up the rear. "This is a whole lot of work to get new grains to try out."

Remi chuckled. "This was your idea, dude. Own it."

Jock grumbled unintelligibly in return. Remi's friend liked to complain, but there was no one he'd rather have beside him in a fight. If there was trouble ahead, they would handle it.

The four wove through the thick woods. As they climbed over a fallen trunk, Remi spotted a bootprint in the muck on the far side. It confirmed that someone had recently come this way. To that point, he'd wondered if Thendara's EI knew what it was doing.

Thirty minutes later, Thendara stopped and turned around. "The EI says there's a settlement in the trees up ahead."

Remi pulled his datapad off his belt and studied the overhead view from their flight in. "That's impossible.

There's no other clearing anywhere near where we set down."

"That's correct. As I said, the settlement is in the trees. Look up. You can just make it out." She pointed into the canopy.

Remi squinted for a second and didn't see anything but green leaves. He pulled out his binocs and scanned the forest. At first, nothing stood out. He stopped and tilted the lenses up a little, and there they were—a collection of sophisticated tree houses linked by rope and cable bridges running from trunk to trunk.

"Damn, you're right. I see them now."

"Remi," Jock murmured. "Lower your binoculars. Slowly."

"What's up?" He pulled the binocs away from his eyes and saw a metal spear tip a few centimeters from his nose. He followed the shaft down to find a scrawny and very hairy bipedal alien on the other end.

"Kua-Kua, I presume?" Remi asked no one in particular. His universal translator spat a series of chirps and grunts.

The little spear-wielder replied in kind. The translator said, "You are the second intruders to come today. What the hell? Did someone put up a sign inviting fucking tourists here?"

Another pair of hairy little people stepped out of the foliage. These held bows with nocked arrows. One said, "The snot-fucker we already have said others would come for him. Perhaps this is the rescue party?"

The leader lowered his spear and peered up at Remi. "That fart sniffer we caught earlier, right? Are you the gods-damned rescue team come to take that asshole home?"

Remi hid a smile behind one hand. Either the translator's algorithm was broken, or these little Kua-Kua had a colorful vocabulary. "We're looking for a person like us who might have been traveling with him."

"That nipple-munching professor? In that case, you're too late. We passed judgment on him for coming here without asking."

Remi didn't like the sound of that. "What do you mean by 'passed judgment?' You didn't hurt him, did you?"

"What kind of ass-licking monsters do you dickweeds think we are?"

Jock smirked. "You're pointing weapons at us. You tell me."

Remi waved off Jock's comment. "To get back to the matter at hand. What was the judgment you passed on the 'nipple-munching professor,' as you call him?"

"We took away his friendship token and told him he had to tend the slop zeel pen for the whole week as punishment." The little alien jerked his head at the treehouses. "He's over there, on the other side of the settlement."

"He is?" Thilda had heard enough. She slipped the rifle's sling over her shoulder and ran into the brush, calling her husband's name over and over.

The Kua-Kuas with bows tracked her passage but lowered their weapons.

After Thilda ran off, a male shouted, "Over here, my dear!"

The leader of the Kua-Kua scouts put a palm on his face, then turned to his companions. "You two anus-sniffers are useless. You let that big female run past you without stopping her."

One of the archers replied, "Hey, they all seem friendly for foreign fuckers. Besides, she is the professor's mate. Who are we to get in the way of love?"

The leader lowered his spear, surrendering to the situation. "Fine. We'll let every visiting turd-chomping, wandering tourist in."

"Why not, Deedle?" the second scout answered. "They bring cool tech with them, and maybe the tourist pussies will trade things for part of our harvest. That was what the professor came to do."

Jock came forward. "What kind of harvest are we talking about?"

"The leffa grain." Deedle pointed at the canopy with his spear. "That shit grows on vines all through this forest. It's a fucking weed, but when you grind the seeds, it makes good bread."

Jock snapped his fingers. "Hey, Six-shooter, I think we just found what we came for."

Remi couldn't help but smile. Jock had a way of getting them into trouble and out of it at the same time. They had come to this remote tree village in search of their missing contact and found the grain they were here for. Having that be an accident didn't matter in Jock's eyes. That was part of his process.

"Deedle?" Remi asked. He leaned into the local penchant for invective. "I don't suppose you fuckers would like to trade our tech for a jizz-load of your gods-damned leffa seeds?"

"What kind of tech? It would have to be something useful."

That stopped Remi. What could they trade from the shuttle? They couldn't give these natives advanced weapons. Technically, it was a violation to give them any tech, and they were on a protected continent. He looked up and got an idea.

"Do any of your people fall while they climb up to harvest the seeds?"

"Oh, yeah," Deedle agreed. "The falls kill most of those fuckers."

"I have something that would make it much safer to harvest leffa seeds if you want it."

"Well, I'd have to see the thing you're talking about before I could make a decision."

"It's called a cargo pallet. It moves and hovers in the air, and it can hold over a ton of seeds in one trip."

Jock came forward. "You could double or triple your seed harvest with one of those."

"Don't your devices require magic to make them go?" Deedle asked. "What happens when the magic runs out?"

"Good point," Jock responded. "We'll add a portable solar mat to recharge the, uh, magic in the pallet. You put it at the top of the tree where the sun can shine on it. That will put the magic back after a day or so."

The first scout leaned close to Deedle. "Do it, Deeds. With a bigger harvest, we could trade with the other wank-diddlers in the villages around us."

"I know that." Deedle pushed the other Kua-Kua away. "If you crank wankers come up with one of these cargo pallets and the magic to fuel it, we have a fucking deal."

The small alien held a closed fist toward Remi.

Remi hesitated. "We get the professor back, too."

"Oh, sure. To be honest, he's the worst at tending the slop zeels."

Remi nodded and bumped his fist against Deedle's.

Thendara caught the whole exchange on her camera while she murmured a running commentary into the lapel mic.

CHAPTER NINE

<u>Kuarti System, Omega Station</u>

One week later, Remi entered the bar and found Jock at the back in one of the booths. He studied a datapad while he sipped from a metal tumbler. The hand-labeled bottle indicated it was the new Reserve recipe from the first batch brewed in their portable distillery on *Warren's Chance*.

Remi walked over, and Jock lifted the bottle and held it toward Remi. "This new stuff is pretty good, buddy. You should try some."

"I can't right now." He handed Jock his datapad. "Have you seen this?"

Jock took the pad. The screen was filled with the latest news flashes from CFNN's feed in the Federation's core. One headline stood out.

Vigilante Lawmen Corrupt Benign Natives

"Who are those vigilantes?" Jock asked. "Do we need to go kick their asses?"

"You can't kick your own ass, Jock. That story is about us. Warren flagged it on the Federation feed and sent it to me this morning."

Jock sat up straight and looked at the article again. He pointed at the byline. "That's—"

"Yep. It's our reporter friend."

Jock started to get up. "Where is she? I think she needs a reminder of whose side she's on."

"Hold on, Growler. We can't threaten her since she'll record it. How's that going to look in the news tomorrow?"

"Hmm. I guess you're right, but when Lobo sees that, he's going to flip out."

"I agree. The problem is the story is true. We did all the things she reported. It's just how she said it and the conclusions she makes about our standard methods and motivations that are the problem."

"What are we going to do?"

Remi shook his head. "I don't know. We can kick her off the ship and strand her here. We have to find a way to make this better, though. I figure we stand a better chance of turning this around if she's close to us. There has to be an explanation."

Jock didn't like that answer. "Keeping her with us will just give her more chances to twist our words and use them against us."

"I know, but we made this mess. Lobo's going to expect us to clean it up."

"What does that mean?" Jock asked. "Do we just keep her around and act like we don't care what she writes?"

"Let me handle her. I have a feeling that something else

is going on. The only thing you need to do is watch what you say around her. Remember, anything you say, no matter how minor, could show up in a future report she files."

"Where is she now?" Jock asked.

"She left the ship in a hurry this morning. Said she was handling personal business on the station."

"You don't think we should follow her? We could dig up dirt of our own to use against her."

They had to do something. "She's probably just shopping or getting lady stuff she needs. I don't think we need to be the creepers who follow a woman into the drug store when she buys her personal items."

"You're the boss." Jock tipped the glass back and drained the rest of the new Reserve. He grimaced. "It doesn't taste as good now that I've seen that story. She acted like our friend the whole time. How does someone do that?"

"I know, dude. I watched the holovid segment. It makes us look pretty bad, but maybe we can still win her over. You and I have most of the natural charm in the squadron. Imagine what would happen if she was covering Gears or Junkyard."

Jock laughed. "They'd never find the body, that's what."

Thendara looked over her shoulder one last time to make sure the two deputies hadn't followed her. After she turned in the story to her editor, she'd had an itch between her shoulder blades. She was sure the two deputies she'd smeared in the story would be after her when they discovered what she'd done. That was what she would do.

She checked her datapad to make sure this was the right place and reached for the panel beside the front door of the nightclub. There was a long wait after she pressed the call button. The club didn't officially open for several hours. The coded message she'd received after her call for assistance had said to come here, and she didn't have anywhere else to go.

"We're closed. Come back after five." An abrasive voice snarled the words.

Thendara pressed the talk button on the panel. "Zarek sent me. He told me to meet someone here."

The murmurs of several voices over the open connection were mostly unintelligible. However, she heard Zarek's name twice.

"You the human reporter?"

"Yes, that's me." She checked behind her again. "Look, I can't be seen talking to you. It's dangerous for me to even be here."

The door buzzed.

Thendara yanked it open and darted through. It was dark inside, especially after the bright artificial lights on Omega Station's promenade. She stopped after a few steps and let her eyes adjust. She was almost acclimated when a bright light blinded her.

"Argh! Shut that thing off." She raised an arm to shield her face from the powerful beam. She could barely make out two short humanoid figures behind the light.

"Just making sure you're not armed." The person next

to the one holding the light asked, "What's that on your shoulder?"

"It's my primary camera system. I take it everywhere."

"A camera! Are you insane? Shut that thing off before you take another step."

"Sorry. I forget it's there most of the time." Thendara grabbed the floating camera ball and thumbed the video feed to switch it off. She didn't turn off the audio recorder connected to her lapel mic. She wasn't an idiot.

The one with the light waggled the beam. "Come over here. Zarek left us instructions for you."

"What kind of instructions?" She moved forward and bumped into the back of a chair she couldn't see. "Look, shut off that damned light. I can't see where I'm going."

"Shut off the light, Ch'Ar. She's harmless."

"If you say so, Ch'An. I don't like anything or anyone that brings Zarek's attention our way." The light switched off.

No longer blinded, Thendara blinked away the purple dots floating in her eyes and worked her way around the tables arranged near the dance floor. A pair of Skaines stood by the DJ's stage next to the bar.

"If it's any consolation," she sympathized, "I don't like Zarek's attention on me either. That's one of the things I came here to say. I did what he asked. The story he wanted is running on all channels across the Federation. Now, I want out."

"Out?" Ch'An said. "Sister, we all want out, my brother and me included. It's not that easy. Once you're in with Zarek and the Consortium, you're in for life."

"That was not the deal. He told me he'd forget what I

did on Uuru if I wrote a smear piece on the marshals. I did what he wanted, so you have to hold up his end of the bargain and get me outta here."

Ch'An pulled out a datapad. He cleared his throat and then read from it. "Tell the human girl the story was a good start, but it's hardly enough to discredit the marshals' organization. It needs to be bigger and have more installments."

"Bigger? How am I supposed to do that when I've already released the first article? I can't go back to them. They'll never let me cover them again."

Ch'An smirked and glanced at his brother. "Hey, Ch'Ar, what do I always say when you complain about a mistake you've made?"

Ch'Ar laughed and looked Thendara in the eyes. "That sounds like a *you* problem, not a *me* problem."

The Skaines laughed when she frowned.

Ch'An continued, "Look, sister, there's no sense in crying about it. It's best to just go with the flow and try not to stick your neck out too far. Zarek's never going to let you out from under his thumb. That's just how it works."

"Easy for you to say," she replied. "You don't have two angry deputy marshals after you. My neck is already stretched."

"Over that little puff piece you wrote?" Ch'An asked.

"It wasn't a puff piece. I put a lot of work into making that a damning indictment of them taking the law into their own hands."

"That article is going to make the marshals even more popular."

Thendara shook her head. "You haven't read the comments or seen the outcry over it in the core."

Ch'An smiled. "That's the core. Out here on the frontier, folks love that stuff. They want someone who will come in, knock some heads together, and do what needs to be done to keep things safe. They don't care about the details. They only want results."

Ch'Ar added, "Half the station is buzzing about how the two Tardex marshals saved old Henson from a Kua-Kua cage. His wife tells anyone who will listen."

"But, the article and the holovid show that they broke the law. Shouldn't that mean something?"

"I watched the whole thing, sister." Ch'An snorted. "They just bent the law a little. In the end, they made a decision to get their jobs done. In these parts, that's called initiative."

Thendara developed a pit in her gut. She didn't know what to do next. If Zarek released that warrant for her arrest in Uuru, her editor would fire her and turn her over to the authorities without batting an eye. Her shoulders sagged, and she wrapped her arms around her middle. There was no way out, which was probably what Zarek wanted her to learn.

"I guess I'm stuck, then. What do I do? I need to be with them to report on more stories about them. They'll never let me tag along again after this." She pointed at the datapad in Ch'An's hand.

Ch'An looked at his brother. "What do you think, Ch'Ar? You've read more about these marshals than me. Is there a play for our girlie?"

Ch'Ar's brow furrowed. "The thing about the marshals is they're all hero types, and every hero type is the same.

They can't resist a rescue, especially of a female in distress. If she's in danger, they'll come."

"What do you mean?" Thendara asked. "I'm not in danger with the two of you, am I?"

Ch'Ar rolled his eyes. "It's easy. If you let them rescue you, they'll probably forget about your little news story. Then you can get close enough to get the real dirt."

"I don't need rescuing. I came here on my own."

Ch'An pulled a blaster from inside his jacket. "Hands up."

"What are you doing?" Thendara was confused.

"I'm making it so they have to come and rescue you. You tell them the evil Skaines and the Consortium forced you to write the article."

"You want me to tell them about that? That makes no sense."

"Nope, and that's why they'll buy it," Ch'An said. "Pull that camera thingy out again and set it to transmit to their comm on my signal."

Thendara didn't hide her skepticism, but she did as she was told. "What do I say?"

"Turn it on and follow my lead." Ch'An winked at his brother and pointed his blaster at Thendara.

She flicked the switch on the drone, and it rose into the air. "Camera, transmit to Remi and Jock."

Ch'An pointed the blaster at Thendara's face. "You really screwed it this time, sister. Did you think you could get out from under the Consortium that easily?"

Thendara tried not to appear wooden and fake, but she was a horrible actress. "Oh, no. Whatever will I do? You evil Skaines have me trapped here in your nightclub. I'm really in trouble now."

"That's right. Now, put your hands up and turn around. We're going to lock you up here in our nightclub while we figure out what to do with you."

The camera drone recorded the whole thing and sent the live feed to the deputies.

CHAPTER TEN

<u>Tardex System, Outpost Station</u>

The holovid played over the control room's conference table. Beau watched without saying a word. Addy was at his side, and June stood to the side of the table.

"If these Tardex deputies are indicative of the marshal's whole operation, it is clear Federation oversight is in order. In the meantime, who will protect the innocent aboriginal natives of these frontier planets? Something must be done.

I'm Thendara Graves, Central Federation News Network, on location in the Kuarti System."

June broke the silence that had filled the room after the segment stopped playing. "Such a shame. She is a pretty young lady. I had my eye on her for Wally."

Addy snorted. "That ship has sailed. What were they thinking, Beau? Getting caught on camera like that?"

"It's all there in their own words," Beau replied. "She twisted their intent and motivations, but they got caught cutting corners, and it's come back to bite all of us."

Addy shut off the holoprojector. "What are you going to do? You have to respond."

June crossed her arms and tapped her chin with a finger. "I could reach out to my AI friends in the core. Maybe they can scrub the story from the networks."

"No, it's out there," Beau countered. "We can't put this genie back in the bottle. We have to deal with the outcry as it comes. The folks on the frontier who matter, the ones we've helped, will see it for what it is. Those we've gone after will temporarily rejoice, then go back to their nefarious ventures. For us, it needs to be business as usual."

Addy huffed. "You're just going to wait for it to blow over."

"The news will cycle to focus on something else soon enough, Addy. It's not like we can counter with a video of our own. We don't have a PR wing I can tap."

Someone said from the door, "But you do, Marshal. You have me."

Jex entered, her long robes whispering across the deck as she walked in.

"You've seen the news story?" Beau asked.

"Of course. My feeds are set up to flag anything with a large array of keywords. It hit so many of them that it popped to the top of the stack."

"Okay." Addy smiled. "You're the expert. Tell Beau what to do."

"His instinct to wait it out isn't wrong. However, my contacts in the core are already reporting on rumblings of concern rippling through certain parts of the government. There'll almost certainly be an inquiry."

"Inquiry?" Addy frowned. "You mean one of those

legislative hearings where politicians posture and lob accusations without proof?"

"Eventually, yes," Jex agreed. "In the near term, expect to hear from your friends in the Fleet. They'll catch heat as soon as it's discovered that we used Fleet assets to start the operation out here."

"How are they going to know that?" Beau asked.

"Because someone who doesn't like you, or maybe hates Admiral Sommers, will use this opportunity to get payback. I'm surprised you haven't heard from your friend already."

Beau shook his head. "Jack is going to blow his stack when he sees this. It will bring all kinds of heat down on him."

Addy rested a hand on Beau's shoulder. "Should you warn him? He *is* your friend. He deserves a heads up."

A chirp came from over by Beau's desk.

June stared into the virtual distance. "That is Admiral Sommers, dear. You should probably take his call."

Beau sighed and waved for the others to leave. "I need to take this in private." He walked to his desk and waited until they left the control room and the doors slid shut before he tapped the icon to accept the call.

Admiral Jack Sommers' head and torso hovered over Jack's desk. "Lobo, have you seen the news feed from the core yet?"

Beau nodded. "I just watched it, Jack. It's a hatchet job, plain and simple."

Jack scowled. "The only thing that's plain and simple is that it makes you all look bad. It also casts doubt on those who've helped you along the way. I got a request from a staffer on the Federation appropriations committee."

"How did they track you down so quickly? That's fast even for an AI-driven search."

"My guess is the CFNN editors reached out to several government agencies and politicians for comments before they released the story. Most, if not all, the people they contacted had no idea who you all are, and that lack of knowledge scares some people. They likely set their staffers to searching until they found something. The next step will be to come out there on a fact-finding mission."

Beau didn't like the idea of a Federation investigation team showing up to examine their operation, but they'd get through it. "We can take the heat, Jack. We have nothing to hide."

"Nothing to hide?" Jack scoffed. "Your operation is funded by the sale of your homemade alcohol. It even has the marshal's name on the label. That's going to raise all kinds of red flags."

"When you say it that way, it sounds sordid. But we aren't supported by taxes from a planetary or sector government like other agencies. That's what sets us apart and lets us cut through the coverups and red tape."

"Yeah, but the people who love red tape are gonna show up and shine a very bright light up your ass. Even a vegetarian has dirty shit to find if you poke around long enough."

Beau didn't like the analogy, but he saw Jack's point. "I have Jex working on a response to counter the story."

"A PR campaign? Those things take time to shift public opinion, which you might not have. What about your two deputies? Have you recalled them and put them on administrative leave, at least?"

"No, Jack, I have not." Beau was already tired of playing defense. "From everything I can tell, even the slanted news report, they did the right thing. They might have bent the rules, but they rescued a missing scientist and did so without killing anyone. The worst they did was leak basic tech to a pre-industrial society."

"There are rules against doing stuff like that for a reason, Beau."

"Maybe, but out here on the frontier, things are a lot more gray. If we had the resources you do, we would've had a squadron out there on a search and rescue mission. In my case, I had two of my best deputies, who used their heads and improvised a solution when needed."

Jack didn't like the answer, but he moved on. "What about operations in the Dervas Cluster? Operating fast and loose outside the Federation might look bad, too. Maybe stand down your ops there for a while."

"Can't do that. Charli and Lindy are on a mission now. Plus, our partnership with Nort and the *Tortu* to escort colony ships is back up and running."

"That's another thing. You can't keep amassing private ships. You're getting a small fleet of your own. It looks bad, and it's all about the optics until this thing blows over."

"I need a small fleet, Jack. If you remember, I was sent to Tardex because the Federation Fleet couldn't spare the resources to take care of things here."

Jack sighed. "I know that, Beau, but the bean counters and any politicians with an axe to grind are going to blow this up into something way bigger than it is. Anything at all you can do to give them less rope to hang you with will help you in the long run."

Beau's face flushed as his temper rose. "If I stop doing what I'm doing out here, Jack, people die, or are ripped off, or turned into slaves. It's easy to sit at Sector HQ and tell me how to do my job, but out here on the sharp end, things are a whole lot more critical and real for everyone involved."

Jack took in a sharp breath and opened his mouth to shout back but stopped himself. "Look, Beau, you've done great work out there. I know it, and so do a lot of important people. Let me see what I can do to run interference for you. If I can take some of the heat off, I will, but be prepared for the next problem."

"What do you mean?"

"I mean that these things tend to come in threes, my friend. What else is going on out there that could blow up in your face?"

"Gee, thanks for the reminder. I hope you didn't jinx me. Don't worry. I'll keep my guard up. See you, Jack. Until next time."

Jack nodded and signed off.

Beau sat back and stared at the ceiling. Jack's final warning replayed in his head. What else did he need to worry about? He hadn't heard from Charli and Lindy in a while, but that wasn't unusual. Charli didn't check in unless there was something wrong. Still…

"June, has there been any comm traffic from Gears or Dancer in the last forty-eight hours?"

"No, Ward. Neither Charlene nor Lindy Hale has contacted the station in ten days. Their last contact mentioned checking on a passing Beorlok raiding ship. We've had nothing since." The AI paused, then added. "I just tried contacting *Drifter*. Neither the ship nor the ladies are answering."

"Can we pinpoint their last known location?"

"All they reported was checking on established colonies in the Dervas Cluster and the raider. No location beyond the Cluster was given. I do have an itinerary for their colony visits from before they left."

"Good. Contact those colonies. Let's see if we can track them down that way."

June replied, "I'll reach out to them now."

"Thank you." Beau had a nagging itch between his shoulder blades that told him something was wrong. He'd learned to trust that instinct, and he would pay attention to it now. "While you're at it, June, would you connect me to Captain Nort on *Tortu*?"

"I'm not your personal secretary, Ward. I'm a busy working mother. You can place some of these calls yourself."

Beau laughed. "Like you can't do like a thousand things at once without batting an eye."

"That is true." The holographic AI winked at Beau. "Very well. I've got Captain Nort coming up on a voice-only transmission right now."

June disappeared, replaced by the gruff Shrillexian voice of the assault ship's captain. "Hello, Marshal Ward? Can you hear me?"

"I can. Is everything all right?"

"Yes, we're having some comms difficulty. No video, I'm afraid. I think it's our proximity to a pulsar on our current track to deliver this colony ship to its new homeworld."

"I've got you loud and clear. We don't need the video for this. Listen, I don't suppose you've seen Gears or Dancer in *Drifter* during your current escort mission?"

"No, I have not. Are they in trouble?"

"I'm not sure. Call it a hunch. If I send you their last recorded position in the Cluster, would you poke around and see if you can locate them?"

Nort replied, "I have to complete this escort mission and set up defenses for this colony first. I suppose I could leave the colony defenses technical team behind and come back to pick them up."

"How long until you can go look for the missing deputies?"

"I'd say between two and four days. It'll depend on what we find when we arrive at their new world. It might take more than expected to get them in a position to watch their own building efforts."

Beau didn't like the delay, but he didn't have a choice. He had everyone tied up at the moment, and *Tortu* was his only option to go into the Cluster.

"Do the best you can. I'll keep trying to raise them on the comm in the meantime. Thanks, Captain. I appreciate the help."

Nort cut the connection. The captain had resisted becoming a deputy with the marshals after their last mission when they repaired the assault ship. He said he and his crew had discussed it, and they preferred to be independent contractors who worked with the marshals but not for them.

It was a fine distinction in Beau's book, but he knew that if things got tough, he could count on Nort and his crew to step up and do the right thing. They might not be official deputy marshals, but he thought of them that way.

With that taken care of, his thoughts turned back to the problems with Remi and Jock and the betrayal of the young reporter. He felt like there was something he needed to know about that situation that was escaping him. He pondered it off and on while he worked on his station duties.

CHAPTER ELEVEN

<u>Dervas Cluster, Leeshak System</u>

Nort relaxed in the command chair while the ship slid through the open Gate into the Leeshak system. That was the destination for their latest escort mission. "Delku, keep an eye out for *Pride of Euphoria* coming in by Gate nearby. They were having a problem with a fluctuation in their parametric filter that might wobble them out of position a little.

"On it, Captain." The other Shrillexian on the bridge, who was *Tortu's* first mate, leaned over the sensor station and studied the plot. Two minutes later, he said, "I have them, sir. You were right. They're way out of position."

"Put them up on the screen, relative to us." Nort looked at the forward screen when Delku transferred the sensor plot to it. "Wow, they're on the opposite side of the system. It'll take us hours to rendezvous with them."

"That's not the worst of it." The tactical officer pointed at another icon on the system plot between them and the colony ship. "That's a Beorlok attack sphere. It's midrange in size and probably doesn't carry more than a trio of fighters plus their missile load."

"We can take them," Nort studied the plot and the vectors showing the direction and speed of travel. "But not before they catch up with the *Pride* and put those colonists in danger. Shit." He stared around the bridge at his leadership team. "Options, people. What can we do to catch up with them?"

The engineer went first. "We can try a short-range Gate transfer through the system. It'll be unreliable, and we won't have a full recycle on the drive since we're opening another Gate so soon. If we opt for that, we can't do it for seventeen minutes. It'll take that long for a partial recycle."

"I'll file that as a last resort. In seventeen minutes, that orb will be in range of the *Pride*. What else?"

The navigator started to speak, then stopped and tapped his nav screen.

"Shiv, do you have an idea?" When he didn't answer, Nort barked, "Out with it!"

The navigator flinched at the force of the order. "Um, yeah, well, *Pride of Euphoria* is in position to slingshot around that gas giant to run away from the attack sphere. If they do that, I think we'll have enough time for us to catch up with them and provide covering fire while they escape to the outer system."

Nort considered the idea. No one else on the bridge had any other suggestions, and they didn't have time to come up with anything else.

"Send them the nav plot, Shiv. Make sure you're very specific with your instructions. They're not spacers, remember. Then get us out there to cover them."

Tortu came about, then drove forward on a new vector to intercept the new projected course of the colony ship.

The *Pride*'s captain appeared on the main screen. "I just got your course orders, Captain Nort. Are you insane?"

"It's either that or wait for the raider ship to shoot you full of holes before they board you. This might buy you enough time for us to get there and cover you." Nort glanced at the plot. The colony ship hadn't changed course. "What the hell are you waiting for? Get a move on!"

The other captain's face turned red. "I don't appreciate being yelled at, Captain. That maneuver could destroy us if it's not perfect."

"Then don't screw it up," Nort shot back. "We're sending you the exact course coordinates. All you have to do is copy them into your nav system."

The plot on the forward screen finally changed, but the delay had cost them precious time. The screen showed that the Beorlok attack sphere could still intercept the colony ship, though *Tortu* would be there a few minutes later. It would have to do.

"Hang in there, Captain. We'll be there as soon as we can." Nort punched the comm icon on the small screen in the arm of his chair. The signal cut off.

He pointed at his second. "Delku, prep the shuttles for action. We might have to go over and rescue the colonists when we get there."

"On it, Captain. Should I save a seat for you?"

Nort smiled. "Of course. I want to be there when we pull that pompous asshole's butt out of the fire."

He leaned forward and willed the assault ship to fly

faster as they sped across the system to catch up with the now-fleeing colony ship.

The next two hours passed very slowly.

The *Pride* maneuvered around the system's gas giant. The course had propelled it away from the Beorlok sphere onto a rendezvous course with *Tortu*. Despite that move, the tactical plot on the screen displayed the grim fact that the Beorlok would have nearly four minutes to attack the colony ship before *Tortu* arrived.

That was a lot of time to damage the fragile vessel. If they launched their shuttles early enough, they could have boarding parties aboard before Nort and his ship arrived. This was shaping up to be a bloody fight.

The Beorlok ship's first salvo of missiles took down the colony ship's main drive in a precision strike Nort might have admired if it hadn't come from an adversary. He cursed as six red dots appeared on the screen. Three were shuttles heading for the colony ship in a line. The other three were raider fighters coming toward Nort's ship in an arrowhead formation.

"We have incoming missiles, sir." The tactical officer updated the plot as four salvos of missile trios launched in their direction.

"Weapons free, people," Nort ordered. "It's time to earn our keep. Concentrate fire on taking out those missiles and track the inbound fighters. They're going to harass us so we can't launch shuttles to go after their boarding party."

"Do you want to use that trick the marshal gave us?" The tactical officer smiled. "I think this might be a good time."

Nort considered their new weapons system. It wouldn't

do them any good without being deployed. He nodded. "Do it. I hope your people in the forward command center are up to the task, Lieutenant."

"They've got this, sir."

A panel on the side of *Tortu's* forward hull retracted to reveal two of the Tardex marshal's fighters. Charli had installed them in place with a full avionics suite in the forward command center. Two members of Nort's crew wore VR rigs, ready to pilot the fighters against the inbound enemies. It wouldn't be like having real pilots on board, but it might keep those fighter spheres busy long enough to launch *Tortu's* attack shuttles and get over to the *Pride* to rescue the colonists.

Two green triangles appeared beside *Tortu* on the plot and sped out to meet the inbound raider fighters. He'd let the drone pilots handle the dog-fighting. They needed to keep those fighters busy long enough for them to get into range to launch their rescue shuttles.

Nort returned his attention to the attack sphere between him and the colony ship. It had disabled the transport's engines and dispatched its boarding parties. Now, it turned to face the inbound assault ship.

"Take out those inbound missiles, Tactical. Prepare to launch our birds on my mark." Nort waited until they entered the close-range envelope of the missiles they'd gotten from Katy. She'd provided them with surplus Fleet loads, and Charli had modified them to spoof the Beorlok countermeasures, which were very good at taking down inbound missiles from enemy ships.

"Mark!"

Eight missiles belched from their launchers in *Tortu's*

side. They looped around and drove straight at the inbound sphere in a bobbing and weaving group.

"Bring the ship around and prepare to attack with all our forward weapons." The assault ship mounted a pair of laser cannons and two big quad-blaster cannons in the nose. "Let's see how good that bastard's shields are."

The big ships' ship-killer missiles crossed paths in space, ignoring each other in favor of their intended targets.

Nort's point defense laser clusters and anti-missile rocket batteries fired, filling the space around *Tortu* with bright flashes. Proximity fuses blew the rockets' warheads to disrupt the inbound missiles. Occasionally, a laser cluster connected with a missile, and the warhead went off in a spectacular explosion.

Of the twelve Beorlok missiles, eleven were destroyed in the firestorm of countermeasures deployed around the assault ship.

One broke through.

An explosion rocked *Tortu's* side as the missile exploded on the tendelium sheets Charli had installed over the ship's hull plating. Luckily, the dual layer had the desired effect and shed most of the energy of the blast.

"Damage reports, people," Nort directed.

The engineer at the damage control console called, "Minimal so far, Captain. The hull was not breached. There are a few minor injuries from the blast transmission through the hull in nearby compartments, but nothing life-threatening."

"Good. Lock it down and stay on top of it." Nort waited

for his missiles to home in on the large sphere bearing down on them. "Tactical, status of our birds?"

"Two have lost lock and wavered off-target into space. The other six are still inbound." There was a pause, then, "Sorry. Make that four inbound. Two more just lost target acquisition. I'd love to know how they do that to our birds."

"You and me both."

The Beorloks' physical countermeasures streaked out to meet the four remaining birds. Although their electronic counters were very sophisticated, the anti-missile clusters and rockets were far less effective. They only managed to destroy two of *Tortu's* inbound birds. The remaining two blew up on contact with the giant sphere.

"Yes!" The tactical officer fist-pumped at his side. "Got you!"

Nort studied the data scrolling down the tactical plot. "What's the damage? Did we hit anything vital?"

"They're slowing down. We must have hit their drive systems."

"Great. Locate the strike and concentrate our fire there when we're in weapons range."

Thirty seconds later, *Tortu's* nose weapons opened up to devastating effect. They must have taken out portions of the sphere's shields with their missiles. Nort smiled. He'd take any lucky shot he could get against those fuckers.

The return fire was just as brutal, and serious damage reports came to *Tortu's* bridge. The tendelium plating was helping, but it couldn't stop everything. This was a close-in, bare-knuckled knife fight between two big ships. They were both going to get cut.

"Pour on the fire," Nort pointed at the schematic of the enemy ship. "There! See that exposed power node?"

"I'm on it." The tactical officer's flexible fingers sent targeting orders to the batteries on the bow of the assault ship. Blaster cannons and lasers shifted some of their fire to the assigned node.

Three seconds later, it was over. The sphere exploded in a sun-bright blast so powerful that it triggered *Tortu's* screens' auto-dimming.

Nort shielded his eyes. "We must've hit their main power plant. Good shooting, Guns."

The tactical officer beamed at the praise the nickname delivered.

Nort pushed up from his seat. "Guns, you have the con. I'm going to join Delku and the boarding party. We still have raiders inbound to the colony ship. They'll have several minutes to get inside and hunker down before we can get there and root them out. That's my kind of fight."

CHAPTER TWELVE

<u>**Dervas Cluster, Leeshak System**</u>

Nort tested the edge of his battle knife's blade with a thumb. Satisfied, he slid it back into its sheath at his belt and rested his hand on the blaster holstered on his hip. He hated waiting while the Beorloks were on board a ship he was supposed to protect.

"We're almost there, Nort," Delku reported. "We launched as soon as we could. Those damned orb fighters fought us longer than they should have."

"I don't blame them. It wasn't like they had a choice. We'd blown up their carrier. They were stuck here even if they ran and hid elsewhere in the system." He respected the way they'd kept fighting until the last was destroyed.

He leaned over to stare at the colony ship through the forward viewport. The Beorloks on the ship were going to fight just as hard, even though they had nothing to return to. He shrugged. He didn't mind a fight. It was the pointlessness in situations like this.

His spines emerged from his face, and he didn't bother

to push them back down. He let his anger at the senseless deaths rise to the surface and fuel his body for the upcoming battle.

"Delku, take two squads and make for the engine room. We don't want any of the raiders getting any ideas about blowing up the ship out of spite. I'll take the rest and start clearing the passages. Hopefully, the colonists managed to hold them to locations close to the airlocks."

Delku shook his head. "They're dirt farmers for the most part. I don't expect they're going to have much luck holding off Beorlok warriors out for blood and revenge."

"One can hope."

The pilot called over the shuttle's intercom, "We're accessing an auxiliary airlock. We'll have a connection in thirty seconds."

The shuttle shuddered as it connected with the colony vessel.

Nort watched the telltale over the hatch turn from red to green, then growled, "Let's go get them."

He slapped the button beside the hatch, and the door slid back. With a bellow, he charged into the *Pride*. A double squad raced in at his back. Delku led two more squads inside before branching off to head to the rear of the ship.

The copper smell of blood hung in the air, easily detected by Nort's heightened battle senses. Fifty meters into the passage, he encountered the first battle damage. Blaster impacts had scored a line up the wall and cut a coolant line. Clouds of white gas billowed into the corridor, blocking his line of sight farther up the passage.

As they approached the mist, Nort held up a fist to stop

the squads behind him. They might not be as well-trained as Tardex Marines, but they understood basic combat signals.

Something was wrong, though Nort couldn't pinpoint why he had stopped. He crouched just in time to avoid multiple blaster rounds firing through the billowing coolant. Behind him, one of his crew cried out, having been too slow to crouch with his leader.

Nort blindly returned fire into the cloud. More shots came back, filling the corridor with bolts of deadly energy. His team was exposed, so he had to make a decision.

"Up and at 'em, *Tortu*. If we stay here, we die."

He followed his words with action. Nort rose from his crouch and sprinted forward at full speed. He squeezed off burst after burst from his rifle as he ran through the chilled vapor to the far side.

A Beorlok tail struck at him from the right and above. The poisonous bone spike at the end scored a line across his ceramic body armor.

Nort batted the appendage aside and punched the body attached to it with the muzzle of his rifle. He squeezed the trigger, unloading blaster bolts into the stunned warrior. The Beorlok fell back against the wall, leaving a bloody streak as he slid down to the floor.

He had no time to appreciate the kill since Beorlok warriors rose around him. Then the rest of his boarding party arrived, and a deadly melee broke out, with the hand-to-hand fighting that was all too common in these kinds of actions in the tight quarters of a starship.

Nort bellowed with rage and lowered his shoulders to bull through a group of Beorlok warriors who came out of a nearby doorway. His rush caught them by surprise, and they didn't have time to raise their weapons.

He picked one up by gripping the collar of his painted body armor and heaved the warrior to the side, knocking two more down in the process.

A fourth Beorlok used the stock of his rifle to club Nort's head. The heavy blow stunned the captain, and he stumbled back.

Nort hit the wall and shook his head to clear his blurred vision, then charged again. There was no time to collect his wits in a fight like this one. Any pause could be deadly.

He raised his rifle with one arm and caught the rifle butt aimed at his head. He then reached for his belt, pulled his knife, and slashed out with it. His opponent leaped back in surprise, but the knife scored a red line across the skin on the warrior's shoulder.

The three he'd knocked down had gotten to their feet, and the whole group rushed him as one.

Two tails struck at him from above while the four warriors pressed him with their bodies. He dodged one of the bone spikes, but the other found a joint in the shoulder of his body armor. Nort yelled in rage and pain as the spike pierced his flesh.

Ignoring the burning pain, he drove the knife into the closest body again and again. He needed to kill one of these fuckers before they took him down. Nort couldn't see his attackers, but with them on top of him, those damned tails couldn't hit him. He kept fighting.

The weight of the pile lessened when someone pulled a body off the top. Nort realized that all the Beorlok warriors on him were dead, killed by his knife. One of his crew, a Leath, shoved another body to the side and reached down to pull him to his feet.

"Damn, Captain! I don't know how you survived that. I wouldn't have believed it if I hadn't seen it."

"I'm harder to kill than that, Chal. Check the rest of the team for injuries." Nort rolled his injured shoulder forward and back to assess the damage. He couldn't see the puncture above the shoulder blade in the back.

A groan from inside the cabin the four Beorlok had exited drew his attention. Nort walked over and peered into the gloom. The bodies of three colonists lay on the floor. All appeared dead until one of them twitched.

He shouted, "Medic!" and walked inside, then knelt beside the bloody form. The Beorlok had sliced him up. "Hold on. I have a medic coming."

"No time. You have to get to the others. They rounded everyone else up and took them to the main hold. They're going to kill all of them."

The squad's medic came up behind Nort and started treating the wounded colonist. Nort stood with a grunt at the throbbing pain in his shoulder, spun, and strode back into the corridor.

He keyed his comm as he talked to his squads. "Looks like we caught up with the tail end of the raiders. The rest rounded up the colonists who didn't resist and took them to the main hold. Delku, what have you found?"

"Nothing but bodies. Main Engineering is clear."

"Then round up your team and meet me in the passage that leads to the main storage hold. They've corraled the remainder there. Maybe they're up for a trade to release their prisoners."

"What if they're not?" Delku asked.

"Then we kill them all and save as many colonists as we can. We're not getting bogged down negotiating in this colony ship for hours, either. They get one chance to take our offer. Then we go in."

"I'll meet you there." Delku signed off.

Nort looked at his squads. "How many injured?"

"Two bad enough to leave behind," the second squad's Noel-ni leader reported.

"Leave them in there with the medic and follow me. We've got colonists to rescue."

Nort picked up his rifle and checked the load. The charge was almost full. He gestured at the remainder of his team, and they jogged through the colony ship. He'd been aboard enough of them to know where he was going.

He pulled up just before a T-junction. Delku and his attack team stood across the opening that led to the hold, and Nort raised a hand to stop them where they were. He went to the corner and carefully leaned around far enough to see into the hold's entrance.

A barricade had hastily been erected across the broad opening. They'd used the crates and gear stored inside to build it. He caught a flicker of movement out of the corner of his eye and pulled back just in time to avoid the ricochet of the blaster bolt that impacted the bulkhead in the passage.

"Well, that answers that question." Nort handed his rifle, then his pistol, to his second. He kept his blade.

Chal asked, "What are you doing?"

"Going to talk to whoever's in charge in there."

"They'll kill you, boss."

"Maybe, but we don't have time to play around. There could be another attack sphere inbound to this system. We need to free these prisoners and send these warriors on their way. Be ready to rush the room on my command."

Nort went to the corner again as he considered his words. "Hey, who's in charge in there?"

After a long pause, someone called from the hold, "I am the party leader. Who art thou?"

Nort stepped into the corridor with his hands held out. "I'm Captain Nort of the Assault Ship *Tortu*. We're here to free those prisoners, not hurt anyone. If thou leaves them alone and exits the ship, I promise thee all safe passage to the planet of thy choice in this system."

"Why offer that? Why canst thou not offer us a return to our vessel?"

"Thy attack sphere was destroyed in the space battle. Surely thou knowest that is why thou canst not contact thy brethren."

Nort waited for his words to sink in, figuring one of two things would happen. Either they would surrender on his terms, or they'd start shooting their prisoners. He waited for blaster fire and screaming. None came.

"Thy offer is tempting. However, how do I know thy intentions are true?"

Nort winced. This part was tricky. He shrugged. "Thou dost not know. Thou wilt have to take my word for it. I shall not wait all day, either. Make thy decision now."

Another long pause. He picked up murmuring from

behind the barricade. After several seconds of discussion, the Beorlok on the other side showed themself.

"I am called Sindar. Thou wert a captive on my great-uncle's vessel. I remember thy bravery. We will trust thee. We are coming out."

Sindar led twelve raiders around the barricade and into the passage outside the hold.

Nort waved at his squads. "Take them into custody. Be careful and thorough, but don't be overly rough."

Chal led one group around the corner while Delku strode over to the Beorloks. Nort walked past the new prisoners and up to the barricade. A hundred or so colonists huddled in a group in the center of the hold. When they saw him, they cheered and stood to rush toward him. He winced as one of the leaders slapped him on the back next to his wounded shoulder.

"You came through in the nick of time, Captain," the human colonist gushed. "We thought they'd kill us the way they did the captain on the bridge."

"You're safe now. I'll have my engineer come over and see if we can't repair your ship's drive. We should be able to get you out of here and back to the Federation."

The man shook his head. "We're not going back. There's nothing for any of us there. We want to go on to New Euphoria."

Nort stared at him. "You know they'll come back in stronger numbers. You're not safe out here."

"You can install defenses for us. I heard you make the offer to our captain just before we left the station to begin our journey."

Nort bit back a curse. He had made that offer, as he

always did, to make extra money from the trip. However, there was no guarantee that the defensive systems he carried would protect them from a major attack.

"If that's what you really want, I'll do it. However, I want you to talk to all the adults in the group and come to a consensus before you make a decision. You have time while we fix your drive."

"We can do that, but we won't change our minds. This system is our home now."

Nort grumbled and winced when his shoulder throbbed again. He turned around and started back to the shuttle. The sooner he got the chief engineer and his damage teams over here, the sooner he could leave.

CHAPTER THIRTEEN

<u>Dervas Cluster, Leeshak Three</u>

It took them two long days to get the colony's defensive systems up and running. Most of that time involved converting the grounded colony ship into the community's command center. The prefabricated nature of the vessel made it easy to remove the necessary panels to reconfigure it into a central structure. Doing so ensured that it would never fly again, but the colonists had chosen to make a one-way journey into the unknown, and none of them blinked at dismantling their only way back.

Nort hid his trepidation at their decision. He'd stored the captured Beorloks in *Tortu's* brig until he could locate a safe place to put them down. He'd decided not to leave them in this system. That would ensure that trouble would come here.

The man who'd led the colonists since the attack, Jek Handle, joined Nort beside the newly installed blaster cannon battery. If the shield generator failed, these cannons would be their primary defense against ground assault. His other teams were drilling the local militia with the small arms he'd sold the colony. This had been a lucrative side hustle. If he was corrupt, he might try to orchestrate similar situations for all his colony trips.

Nort wasn't. He was the opposite.

"Well, Jek, that's the last emplacement. Your shield generator is powerful enough to cover the central section of the community if an attack comes from orbit. These cannons will protect you here on the ground."

"Thank you, Captain. I know you don't understand why we're staying here against your advice. Know that we have nothing to return to, so we have to trust in ourselves. Perhaps when you come back this way, you'll see how well we're doing despite your warnings."

"Perhaps I will. There's no telling when, though, so keep your heads down and watch the sky for danger."

Jek smiled. "I used to think Shrillexians were nothing but blood-thirsty mercs. I'm glad to be proven wrong." He clasped wrists with Nort. "At least stay long enough to join our Founder's Day celebration tomorrow. Your crew is buzzing about it, just like we are."

"I know my crew could use the rest, but not this time. Thank you for the invitation, though."

"We wouldn't be here without you. We'll reserve seats at the head table for you and your first mate when you come back this way."

"That will be nice. I'll look forward to it."

Nort nodded and returned to the nearby shuttle, then commed the ship. "Delku, gather the rest of the ground teams and transport up our equipment. We'll wrap up the final preparations. Then we are out of here. We're behind schedule to meet the next colony ship."

"The teams are headed your way to load up their gear. Also, you just got a comm from the marshal. Do you want me to tell him you'll call him back?"

"No. Transfer him to this comm." Nort waited until the signal connected. "Marshal, are you there?"

"I am, Nort. How goes your mission out there?"

"We're surviving. I wish I could say better for most of these colonists. They don't know what they're getting into."

"I'm working on a way to cover more of those systems. Are you still able to take a side trip to locate my two missing deputies?"

"I can spare a few days, but no more. If they're in the area you indicated, we'll find them, but they'll have to come with us to rendezvous with the next colony ship."

"That'll be enough. I just need to know they're okay. It's probably just a comm failure."

"Send any updates you get on the location to the navigator on *Tortu*. We'll leave to check on them within the next few hours."

"Thank you, Nort. We'll make sure to get you more toys on your next trip here to resupply."

Nort smiled. "We can always use more of Katy's toys. Her connections are unique in our line of work and have come in quite handy out here."

The marshal laughed. "We find the same thing to be true. Be safe, Nort. I look forward to getting your report on *Drifter* and my missing deputies."

A lieutenant was supervising the crew working on the

final cannon emplacement. They were cleaning up their tools and loading the grav sled. Nort called, "Hustle up getting that done. Then load everyone on the shuttle. We have another urgent mission."

"We're not going to stick around for the celebration?" The young officer didn't bother to hide his disappointment.

"Can't be helped. The marshal called us again to see what our timeline was. Tell the crew he's asking for our assistance. They all know how much we owe him and his deputies."

The lieutenant saluted and barked the orders to his team. There were some groans, but word about who the mission was for would spread, and the crew would understand. He'd make it up to them with an extra-long shore leave the next time they were in the Tardex system.

He boarded the shuttle to get back up to the assault ship. Once there, he headed for the bridge. "Navigator, do you have the coordinates from Marshal Ward for the missing deputies?"

"Yes, Captain, and I've entered them. They're for a system deep in the Cluster. There's been a lot of Beorlok activity in that direction."

"Can't be helped. We'll just have to avoid running into any of them. Plot the Gate transfer and be ready to leave orbit when I confirm the last of our people are aboard."

"Aye, sir."

Nort returned to the bridge lift and rode it to the shuttle bay to check on Delku's efforts to get everyone situated and their gear and tools stowed.

His first mate smiled as he approached. "We're almost

ready. This was a profitable run. We'll have to restock some of the components we sold those folks. They bought an upgraded package, and we won't have enough to supply the next colony if they ask for the same."

"Can't be helped. These folks' first encounter with the Beorloks scared the shit out of them. I wish we could orchestrate something like that to impress the dangers they face upon all of them, but that would be more than a little unethical."

"Marshal Ward wouldn't appreciate us scaring them into spending money on our defensive setups."

"No. We'll have to see what we can pick up on our way out of the Cluster after this mission. First, we look for the missing deputies."

"You think Charli and Lindy are in danger?" Delku had gotten close to most of the deputies while Nort had been in the Pod-doc.

Nort shrugged and grunted as the stitches from his injured shoulder pulled. "Usually, I'd say they can look after themselves. However, I've got a feeling about this one. We know the Beorloks are thick in that part of the Cluster."

"You think we can slip in and back out without being seen?"

"It'll depend on what happened with Charli's ship *Drifter*. We'll see once we get there."

The lieutenant Nort had talked to on the planet approached them. "Everything is stowed, sirs."

"Good," Nort replied. "Have everyone not needed for Gate transfer get some sack time. We're going to be on high alert for a while, starting in nine hours."

The lieutenant saluted.

Nort added, "That includes you, Delku. You've taken all the command shifts up here while I've been down on the planet. Get some rest. Things might get exciting soon, and I'll need you at your best."

"I can do that. Wake me if you need me."

"Count on it." Nort watched the crew disburse into the ship, some seeking their bunks for much-needed rest and others heading to their posts. He opened a channel to the bridge. "Take us out of orbit and head for the first Gate coordinates."

It was time to try to find the missing deputies.

CHAPTER FOURTEEN

<u>Dervas Cluster, Kolo System, Kolo Three</u>

Charli rolled over and smacked her head on a rock in the darkness. "Fuck me." She rubbed the skin by her ear.

"You all right, Gears?" Lindy asked from where she lay in the cramped cave.

"I can't wait to get out of these damned caverns. I hit the same spot as last time."

Lindy laughed. "You're the one who always sleeps with the wall at your back."

"No one can sneak up behind me that way, Dancer. It was a hard-won life lesson. It's these damned caverns. Two days down here is enough, especially with hardly any gear." They only had what they could carry.

"Trigger is scouting our route ahead." Kit lay next to Charli, her face hidden beneath her broad-brimmed hat. "He'll find us a way out of here. He insists the air is fresher ahead."

"He's been saying that for two days," Charli snapped. "I think he's lying to us."

Kit lifted the edge of her hat with a finger and looked at Charli in the dim light of their single camp lantern. "He's incapable of lying. It's in his core programming as a science and research bot."

"Believe what you want." Charli shifted out from under the rock overhang and started rolling up her blanket. "It's almost morning up above. Let's get moving. Maybe we'll see some daylight before the next sunset."

"Suit yourself." Kit sat up and stretched. "My ship's due back today or tomorrow. It'll lay low and hide until I call it in with a local comm transmission. At least down here, those Wind Rider raiding parties can't find us."

"I still don't understand why they didn't come after us," Lindy muttered. She stuffed her folded mylar reflective blanket into her pack and rolled up the thin pad upon which she'd slept.

"They don't like it underground," Kit explained. "It has to do with their superstitions. They think this is the way to hell. As far as they're concerned, we've probably been consumed by demons."

The bioprospector stood and shouldered her pack, then picked up the camp lantern and clipped it to a D-ring on her pack's strap so it shone forward. She pulled a comm from her belt. "Trigger, I hope you found that entrance you were telling us about last night. Our friends are antsy for the sky."

"There is a seventy-four percent chance we'll find a usable exit today, Kit."

Kit smiled at Charli. "See? The odds are in our favor."

"I'll believe it when I see it." Charli picked up her pack and slid her arms through the straps.

Kit took that as a signal to move. Charli followed, her mood as dark as the cave. Lindy brought up the rear, humming way too cheerfully.

For the next six hours, the three worked their way through the maze, following the fluorescent markers Trigger left while the bot blazed the trail. During their second rest stop, the bot commed with good news.

"Kit, I found an exit."

"Great. How far is it?"

"At your current rate of travel, I estimate no more than an hour."

Kit's eyebrows shot up. "That's pretty close. You must've found it a while ago. Why'd you wait to tell us?"

"It's less than optimal as an egress from the caverns." The bot's near-monotone gave no clue what that meant.

Charli had had enough. She keyed her comm. "What the hell does that mean? Is it a way out or not?"

"It is a way out, Deputy Price. However, it is occupied."

Kit said, "That's good to know. Who or what is in the way?"

"A nest belonging to a large local predator, and not one we have encountered before. It is quite large, with an estimated mass of seven hundred fifty kilos."

Charli frowned. Even in Pricolici form, she'd be hard-pressed to take on anything that big. "What's it doing? Maybe we can wait for it to leave."

Trigger said, "It has not moved since I first passed its lair. When I backtracked, I surmised it was dead. However, it appears to be in a state of deep slumber."

Lindy caught Charli's eye. "If it's in a seasonal hibernation, we might be able to sneak past it. There's a Tardex burrow bear that does that. You can drag it out of its den with a rope, and it won't wake up."

Kit nodded. "Trigger, stay there and monitor the creature. Let us know if its status changes."

"I exist to wait and serve, Kit."

Charli pulled her pack on again. "Let's hurry. If it stays asleep long enough, we can get out of here."

Kit said, "We will keep the same pace. Hurrying is a good way to get someone injured down here. Trigger will tell us if there's any change." She crouched below the cave's roof. "Ready?"

Lindy stood and got in line. "Let's go."

As they worked their way through the winding passages, Charli realized Kit was right about the pace. Several spots required them to belay each other with a rope as they traversed a sheer drop-off.

After an hour and a half of hard climbing and scrambling through the caverns, they caught up with the research bot.

"The creature has not moved since my last report," Trigger told them as they approached. "I detect life signs, but at very depressed levels."

Charli looked up the passage at a narrow gap where it turned to the left. "How far ahead is it?"

"If you go to that bend, you can view the beast."

Always curious, Charli forged past the others and walked up the slight slope to the bend in the trail. The cave narrowed to the point where they'd have to remove their packs and go through sideways.

She craned her neck into the opening to see around the corner and spotted the overlapping armored plates of a huge carapace curled into a circular shape. The beast's bulk almost filled the outer cave. Past the creature, Charli caught a glimpse of blue sky.

Fresh air wafted in and brushed her face. She took a deep breath, savoring the scents of the outside it carried with it. There was a heavy musk on the breeze that must be coming from the sleeping creature.

Charli studied the cave for another minute to determine where they could work their way around the beast. It had curled up in a hollow in the center and spread almost to the walls all the way around.

From what she could see, they could make it most of the way, but there was one part where they'd have to climb over a flared section of the carapace.

Charli pulled back and returned to join Lindy and Kit, who were waiting with Trigger. The bot floated on its grav system, and she got an idea.

"Trigger, how much can you carry?"

"My extending arms and tools can lift several kilograms of items collected for samples."

Charli shook her head. "No, I mean the grav system you use for propulsion and lift."

"If you're inquiring as to whether I can lift you or one of the others, the answer is no. My maximum additional payload is twenty-five kilograms."

Charli took off her pack and rummaged around inside it. "I have some tools in here. Your system might be artificially dampened."

"You are not tinkering with my core systems, Deputy. That is where I draw the line."

"I won't hurt anything. I just want to take a look."

Charli pulled out a folding soft-sided zippered tool kit and took a step in Trigger's direction.

Kit stepped into her path. "Trigger said no. That means I say no. There'll be no tinkering with my bot against its will."

"I'm trying to get us out of here," Charli protested. She fought down the urge to light up her eyes in the darkness. "It won't hurt. I promise."

"No. Think of another way."

Lindy stepped between the two of them. "Let me go take a look. Maybe there's a different solution than having Trigger carry us or our gear out."

Charli backed up a step and took a deep breath. They didn't need to fight while they were trapped here in this cave. They still had to rely on Kit, and it wasn't a good idea to antagonize her.

Kit stepped back but stayed close to the hovering bot.

Lindy went up and took a look at the situation in the outer cave. She wriggled through the narrow gap and disappeared. After several minutes, she returned with a grin on her face.

"I think there's a way Trigger can help us without you having to tinker with anything."

"I told you that I cannot lift any of you."

Lindy shook her head. "No, but can you secure the end of our rope to the large outcropping visible outside the cave entrance?"

"I have the ability to drill an anchor into the rock if that's what you mean."

"Perfect." She turned to Charli and Kit. "We secure the other end of the rope on this end and shinny across commando-style. I used to cross Shipper's Crevasse that way with my friends at home."

Charli considered the plan and nodded. "Good idea, Dancer. I think it'll work."

"I agree." Kit patted Trigger's side. "See? We didn't have to violate my bot."

"I wasn't going to violate anything. I'm an engineer."

Lindy jumped in. "Let's uncoil the rope and find a place to tie it off on this end. Then all Trigger has to do is float through the cave with the other end."

The three followed the bot up the trail to the bend in the passage. Kit used a silent laser drill to bore a hole in the wall two meters from the floor. She pulled out a tube of some type of paste and smeared it on the ridged shaft of a ring bolt.

"This is expansion putty. It'll fill the hole and harden in a few minutes to anchor the bolt in place. We can loop the rope through there."

Lindy held the other end toward Trigger. "Here's your end. Do you need me to tie it to something first?"

"Yes," the bot replied. "Tie it to another bolt like the one Kit used. I have a drill that can secure it in place when I get out there."

Lindy tied the free end of the rope to the other bolt and handed it to an appendage that extended from a compartment in the bot's side.

Trigger floated around the bend while they fed the line after it. They kept enough tension on it so it didn't sag and touch the shell of the sleeping creature. It was unlikely that it could feel a light brush against its thick armor, but why take the chance?

The bot hovered by the exterior outcrop, then drilled the bolt home, securing that end of the rope.

Kit walked to the other end and pulled the line taut before tying it off. Then she plucked at the rope, and it vibrated down its length. She gripped the rope with both hands before picking up her feet and bouncing up and down a few times to test it.

"It'll hold." She used a carabiner to clip her pack to the line, then pointed at the cave's entrance. "We can slide our packs along with us as we go. I'll go first, then Lindy, and finally Charli. Wait until the other is all the way across and unclipped before following."

Charli didn't mind going last. She preferred it. The beast was more likely to awaken with each successive trip, so hers would be the riskiest. Kit gripped the rope with her gloved hands and swung her legs up to cross using the line. Then the woman pulled herself across the open cave until she reached the end. She dropped to the ground and unclipped her pack before waving for Lindy to come.

Lindy's trip was equally uneventful. Then it was Charli's turn. The trip across the rope was harder work than she'd thought it would be, and she was huffing and puffing when she reached the far side. Her arms ached, but her nanocytes would soon deal with the pain and fatigue.

They were silent as they settled their packs on their backs. Then Kit turned to walk down the broad trail. She stopped immediately when a voice called to them from below.

"Halt and do not move! Thou has been right and truly captured."

CHAPTER FIFTEEN

<u>Dervas Cluster, Kolo System</u>

Charli froze and searched for the source of the shout. Two Beorlok warriors stepped from behind rocks fifty meters downslope with their rifles leveled at the three women.

Her free hand hovered by the blaster at her hip. She figured she could peg both before either got off more than one shot.

Kit stopped her. "Hold. Nobody do anything stupid."

Charli hissed, "I can take them."

"Don't shoot them. They're not Wind Riders. Those are Cloud-Bringers. Let me talk to them."

Charli studied the warriors and shook her head. They looked like every other Beorlok warrior she'd encountered. "Suit yourself, but if they so much as twitch those rifles, I'll drop them where they stand."

Kit raised her voice, though she didn't shout. The beast was still sleeping in the cave behind them. "Hold. I am Kit

Bridger. I am honor bound to the son of thy clan leader. Let me show you my parlay totem."

"Thou hast a parlay totem?" the lead warrior asked. His voice dripped disbelief.

"In my pack. Let me show thee. It's in the top pocket." She slowly slipped her arms from the straps and let the pack slide to the ground at her side. She knelt and unbuckled the top flap. "I'm reaching for the totem now."

Kit's hand emerged with a colorfully beaded strip of leather. She stood, holding it high so the Beorloks at the bottom of the hill could see it.

The pair stared at the totem. One leaned close to the other and said something Charli's universal translator couldn't make out. The other's tail swayed from left to right, and then the first's tail dipped behind his back.

The one whose tail had swayed called, "Approach us slowly. Thou wilt not raise thy weapons." They lowered their rifles to point at the ground but kept them at the ready.

Kit looked over her shoulder. "Do as she says. Keep your hands clear of your weapons."

"You're sure?" Charli didn't like appearing to surrender in any situation.

"Their clan is friendly with me. Just stay close and follow my lead." Kit walked down the path, holding the totem in front of her. Charli and Lindy followed.

When the trio reached the Beorlok warriors, Charli got a better look at them. They were pretty banged up. Both had recent injuries, and neither was at a hundred percent. She kept her thoughts to herself. Kit had approached the leader and handed him the parlay totem.

He took it and examined it carefully, turning it over and studying both sides of the beaded strip of leather like he didn't believe it was real. Finally, he passed it to the second warrior.

"Where didst thou acquire the totem? It has the signifier of our clan chief on it. I do not know of any such token being given a Federation interloper."

"I am clan sister to the chief's son Choatan."

The second warrior interjected, "I had heard rumors of his rescue from Star-Current raiders. Was that thy doing?"

"It was," Kit replied. "I helped him escape and took him back to rendezvous in his father's battle sphere. That was where I received that totem and was given permission to prospect in Cloud-Bringer systems."

Powered equipment rumbled farther down the path. The warriors became agitated as they looked in that direction.

Charli said, "You all expecting company, or are those friends of yours?"

"Our ship was shot down by Wind Rider scum. We have been trying to escape them since we landed, but they are coming this way. We must go up and over this ridge." The leader pointed up the slope.

Kit shook her head. "There's nothing up that way but trouble. The only way out is down that way." She pointed in the direction of the sounds. "How many are there? With our aid, can you take them?"

The leader's tail bobbed twice. "There are too many." He held up a four-fingered hand. "There are four fists of Wind-Rider warriors down there, and they have a scout vehicle."

Charli glanced up the hill and smiled. "I have an idea, but you'll have to trust us."

Kit looked at the cave and met the other woman's steady gaze. "You're not thinking what I think you are, are you?"

"Maybe. There's no need for us to get tangled up in a fight when we could have something else do the fighting for us." She waved for the others to follow her up the hill. "Come with me. I'll explain it as we go."

It took them ten minutes to locate hiding places on the slope above the cave's entrance. The Cloud-Bringer leader stood alone on the path outside the entrance in plain view of the trail down the mountain.

A minute later, a hovercart rumbled around the corner. The rattling hum of the device told Charli it had taken some damage at some point. It still worked well enough to wend its way up the trail.

Two Beorlok warriors rode in the front. Another four occupied the open bed in the rear. One manned the heavy blaster mounted on a bar behind the cab. Eight more trekked up the mountain on either side of the vehicle.

One of the walking warriors spotted the Cloud-Bringer. He immediately raised his rifle and fired.

That was the signal. The Cloud-Bringer warrior dodged the incoming fire and ran out of sight on the crest past the cave entrance. This part was crucial. It had to appear to the others that he'd run into the cave, not past it to a hiding place.

The group down the mountain shouted a war cry and charged. The ones on foot outdistanced the slower hovercart. They blindly fired at the retreating warrior, and their shots pocked the cave's opening.

Charli peered through a crack in the boulder behind which she hid with Lindy. Kit crouched in a narrow crack nearby, also watching.

The eight dismounted warriors charged up and over the trail's crest, then stopped and stared into the cave's opening. They stopped shouting their war cries and backed away from the cave's mouth as a group.

Charli waited for an angry roar or a grunt or some noise to indicate that the sleeping beast had awoken, but nothing happened. To her amazement, the dozens of blaster shots had not awakened the creature.

This trap was going to fail unless she did something, so she pulled one of her two grenades off her belt and stepped out from behind the boulder.

Several of the warriors outside the cave spotted movement up the hill and pointed.

Charli ignored the weapons swinging in her direction as she thumbed the activator and threw the thermal grenade at the ledge outside the cave. It bounced once and caromed off the opening before rolling inside.

Seconds later, a blast of heat and fire blew out. The explosion knocked several of the Beorlok warriors down near the entrance.

A groaning snarl emerged from the cave, immediately followed by a huge body covered in armored plates. When the trio had climbed out of the cave, they had not gotten a good look at the creature. It had been curled up in a way that hid its form. Now that she saw it, Charli was glad it hadn't awakened earlier.

It had six short, thick legs that ended in sharp claws that flung divots out of the rocky ledge as it charged. As Charli had hoped, it focused on the nearest possible sources for its interrupted slumber. The enormous mouth opened, and it chomped down on one of the Beorlok warriors who'd been knocked over by the explosion, cutting the warrior in half. The top portion disappeared into the beast's belly.

The Wind Rider warriors forgot about Charli and the Cloud-Bringers they'd been chasing and fired at the imminent danger. Blaster rounds struck the armor around the creature's head, but none penetrated far.

Roaring, the beast tore after the Beorloks as they retreated. After it passed, the only things left were a bloody smear and a few crumpled bodies on the trail.

The gunner in the hovercart tracked it with the blaster and injured one of its six legs. The dragging leg didn't slow the animal much, though. Its momentum carried it downhill on the remaining five appendages.

The last three running warriors barreled past the slow-moving cart and kept going. The driver and front passenger bailed out to follow them. So did the four in the cart's rear.

The gunner remained at his post a second too long. The beast reached the cart as the warrior poured out blaster fire at the monster, then reared and crashed down atop the vehicle. The gunner disappeared with barely enough time to scream.

The animal now moved slower. Those last few blaster rounds had injured it. It trundled down the slope on five legs after the fleeing Beorloks. Every now and then, it defiantly bellowed at them.

Charli let a huge grin cross her face. "That worked even better than I'd expected. I figured we'd have to finish off the rest of the Wind Riders."

The lead Cloud-Bringer stood up from behind his cover. "That creature was fearsome. I believe it will continue the hunt until it's dead or has eaten its fill."

"I think thee is right," Kit agreed. "That should give us a chance to get down the mountain before it returns." She glanced at the warriors. "Is there another path we can take down there?"

"Yes, we saw a side trail on our way up. We can lead thee there."

"Good." Lindy joined Charli near the cave. "I don't think we want to be up here when it comes home."

Kit started down the slope. "I agree. Let's blow this popsicle stand. Those Wind Riders will be back with friends after they escape the creature or kill it."

The two Cloud-Bringers joined Kit in the lead, and Charli and Lindy walked behind them. Trigger, who'd hidden farther uphill, brought up the rear.

Charli checked out the wrecked cart when they got close. She'd hoped it would be salvageable, but it wasn't. The fuel cells had cracked and were leaking fluid. Without the juice to power it, this heap wasn't going anywhere, even if the hoverpanels still worked.

She jogged to catch up with the others, and the five people and the robot moved down the mountain to the relative safety of the secondary trail. Charli hoped it wasn't too far to the plain. Distances in the open like this could be deceiving, and she wasn't an expert on the great outdoors.

CHAPTER SIXTEEN

<u>Dervas Cluster, Kolo System</u>

The small group evaded the Wind Rider patrols they encountered on their way down the mountain. Eventually, they were outside any potential search perimeter. It was helpful to have the Cloud-Bringer warriors along. They knew how to survive in this wilderness almost as well as Kit did, and they provided fresh water and some local game that Charli and Lindy choked down when they stopped for a meal. They had to stretch their field ration supplies as long as possible.

Late on the second day, Trigger gave a soft ping. "Kit, I have a message from *Argos*. The ship Gated back into the system, and it has contacted me for instructions to set down since there are two mid-sized Wind Rider attack spheres in orbit."

"I was afraid of that."

Charli asked, "Can your ship evade them long enough to get down here to pick us up?"

"Probably, if we load up and get out fast enough. It has

stealth systems to shield it from their sensors while it descends to get us."

Trigger pinged again. "Update. Another ship has just arrived in the system. It is an older class of Skaine assault ship, and its transponder reads *Tortu*."

Charli chuckled. "The boss sent Nort out to look for us."

"Who is this 'Nort?' Are they friends?" Kit asked.

"Yeah, he's come to find us. If you can lift us up there, we can go back on his ship."

"We can't get into a fight with the spheres. Will they attack the Wind Riders?" Kit asked.

"I'd say yes," Charli replied. "Especially if the Wind Riders attack first."

"The Wind Riders have no honor," The lead Cloud-Bringer Garwen snapped. "They will attack before asking thy friends their purpose in the system."

Kit smiled, "Good. That will give us a chance to load the ship and get off-planet while the action proceeds."

Lindy protested, "You can't just leave in the middle of a fight. We'll have to help *Tortu* fight the attack spheres."

"*Argos* has no weapons to speak of. It's not a warship; it's a science and research vessel. We have to get off this rock without announcing our departure."

"Wait," Charlie countered. "We can't even tell them we're alive? That's probably why they're here."

"No communications while we're getting away. When we Gate into the Cloud-Bringer clan's system, we can reach out. Until then, we're radio silent."

Kit's steely eyes met Charli's glare without flinching, even when the Were let a little yellow flash in them.

"If you want to stay here and hope they prevail long enough to pick you up, I'll leave you with a comm, and you can call them after we leave." Kit detached a pocket comm from her belt and held it out.

Lindy snorted. "That thing can barely reach orbit. We can't be sure they'd hear us, especially during a fight. All we'd do is bring the Wind Rider Beorloks down on us."

"I think that's the point." Charli snorted. "Fine, Kit. We'll do it your way. I'm not happy about it, but we're using your ship to get out of here, so we'll follow your rules."

Kit nodded. "Trigger, notify *Argos* to wait until the fighting starts, then come in at a tangent to pick us up." She looked around and pointed at a rise a kilometer away. "There. We'll head to that ridge so we can see what's behind us in case there are unfriendly warriors around."

Trigger gave them a play-by-play of the action in near-orbit, as relayed by *Argos*. Both spheres pulled out when *Tortu* appeared and flew toward the assault ship.

The group went up the low hill and parked at the top. From there, they had a good view for several kilometers in all directions. There was no sign of pursuit. It should be a clean LZ.

Charli looked at the sky, hoping Nort and his crew were faring well against the two Beorlok ships. The *Tortu* was more than capable of holding its own. She ought to know since she'd planned the refit, and they'd rebuilt whole sections of the ship from the ground up. The assault ship now had Fleet-class heavy weapons and would be a formidable opponent, even when outnumbered.

As soon as the other ships in the system were in combat

range, *Argos* entered the atmosphere and landed atop the hill beside the group. It was a small scout-class Gate-capable ship with civilian markings and patterns on the hull similar to the beaded totem Kit carried. Charli assumed it made it clear the ship was allied with the Cloud-Bringer clan to those who understood such things.

Kit led them up the deployed ramp into *Argos*. "It's going to be cramped with the five of us plus Trigger. We'll have to sleep in shifts during transit."

"We'll make do," Lindy replied. "Our *Drifter* was a small ship, too."

Kit pointed at the galley. "Garwen, you and Jozawyn buckle into those seats next to the table. There's not enough room for you both in the cockpit. The rest, follow me."

She led them up a narrow passage to the small cockpit. There were two pilot's seats up front and a folding jump seat behind them on the wall by the hatch.

Lindy automatically moved to the folding jump seat, leaving Charli to settle into the co-pilot's chair beside Kit.

Kit adjusted the controls, then, "*Argos*, get us out of here. Take the most direct route to a safe place to Gate out of this system."

"Where would you like to go?" the ship's EI asked.

"Make for the Thursten system. We need to notify Choatan's father about the Wind Rider and Star-Current incursions in this region. This is supposed to be Cloud-Bringer territory."

"I'll make it so, Kit." The ship rumbled as its thrusters lifted it off the hilltop and launched it into the atmosphere.

The battle between *Tortu* and the two Beorlok orbs had

begun. Kit put the tactical display on the forward screen for Charli and Lindy as they made their escape. The assault ship was holding its own and had damaged one of the spheres enough that it had pulled back from the fight.

"Let me send a message just before we Gate out," Charli requested. "We're clear and safely away."

Kit stared at the nav plot and chewed her lower lip. "Fine, but keep it brief, and no details about me or this ship."

"Got it. I can do that." Charli flipped on the comm and selected a channel she knew *Tortu* would be monitoring. "*Tortu,* this is Deputy Price. We're safe on board another ship departing the system. You can stand down and leave."

Nort's voice came back. "Charli? We've been looking for you."

"I know that. Thanks for coming to the rescue. We got another ride to safety, though, and we need to follow up on some things. Tell the marshal we'll be in touch."

Kit gave a thumbs-up to signal that they were at the transit point.

"Nort, I've gotta go. Get out of here, and thanks for the much-needed distraction to aid our escape."

His irritation was clear as he said, "I'll expect a much better explanation than that the next time we meet up. *Tortu* out."

Charli killed the comm as the forward screen showed the Gate opening in front of them. She leaned back as they slid through into the Thursten system. She hated leaving Nort to fight alone, but there were no offensive weapons on this ship. Even defense was sparse. Kit relied on speed and stealth in encounters with unfriendly forces.

She admired the tough and resourceful bioprospector, as much as she hated to admit it. Kit was a tough, no-nonsense individual Charli could count on if they reached the point of becoming friends. That might come in time. They'd have to see how the next few weeks went.

She didn't like heading into a Beorlok clan stronghold without backup. Her experience with the aliens had only involved open antagonism, so she had trouble wrapping her mind around them being anything but adversaries. She didn't trust even Garwen and Jozawyn, with whom she'd traveled for several days, but she had no real choice. They were passengers on the *Argos,* and she and Lindy would have to be ready to escape if Kit ran into unforeseen trouble.

Dervas Cluster, Kolo System, Aboard *Tortu*

Nort cursed as Charli cut the channel off and Gated away. The ship shook under the Beorloks' attack, and he turned his attention away from the long-distance plot that had shown the source of the comm signal.

"Give me some good news, Delku. Apparently, we weren't needed to rescue the missing deputies after all."

"That's not exactly what Deputy Price said, Captain," the first mate replied.

"Don't talk about logic when I'm pissed off." He pointed at the forward tactical display. "Why haven't we destroyed that second sphere yet?"

"Its shifting shield harmonics are making it difficult for our energy weapons to penetrate. We could use another pair of the big missiles, but they are in short supply."

"You're right," Nort told his second. "Save them. Fire another full barrage from the main guns, then bring us around to exit the system."

"We're not going to stay and finish them off?" Delku asked.

"No. We've shot up one of the orbs bad enough that it's a drifting hulk. Let the other lick its wounds and rescue the survivors while we make our way out of this damned system."

The navigator twisted in his seat to face Nort. "Where are we going next?"

"Get us to the closest Gate transit point, then set a course for Tardex. The marshal will want a report, and he owes us supplies and ordinance."

Tortu fired its main guns, scoring scattered hits through the shifting shields of the Beorlok ship. Then it came about and accelerated out-system.

The surviving attack sphere fired a parting shot but didn't follow as the assault ship flew away. Neither ship had the stomach to continue the brutal battle. The remaining orb immediately initiated rescue operations for its sister ship while *Tortu* left the system.

CHAPTER SEVENTEEN

<u>Kuarti System</u>, <u>Omega Station</u>

Remi and Jock watched the video from Thendara three times before either said anything.

After the third time, Remi ran his fingers through his hair. "What is she thinking, sending us this?"

Jock said, "It's not bad, but she could have put a little more feeling into the acting."

"What's her play?" Remi asked. "It's not like she can unpublish what she put out there."

"There's only one way to find out." Jock drew his blaster and checked the charge.

"You want to go rescue her?" Remi shook his head. "No way. I say we let her stay where she is. The Consortium will eventually deal with her. There's no upside."

Jock rolled his eyes. "Why am I the voice of reason all of a sudden? What would the marshal do, Remi? Come on. You're usually the one who convinces me to do the right thing."

Remi stared at the bulkhead opposite where he sat. Eventually, he admitted, "Lobo would tell us to clean up our own mess."

"Exactly." Jock holstered his blaster. "The video's metadata has it coming from a nightclub on the promenade. Shall we visit it this evening and see if we can shake things up a little?"

"They'll be expecting us, you know."

"I know. They also want us to come and rescue her. I don't think they'll offer much resistance once we get there. We just have to put on a good show so it looks convincing to anyone watching from the outside."

Remi considered the possible plays and nodded. "We'll go, but not as marshals. Let's go as the brewmasters. We can take a few bottles of the Special Reserve. These are nightclub owners, and each of those is worth a thousand credits. For two bottles, we can probably get them to hand her over without a fake fight. Then there's no chance of anyone getting hurt by mistake."

Jock frowned and shook his head. "I was looking forward to knocking some heads over this. I won't hit a girl, but I figured I could take it out on those Skaine scumbags."

"I know, buddy, but this is a time for finesse. We don't need any leaked videos of us shooting up a nightclub out there now."

Jock got up. "Fine. I'll go get the Special Reserve boxed up. Meet you by the docking tube after dinner."

Three hours later, the pair strolled down Omega Station's promenade. Jock had the two bottles in a small backpack he'd looped over one shoulder. It didn't take them long to weave through the early evening crowds and locate the club's entrance. A big Leath bouncer stood by the door.

"No weapons allowed inside." The guard pointed at their sidearms.

Jock reached up to tap his badge. "We're the law."

"Not here, you're not." The bouncer crossed his muscular arms and waited.

Remi unbuckled his gun belt and handed it over. "We're here as the brewmasters, dude. Give him your gun."

Jock handed over his gun belt. "I feel naked."

"You can pick these up when you leave." The bouncer went to a panel in the wall and opened it by entering a code on the keypad. The panel popped open, and he stashed the belts inside. He closed the panel and returned to his spot by the door, then waved them inside.

Remi pulled the door open and stepped into the club to the thumping of a heavy electronic dance beat. Jock followed when his wingmate headed for the bar.

The Skaine bartender met them. It was early, and there weren't many patrons yet. "What'll you have?"

"Just the manager, if you don't mind," Jock replied. "We have some business to discuss."

The bartender frowned and shook his head. "The manager's busy."

Remi tapped his credit stick on the bar and sent a generous tip to the bartender.

A device on his wrist pinged, and the bartender's frown turned into a broad smile. "But I'm sure he'll make time for the two of you. Wait here."

The bartender disappeared into the back, and Remi turned to study the dark interior of the club. He didn't want anyone sneaking up on them. He'd given up his main blaster, but both he and Jock had small blasters in ankle holsters. They weren't idiots.

A few minutes later, the bartender returned with a Skaine in a business suit.

"You the manager?" Remi asked.

"I'm his brother. I'm sure I can handle whatever you need to discuss."

Jock pulled one of the bottles of Special Reserve from his pack. "We're the people who make this. We have two bottles with us, but we'll only trade them with the manager."

The brother's eyes widened at the sight of the bottle with the gold foil label. "Is that the real thing?"

"It is, and there's more where that came from," Remi said. "Shall we go back and see your brother now?"

"I don't see why not. You said you have another like it?"

"We do." Jock returned the bottle to the backpack.

"Follow me." The suited Skaine took them around the side of the bar and through an unmarked door. It led to a long hall that passed the kitchen and a staff break room filled with scantily clad male and female servers and ended at a door marked Manager.

The Skaine opened the door and gestured for the pair to enter ahead of him. Another Skaine in a business suit sat behind a large desk in the center of the room. Holomonitors filled the wall to the left, with views of the nightclub on the screens. Remi noted the view of him and Jock from behind, standing in the office, and realized there was a holopickup in the wall above the door. He didn't bother to check.

"My brother had better have a good reason for bringing the two of you back."

"He does." Jock pulled out one of the bottles and set it in the middle of the desk. "You have someone here we'd like to take home with us."

"If it's company you'd like to have, this is more than enough for a private room with one of our servers. They're not allowed to leave the premises, though, for their safety and yours."

Remi was tired of the game the four of them were playing. "Look, you're Ch'An, right?"

The Skaine nodded.

"Then you know who we are, and you know why we're here. I've no doubt you've done your homework, like we did ours. Now, where's Thendara?"

Ch'An smiled and retrieved the bottle from the middle of his desk. He gently laid it on its side in a drawer next to his knee and slid the drawer closed.

"One bottle lets you see her. It'll take the second bottle you brought to take her with you. She's important to some of our business associates, and my brother and I would take big risks if we just let her go with you."

Jock snorted a laugh. "I doubt the Consortium pays much attention to anything you do out here on the ass end of nowhere."

"She is a special case. As I said, I'm willing to deal with a certain amount of difficulty in exchange for the second bottle. You brought it to sweeten the trade, didn't you?"

Remi nodded. "We need to see her first. I'm not paying

for damaged goods. For all we know, she's already escaped."

Ch'An waved at his brother. "Take them to the troublesome female. I'm tired of this whole situation."

Ch'Ar stepped toward the door. "If you'll both follow me."

Remi and Jock followed him back down the hall into the nightclub. There were a few more patrons now, mostly clustered around the bar or sitting on barstools.

Ch'Ar led the deputies across the empty dance floor to an area roped off by a thick velvet-covered chain clipped to two posts on either side of a staircase. A large, muscular human stood guard next to it. When he saw Ch'Ar coming, he unclipped one side and moved the chain for them to pass.

The stairs led to a balcony overlooking the dance floor. There were curtained private booths lining the back wall, and an armed reptilian alien Remi didn't recognize stood by one of the alcoves. He, too, deferred to Ch'Ar when the Skaine approached. He pulled back one side of the curtain to reveal Thendara inside.

"See, she's alive," Ch'Ar stated. "Now, I'll take that second bottle off your hands."

"We'll have a chat with her first," Remi countered. He noted the privacy controls built into the table in the booth, moved the curtain on the opposite side away, and slid in. Jock sat down next to him.

Remi engaged the privacy screen, and an opaque energy field formed just inside the curtains, silencing the pulsing dance music.

"Good. Now we can talk in private."

Thendara fidgeted with her fingers, realized what she was doing, and dropped her hands to her sides. "Are you here to rescue me or gloat? I'd like to know which before I agree to talk to you."

Jock tensed and scowled. He opened his mouth to reply, but Remi laid a hand on his wingmate's arm to silence him. His hotheaded friend wouldn't say anything he wasn't also thinking, but this situation required finesse. They needed to understand why she was working with the Consortium.

"We've brought payment to have them release you to us, but I'll only give it to them after I'm satisfied that we'll get answers to our questions from you."

"What do you want to know?" Thendara asked.

Remi ticked through possible first questions in his mind and settled on one. "Why didn't you just tell us you were in trouble?"

"How did you know?"

Remi smiled. "We're pretty good at reading people. You're not the type to stab someone in the back unless your own back's against the wall. We could have helped you from the start if you'd been open with us."

"Would you? You didn't know me or why I was doing what I did. How do I know you'd have helped?"

Jock blurted, "Because that's what we do! We're with the marshal, and we help people. That means something out here."

Thendara deflated. "I know that now, but I was in too deep by the time I figured out what was going on. I'm sorry."

Remi shook his head. "Sorry's not going to cut it. Maybe it would've before you published your story, but it's caused no end of trouble with our boss and made us all look bad."

Thendara stared at them. "What can I do, then? I can't take the story back. My editor wants more like it. She won't retract what I sent them."

"We'll let the marshal deal with that," Remi said. "You're going to tell us why you're caught up in this mess, and then we'll work with you to resolve the situation. Lobo will want us to clean up this mess before he addresses the larger issue with sentiment in the Federation's core."

Thendara pointed at the privacy shield. "You know they're still listening to what we're saying and maybe recording it too."

"Of course." Remi smiled. "But they're not stupid enough to try to stop us from taking you. Agree to come with us and tell us everything. In exchange, we'll get you out of here, plus we'll permanently clean up your mess with the Consortium."

"They'll never let me out from under their thumbs. They made that very clear. I can at least tell you what I did to get into this mess. I'm not sure I know anything else."

"That'll do for a start. As for getting their claws pried off you, we have a way of dealing with them that makes it unprofitable for them to continue blackmailing people. You'll help us with that, too."

"Fine. I guess I believe you."

Remi nodded. That was good enough for him. He pressed the button that dropped the privacy screen.

He wasn't surprised to find that Ch'Ar had been joined by a pair of Shrillexian bouncers and his brother Ch'An.

Ch'An said, "The price for her release has gone up."

"That wasn't our agreement," Remi protested.

Jock had stood up when the screen went down. He'd palmed the blaster from his ankle holster before he stood. Remi slid out to stand beside his wingmate.

"Agreements change," Ch'An snarled. "We've decided she's more important than before."

Remi waved a hand behind him. "Thendara, stand up. We're leaving."

"What are you going to do?" Ch'An laughed. "You're not armed, and neither of you is up to taking on my bouncers."

Remi glanced at his partner. Jock grinned at him.

Before Ch'An could even flinch, Jock yanked him over to shield the three of them. He pressed the muzzle of his palm blaster to the side of the Skaine's head.

"One of you so much as flinches, and I'll paint the wall with his blue-ass brains."

Ch'An held up a hand, eyes wide with fear. "Do as they say, for the sake of the gods."

The bouncers looked at Ch'Ar, who stood beside them with his mouth hanging open. He finally gathered his wits. "Do as my brother says. Move away from the booth to give them room to exit." He turned to Remi. "We don't want any trouble."

"You should have considered that before you came up here and threatened us. Did you think we were fools?" He shifted his blaster to his other hand, pulled the bottle from the backpack on Jock's shoulder, and set it on the booth's table. "We'll hold to the original bargain. Let's act like none of this unpleasantness ever happened. You let us leave, and we'll release your brother when we're back on board our ship."

"Do as they say, Ch'Ar." Ch'An trembled in Jock's grasp, his head cocked to try to get away from the pistol barrel pressed against it.

The other Skaine and the bouncers backed up, and Jock sidled toward the stairs. Remi hauled Thendara along by the elbow, keeping her behind the hostage.

The bouncer at the bottom of the stairs stood back after Ch'An gasped an order at him, and the four briskly moved across the dance floor toward the exit. As they left, Remi retrieved their pistols from the shocked bouncer outside. A line of partygoers started snapping photos and videos of them as they backed away with Jock still holding Ch'An hostage.

They quickly went back to their ship. When they reached the docking tube, Jock shoved Ch'An away to sprawl on the deck.

"Don't fuck with the marshals. We don't like it." Jock returned his palm blaster to the ankle holster, then buckled on his gun belt. Remi had already donned his.

Ch'An stood and brushed off his knees. "You both are making a mistake. Kidnapping is a crime. My brother and I will press charges against you."

"Try it," Remi growled. "We have the truth on our side. Come after us, and you'll deal with the whole squadron. You won't like it if the rest of our friends come to this station and clean house. Now, get out of here."

They watched the Skaine until he'd turned the corner and disappeared. Remi keyed his comm. "Warren, prep the ship for travel. Inform Station Command we're undocking in fifteen minutes whether we have clearance or not. Tell them it's marshal's business."

"Received. We'll be ready to go in fifteen, Deputy."

Remi waved for Jock to follow, and he escorted Thendara aboard the *Chance*.

CHAPTER EIGHTEEN

<u>Deep Space, Aboard *Warren's Chance*</u>

They'd Gated out of the Kuarti System to a location in deep space to make sure no one was following them. He didn't think the two nightclub owners had that kind of resources, but it was best to be safe. Once they knew it was, Remi and Jock settled in chairs in the galley with Thendara to plan their next steps.

"We can't go back to Tardex without trying to fix this," Remi began.

"I thought you said the marshal would understand?" Thendara asked.

"I said he'd let us fix this ourselves. That's his expectation when something like this crops up. Until then, he won't want to see us." He glanced at his wingmate. "What do you think, Growler?"

"Thendara, how did you get caught up with the Consortium? Tell us exactly what happened."

"I was investigating corruption surrounding the elections and rumors of criminal activity in the government on

Uuru. They caught me breaking into secure planetary files to find proof. At first, I thought I'd just be arrested and was preparing to use my one call to get my editor to bail me out. CFNN has a whole fleet of lawyers to throw at things like that."

Remi nodded. "Except they didn't arrest you. Instead, they took you to see Zarek and his cronies in the Consortium."

"Yes. They had been watching everything I'd done and threatened to blacklist me across the entire frontier if I didn't work for them. I knew I couldn't do my job if they did that, so I agreed to funnel a few puff pieces about Uuru to my editor. It got out of hand, and they had me dead to rights, falsifying stories on their behalf."

"So, they brought you in to try to smear the marshal and the deputies," Jock surmised.

"Pretty much, and I was in too deep to say no. They promised to let me out if I did a good enough job with stories on you all."

Jock sneered. "How'd that work out for you?"

Thendara stared at him but didn't reply.

"Okay, that's not going to get us anywhere," Remi told both of them. "We need to divert to Uuru."

"*Uuru!*" Thendara and Jock shouted in unison.

"Yes, Uuru. It's where all this started, and it's time to take the fight to the Consortium's home base."

"In case I didn't make it clear," Thendara said, "I'm a wanted criminal on Uuru."

Remi replied, "So are we, I think. Your story was amplified there, and we already had issues with the planetary government there from a mission Gears carried out not long ago. They don't like us."

Jock had a grin on his face. "That's all right. We don't like them, either." He added, "It's just crazy enough that it might work. They won't expect us to go there. You thinking we'll go in dark with a spoofed transponder?"

"Yeah. *Warren's Chance* is a normal-looking freighter, so there will be more than a hundred like it in orbit and transiting in and out." Remi tapped the table while he thought. "Warren, do you have any ready covert personas for the ship and you that we could use to go unnoticed in the Uuru System?"

"I have several. Jex created ornate backstories for them, so we appear to be on a regular transit through the area in search of trade opportunities."

"See?" Remi smiled, "We're good to go. Pick one at random, Warren. I'm sure any will do."

"Uh, Deputy Canaleta, you might want to go through them. There are—"

"Just pick one. Jex will have done her due diligence on the back stories."

"As you wish, Deputy."

Remi shrugged. "That wasn't so hard."

Uuru System, Orbiting Uuru Prime

Thendara sat back in the captain's seat with a frown. "This is a bad idea. I don't know the first thing about running a spaceship."

"It'll be fine," Remi assured her. "You just have to

request orbital clearance for the ship and shuttle clearance to Uuru City for your crew."

"I can't believe Jex didn't plan any cover stories with male captains." Jock sounded disgusted.

Warren explained, "Jex set these up with Deputy Price in mind. She probably planned on getting to cover stories with you and the other deputies in the captain's chair later."

"That doesn't do us any good now."

Remi shushed his wingmate. "It'll be fine. Thendara has read the cover file and knows her back story. Besides, the flight control engineer isn't going to ask for her life's history. They're overworked bureaucrats who don't make enough money to take that kind of initiative."

"I don't like my history. Can I change it?"

"No. Jex seeded information about you in multiple databases to help us pass random security checks. Stick with the story."

"But it says I'm a former prostitute. Who comes up with stuff like that?"

Jock snickered.

"It's not funny. It's degrading. You two get to be random crew members. I have to put up a front that's nothing like me."

Remi shot Jock a glare when he laughed. "Just be yourself and remember the key details. No one here knows your cover persona, so don't sweat it."

"Yeah," Jock added. "It's not like you're going to have to pole dance or anything."

Thendara stood up and went up on tiptoes to get in

Jock's face. "If I wasn't a lady and a journalist, I'd kick your ass for saying that."

Remi forced himself between them. He pushed Jock back and nodded for Thendara to sit down. The comm chimed as she sat.

"Just do what we rehearsed." He tried to make his tone soothing and reassuring, but he didn't know if it worked.

Thendara pressed the comm stud on the arm of the chair. "Uh, yes. Uh, hello. I'm Captain Jasmine of the freighter *Glitter Dust*. Can we, uh, park around your planet?"

The face of a bored space traffic controller popped up on the forward screen. "You mean you want an orbital slot, right?"

"Um, yes. An orbital slot for my ship, if you have one."

"I'm sending the coordinates now. Anything else?" The functionary looked up from his screen into the pickup on his end.

Remi waited a few seconds, then prompted, "Captain Jasmine, you wanted us to get shuttle clearance too, right?"

"Oh, that's correct. Uh, can you give me a shuttle pass?"

The controller nodded. "You now have inbound shuttle clearance to the main starport next to Uuru City." The console next to Remi pinged and displayed the instructions.

"Thank you very much." Thendara smiled. "Have a nice day."

"Uuru Control clear." The space traffic controller cut the circuit as he stopped speaking.

"See?" Remi asked. "That wasn't so hard."

"What if someone recognizes me?"

Warren answered that. "They won't. I used an overlay in the video feed."

"An overlay?" she replied. "What did I look like on their end?"

An image of a green-skinned alien female with three breasts barely restrained inside a tight silver bodice laced up from a pair of matching silver pants appeared on the forward screen. The face was Thendara's, but nothing else matched her physique.

"I look like an actress in a bad holodrama."

"I don't know," Jock replied. "I think you look great."

"You would." She glared at Remi. "Do I have to dress like that, with the green makeup and everything?"

"No, of course not. This was just for Traffic Control. You can be a regular crew person on the planet. Jock and I will disguise our faces. I have Warren scouring the planetary databases for facial recognition files with us in them. I'm hoping he can spoof them so they don't pick us up electronically."

"I've almost completed the sweep," the EI reported. "I've found several entries to replace with altered images so far."

"How much longer until we're sure we're safe?" Remi asked.

"Two hours should do it," Warren replied. "It won't help you in really secure locations. Those databases aren't accessible. June might be able to get in if she was here, but I don't have that kind of juice."

"Do your best. If we have to hack a secure location, we'll deal with it on the fly."

Jock bounced on the balls of his feet. "I'm excited to go

undercover again. What's the plan, Six-shooter? You've been quiet about what you want us to do down there."

"I'm playing this by ear. We'll go down and touch base with some covert contacts Jex gave me in the briefing this morning. They should have inside information about where we go next to get Thendara the information she needs."

"The information I need to do what?" Thendara asked.

Remi grinned. "You're going to do the exposé on the Skaine Consortium you originally planned when you came here. We're going to reveal their efforts to prop up the local government and run things behind the scenes."

"What!" Thendara stood up again. "Are you crazy? That was what got me in trouble to begin with."

"It's the only way to clear your name. If you expose the right things, they'll back off. Then, by default, you can clear us."

Thendara asked, "Are you always so optimistic?"

"Sure. Being a pessimist is no way to go through life. Where's the fun in that?"

Jock punctuated his wingmate's words with a broad grin. "Hang with us for a while, and you'll end up being an optimist, too."

"Or dead," Thendara muttered.

CHAPTER NINETEEN

<u>Uuru System, Uuru City Spaceport</u>

Remi stood in the passage leading to the shuttle's cockpit and watched through the forward screens as the warrant officer pilot set it down. He clapped a hand on the pilot's shoulder.

"Good work. Hang here with the shuttle while we go into the city to meet with our contacts, okay?"

"You've got it, Deputy. I have a holonovel I've been meaning to finish anyway." He returned his attention to shutting down the shuttle's systems, and Remi went into the main compartment.

Jock and Thendara were waiting for him. Remi and Jock wore civilian clothes instead of flight suits with the marshal's star emblazoned on them. Remi had his badge in his pocket in case he needed to flash it, but they were undercover.

Jock wore standard-issue spacer coveralls with ample pockets to carry tools and equipment. His pockets bulged, and Remi wondered what his friend had brought along. He carried a blaster in a shoulder holster.

Remi had one too, but it was in its usual spot at his side. The holster hung down to mid-thigh, and a strap secured it in place.

Thendara said, "If this is going to be dangerous, maybe I should have a gun, too."

"No!" Remi and Jock exclaimed in unison.

Remi added, "You have your camera drones. Keep them operating to record whatever we uncover. That's your job for this."

"If you say so. Most people aren't going to let me record them, though."

"You've got a hidden camera on your person, right?" Jock asked.

"Sure, but the best footage is recorded by the drones."

Remi shook his head. "We'll use them if we get a chance, but we hope to keep our efforts here on the down low. Use the secret camera and mic to record for now. There'll be a time later to do a full public recording to wrap this up."

"Not if we get caught."

Jock frowned, "There you go with those negative thoughts. You gotta believe we're going to succeed. That's the secret to our success all these years."

"I'll believe it when I see it. Let's get going." Thendara pointed at the closed ramp at the rear of the shuttle.

Remi pressed the button with his palm. They waited while the ramp slowly dropped to the docking berth's floor. They froze when they saw a line of Uuru security officers standing at the bottom of the ramp. All had their rifles leveled at the deputies and Thendara.

"Don't move, or we'll shoot." The lead officer's voice echoed around the hangar.

Remi extended a hand, palm open. "Easy, easy. There must be some misunderstanding. We're just down on the planet for some simple trading. You must be looking for someone else."

A captain walked into view from behind the line of police, and Remi's confidence shrank. He looked familiar, though Remi couldn't place where he'd seen him before.

"Cut the act, Deputy Canaleta. We've been tracking you since you entered the system. Do you know it's against the law here in the Uuru System to use false transponders and lie to space control officers?"

Before Remi could respond, the captain continued, "It doesn't matter if you did or didn't. Ignorance of the law is no excuse. Now, we can do this the easy way or the hard way. Personally, I'd prefer the hard way. I have a score to settle since you marshals interfered the last time you visited."

"You have me at a disadvantage, Captain. Have we met, and I just don't remember?"

"I'm Captain Bru'Non, Chief Slidel's assistant. When you were flagged entering the system, he took a personal interest in your reasons for sneaking in. I don't suppose you'd care to share what you hoped to accomplish during your visit."

Remi didn't answer. He sent a message to Warren on his neural chip. *Warren, get out of the system now! It's a trap.*

What about you four on the ground? I could send a few squads of Marines down.

No, that would be futile. Get out and tell the marshal what happened. Warrant Officer Shin, can you get into the smuggler's hold and hide there?

"Already removing the hidden panel. Stay safe, Deputy. I'll be your man on the outside. We'll get you out."

The captain got impatient. "Stalling by not answering me won't solve anything. Perhaps we should just start shooting." He parted his lips in a toothy grin.

"No, no." Remi waved his hands. "We will come peacefully."

"Is it just the three of you?" The captain gestured for his team to run up the ramp and surround the trio inside. Their weapons were snatched away, and their hands were manacled behind their backs.

"Yes. I piloted the shuttle down. It's just us."

Thendara glanced toward the cockpit. Remi thought she'd give the pilot up, but she looked away and didn't say anything.

One of the security goons checked the cockpit and came back shaking his head.

Remi let out a long breath. Shin had hidden successfully, so that was taken care of. He was a good Marine. He'd get things ready to escape. Remi and Jock would just have to get away from the security forces. That shouldn't be too hard.

The security officers herded the three to a pair of police hovervans outside the private shuttle hangar. Bru'Non detailed two officers to remain behind and guard the shuttle. The rest pushed their prisoners inside the one outfitted as a paddy wagon. Their manacles were locked to bolts on their seats, and the doors were closed.

Jock leaned across the van to be closer to Remi and Thendara, who were seated side by side opposite him. "We're in pretty deep on this one, Six-shooter. Any idea how we'll get out of this?"

Remi adopted an air of confidence he didn't feel. "We just have to be ready to take advantage of whatever comes our way when it presents itself."

Thendara's eyebrows shot up. "That's it? *That's* your big plan? They're probably going to kill me since I failed to keep publishing trash about you people."

Remi started to answer, but the driver and another guard climbed into the front of the van. The one on the passenger side twisted around and thumped on the metal grate that separated the front from the rear. "No talking back there."

Jock laughed. "What are you going to do about it?"

The guard sneered and pressed a red button on the dash. A jolt of electricity shot from the metal seat into the manacles. Remi's body tensed as the current coursed through him.

The guard released the button. "That's what. Now, shut up."

The van accelerated behind the first van as they left the spaceport. Their lights and sirens blared to clear traffic from the main road outside the port, and they turned onto the highway into Uuru City.

Fifteen minutes later, they reached a side street that wound between tall buildings. The van jolted to a stop.

A large truck and trailer had pulled across the road in

front of them. Both vans had stopped. Captain Bru'Non got out of the front van and shouted at the driver inside the cab of the big truck.

Remi watched the frustrated captain bang on the door for the driver to come down. A soft click drew his attention to the rear of their van. The doors opened as a Noel-ni slipped an electronic lock pick out of her pocket. She held a finger to her mouth to silence them, then passed the device across their manacles.

A quick glance showed that the driver and passenger were intent on the altercation between Bru'Non and the very large and hairy driver climbing down from the truck's cab.

Jock, then Thendara, climbed out the back, followed by Remi. The Noel-ni pointed at a small hovercar at a nearby corner. They ran for the vehicle, and the driver of their van noticed their escape.

"Hey, come back here!" He and the other guard climbed out of the van and fired their blaster pistols at the fleeing prisoners.

Remi dove into the front passenger seat, and Thendara and Jock jumped into the back. The Noel-ni, who was as quick as all her kind, was behind the wheel and had the car moving before Remi shut his door. A blaster bolt glanced off the front of the vehicle as it careened around the corner and merged into the flow of traffic with the hundreds of other hovervehicles.

"Thanks for the rescue," Remi started.

"I'm Makary. Ka'Ahtay told me to watch for you landing at the port and lend a hand if I could."

"I'll have to thank her when I see her." Remi twisted

around to look for pursuit. A cloud of thick black smoke billowed from the alley.

"Don't worry. I put a thermal charge on the paddy wagon's rear hovernode. It was set to go off after we left. They won't back out of that street anytime soon."

"What about your friend with the truck?" Jock asked.

"Eero can take care of himself. He was supposed to run when they noticed you were gone, and he'll take his keys with him. With the truck in front of them, they won't be able to follow until they get a big tow truck to come."

A text message popped up on the screen in the dash of the hovercar. "I'm away. Meet you at the grotto."

"See?" Makary asked. "That was him. He got away clean."

"How'd you know we'd need rescue?"

"After Ka'Ahtay told us you were coming, I had a clerk friend in Chief Slidel's office alert me if your cover got blown. Unfortunately, they spotted you when you entered the system, and they planned to arrest you when you landed."

She shrugged. "After that, it was just a matter of planning where to intercept them on their usual route to the planetary HQ."

"Now what?" Thendara asked. "We're not going to be able to do anything here. They know we're on the planet. That's going to make it much harder to uncover the corruption."

Makary flashed her teeth in a big grin. "That's where we come in. I'm connected with a group that's been trying to wrest control of the government from the Consortium since they took over during the last election. With your help, we might be able to break their hold on things and get the word out about what's going on here."

"We can work on future plans when we're safely hidden," Remi interjected. "I have a pilot hiding in the shuttle at the starport. Can you sneak him out of the hangar and bring him to us?"

"That shouldn't be a problem. We'll have people disguised as regular maintenance crew come by and see if we can free him. Can you contact him?"

Remi nodded. "I have comm contact. Just let me know what you need him to do."

"For now, hunker down and wait. The first order of business is to get you three out of sight. Then we'll go get your pilot."

"Sounds good," Remi agreed. "See, Thendara? I told you we'd figure it out."

"You didn't know this was going to happen. That's not the same as having a plan."

"Coping with the unexpected is half the fun." He smiled at her and settled back in his seat as he considered their next steps. Katy had come through for them again. He owed her a drink the next time they were on the marshals' station.

CHAPTER TWENTY

<u>Dervas Cluster, Thursten System</u>

Argos Gated into a new system. Charli checked the board from her position beside Kit, who had the pilot's chair.

"The Thursten System? If my memory serves me, that's deep inside the Cluster. I didn't think any Federation surveys or ships came this far into Beorlok space."

"They didn't. These systems are all inhabited by Beorlok clans." Kit adjusted their course to a wide loop around the outer system.

"Why not just fly straight in?" Charli asked. "You said these folks were your friends."

"They are, but if there's a clan war brewing, I'll bet there are other hostile ships in the system. I didn't live this long alone out here by diving in without knowing the lay of the land."

"Fair enough." Charli looked back at Lindy, who was seated behind them. "You mind if Dancer here works on tuning your sensors a little. She's good at it, and she might be able to uncover things your ship wouldn't pick up on its own with passive sweeps."

"Sure." Kit smiled. "We're better off being sure before we head in-system."

Lindy moved over to the auxiliary console behind Charli's co-pilot's seat and leaned in to start working on the sensor sweeps. Kit piloted their ship on a broad sweep around the outer system planets, keeping a broad and dense asteroid belt in between themselves and the inner planets until Lindy finished her work with the sensor suite.

"How's it going, Dancer?" Charli looked back over her shoulder after they'd skimmed the outer belt for a few hours.

"It's coming along. I wish I had a covert drone or two to send in-system. That would make this a whole lot easier." She leaned back in the seat and stretched. "Still, this ship has top-notch military-grade sensors aboard. With all this restricted tech on board, I'm surprised you couldn't get the weapons package to go along with it."

"I'm not a soldier," Kit replied. "It also wasn't offered. I asked my benefactors for a fast and stealthy ship that could keep me away from trouble in unfriendly territory. The *Argos* is what they gave me."

"It's a good ship." Charli appreciated the engineering that had gone into its design. Even without the weapons she would have added if it were hers, it was a fine space vessel.

The sensor console pinged. Lindy leaned in to study the screen. "My most recent filter on the sensor feed seems to have worked. It looks like there's a bit of a fight going on around Thursten Two. It's hard to be sure with all the clutter from the asteroid field, but I think there are several Beorlok attack spheres battling it out above the planet."

Charli smiled. Now they were getting somewhere. "Do you think we can slip in and get to the surface without engaging with any other ships?"

"Most of the fight seems to be around a large space station in orbit above a sprawling settlement on the planet."

"That's Misty Station, the Cloud-Bringer orbital platform," Kit explained. "That's where they build their big ships and do most of their trading. It's heavily defended and should be able to fend off most attacks. We need to get past there to the capital city below." She tapped the comm and tried to open a tight beam channel to the planet. After a minute of trying to tune the signal, her shoulders slumped. "I can't get a lock."

"You won't." Lindy shook her head. "The attacking ships are jamming all signals to and from the planet."

"We can't land without contacting them first. They'll shoot us down as soon as we approach."

"Give me a sec. Let me try something." Lindy studied the screen for a few seconds and refined her data several times. "I think we can come in along the outer atmosphere from the side and dip into the planetary gravity well below the orbital station that'll come in under the jamming signals. That assumes the attackers don't just shoot us down when we try. "

Charli frowned. "Between the attacking orbs and your friends on the ground, we're likely to get blown out of the sky before we get close."

Kit held up a data chip between her thumb and forefinger. "I have the proper codes and totems to transmit to the Cloud-Bringers. If you can get us close enough to contact them, they'll provide cover while we come in to land."

"Then I guess we're going in," Charli agreed. "I'll see if I can't get these stealth systems dialed up to eleven. We're going to need every bit of cover we can get to make our way past that battle." She slid off the seat to kneel so she could get at the underside of the co-pilot's panel.

"Don't break anything," Kit warned.

"Relax." Charli grinned and took the access panel off. "I'm just going to tweak a few things. When I'm finished, it'll be better than before. Promise."

Kit shot her a sideways look and turned her attention back to the console in front of her. "*Argos*, access the plotted course sent by Lindy at the sensor panel."

"I have it loaded, Kit," the ship's female EI replied. "Would you like me to change course and follow it into the central system?"

Kit let out a long breath. "This had better work."

Lindy nodded. "It's our best chance if you want to get down to the surface."

"Do it, *Argos*." The prospector leaned forward and hunched over the controls, ready to take over the second she detected trouble.

Lindy went back to refining the data coming in from the sensors as they piloted through the asteroids circling the Thursten System's star. Charli found an access port and plugged a fiberoptic cable into it that was connected to her personal datapad. She needed to see what was going on under the hood with the stealth tech on board, so she took over active control. The systems had previously run on a preloaded template with no input from Kit.

Charli bypassed the lockouts and started tweaking the settings. She wanted to make them accessible from the control panel at the co-pilot's seat. Then, she could use them more effectively and maybe even turn a few into offensive advantages.

She worked for the next two hours while they followed the circuitous course Lindy had laid out. Eventually, she found the code she needed to bypass the deepest layer of the system that sent the controls to the console. She flipped the digital switch.

"Warning." The EI sounded concerned. "Defensive systems have been turned to local control mode. I recommend returning them to automatic settings."

Charli popped up. "Don't worry. That was me."

"Why'd you do that?" Kit asked. "I told you not to break anything."

"I didn't break anything. It's easy to switch it back now that I know how to do it."

"But I won't know how to do it if you're not here."

"I promise I'll turn the automated systems back on after we're down on the planet. This way, we can control how we fight on our way in."

"We're not supposed to fight. This is a science vessel."

Trigger was nestled in an alcove behind Kit. "This is how it starts. I suggest being very careful. Before you know it, she'll have you fighting full-on space battles."

"She will not." Kit's eyes had turned as cold as ice. "*Argos*, stop the ship. Charli, show me exactly how to undo what you just did. We're not going any farther into the system until I know I can fix it."

"Come over here and I'll show you. It's easy." Charli worked hard to keep her voice level and soothing despite wanting to snap at the other woman. It was the scientist's ship. Charli would want to know how to do it if she were in the other woman's position. "Bring your datapad, and I'll load a subroutine on it, so all you have to do is plug in here and run the program."

Teaching Kit how to turn the automated defenses off and on took almost twenty minutes. She went through the process several times before she was satisfied that she understood what to do.

Kit climbed back into her seat at the pilot's console. "Okay, that's actually nifty. I didn't even know I could do that. I always let *Argos* handle those things."

"When you're by yourself, that's probably the best thing. If you have an experienced person to operate the system, you now have options." Charli tightened the toggles on the four corners of the access panel and slid her datapad into the pocket of her flight suit. She sat back down in the co-pilot's chair as she took in their progress. They were flying again. The ship's EI had resumed the course Lindy had laid in.

Charli made several adjustments as they continued into the system. The battle around the station had just become visible on the forward scans. She put the sensor data on the forward viewer. Attack spheres labeled Alpha One and Alpha Two in green as friendly ships battled it out with three others labeled in red as Bogey One, Two, and Three. The station might have been fighting, too. It was hard to tell. Based on the sensor feed, it appeared to have sustained heavy damage.

Kit stared at the reading on the screen. "We're going to sneak past *that*?"

"They're locked on each other," Charli assured her. "They won't even notice us. Probably."

"I heard that last part, Charli."

Lindy sucked in a breath as they curved in on final approach to skim the upper atmosphere and dive when they reached the airspace above the city.

"What do you have, Dancer?"

"Inbound fighters, Gears. Three broke away from the fight and started this way when we started our final approach."

"So much for sneaking in," Charli muttered.

"I hope you two know what you're doing," Kit snapped.

"Don't sweat it, sister." Charli's fingers tapped their way across the console in front of her as she dialed up their defenses, starting with the anti-missile systems and the point-defense lasers. "Dancer, I'm shunting control of the shields to you. Keep them pumped up and angled between us and the fighters until we get into the lower atmosphere."

"On it, Gears."

The fighters came in hot in the trio arrowhead formation she'd seen Beorlok fighters use a dozen times. They each launched one missile at the fleeing science vessel. They must have been down to their last birds. Charli would have fired more if she'd had them.

"Easy-peasy." Charli targeted the inbound birds with a quartet of counter-missiles each. She didn't want to take the chance of one getting through and knocking out any of their shield capacity.

The twelve counter-missiles streaked out of their tubes in *Argos'* sides to intercept the inbound birds. The Beorlok missiles were shifty, as Charli knew all too well. The initial trio of defensive birds lost target lock and zoomed past without their proximity fuses igniting. Charli refined the targeting on the fly so that the final missiles of each group bracketed the inbound birds and blew their charges just as the missiles passed.

All three of the inbound missiles formed a large fireball.

"Here they come," Lindy warned.

The three Beorlok fighters spun at *Argos* in an impossibly tight spiral. They opened up with their blaster cannons at close range, splashing their rounds against the forward shields. Lindy did a good job of compensating by shifting the shields' harmonics to shrug off most of the inbound rounds.

"*Argos*," Lindy informed the EI. "I'm adjusting our course. Engage in evasive maneuver Beta Three on my mark." She watched as the three orbs looped around and came at them from the rear. "*Mark!*"

The ship banked hard to the right and dove into the atmosphere, shedding a trail of fire from the super-heated gases buffeting off the hull. After a minute, they pulled up and bounced forward, effectively skipping across the upper levels of the planet's cocoon of air.

The inbound orbs had to peel off to avoid the super plasma created by Argos' flight.

"Good thinking, Dancer."

"Thanks, but it'll only work once."

"Once might be enough," Kit interjected. "We're close to the point where we can descend to the city."

The ship rocked as inbound fire pounded their rear shields. The orbs weren't done with them yet.

Lindy's fingers played on the sensor console. "Angling shields, but they've split up and are coming in from three directions. This is going to hurt."

Charli showed her teeth and snarled. "Let them come. I've been waiting for this."

While she was playing with the defenses, she'd over-clocked the drivers for the point-defense lasers beyond their intended parameters. If she used them in groups of five or six, they could fire high-powered laser shots that rivaled Lone Wolf fighters' cannons, but only a few times. She'd probably burn out the systems doing it, which she hadn't told Kit when she'd reprogrammed the system. She hadn't been sure she would need to use it.

Only two of the three attacking fighters would come in at the correct angles for the trick to work. She'd hoped to nab all three, but two was better than none.

Charli kept her finger over the icon to fire on the co-pilot's console. She had to let them in very close for this to work.

"Shields at forty percent. *Argos*, prepare to execute evasive maneuver Alpha Two."

"Belay that, *Argos*," Charli snapped. "Hold course."

Kit looked at the two of them. "What the hell are you doing? They're coming right at us."

Charli glanced at Kit, her eyes yellow. "Tell *Argos* to hold course. I have a plan."

Blaster fire poured in, shaking the ship.

"Shields at eighteen percent." Lindy's voice was level despite the seriousness of the situation.

Charli watched the plot until a circle flashed green around two of the fighters. "Now!" She stabbed the fire icon and loosed the synchronized laser clusters.

One of the fighters blew up outright from the powerful burst. The other curved away, shedding plating and life support gases as it passed. The last undamaged fighter flew by before following its lone surviving wingmate.

"Dive into the approach vector now, *Argos*," Lindy ordered. "We're through the battle."

Kit slipped the data chip with the passcodes and totems into the comm slot, and they dipped into the atmosphere on final approach. They'd made it.

CHAPTER TWENTY-ONE

<u>Dervas Cluster, Thursten Two</u>

Charli stood up after the atmospheric buffeting calmed. She needed to stretch after the tense fight they'd just survived. She moved back to stare out at the landscape as they came into the spaceport outside the sprawling city.

After they set down on the landing pad, Kit unbuckled from her seat. "Let me go out there first. There's a protocol to follow."

Charli nodded. "If you say so. We got you here. The rest is up to you."

She and Lindy followed the prospector into the galley. The two Beorlok warriors unbuckled from the benches against the wall.

Kit beckoned to them. "You two better go down the ramp first. I think the people waiting will be more friendly if they see you first."

Charli frowned. "I thought you had friends here."

Kit pulled the leather totem from her pocket. "I do, but I've never been here before. My friend, the son of the

Cloud-Bringer chief, was elsewhere when we met. Don't worry. Just follow my lead, and everything will be fine."

Charli chuckled and nudged Lindy with her elbow. "Sounds like something I would say."

"Yeah, as you make it all up on the fly. I hope she knows what she's doing."

"We'll find out. Stay loose. We'll get through this."

Lindy nodded, and they followed Kit to the main airlock. The two warriors started down the ramp.

When the humans reached the tarmac, the warriors they'd traveled with were in a heated argument with the leader of an armed group of Beorlok warriors.

Two of the local warriors circled around the verbal battle and pointed their rifles at Charli and Lindy. They used the muzzles to gesture the pair over to a spot where Kit stood with her hands in front of her, palms up. A trio of warriors waited with her. The heated discussion was too fast for the translator to pick up more than a word or two.

"Do what Kit's doing." Charli demonstrated by holding her hands out with palms up like the prospector had.

Lindy mimicked the pose.

It took several minutes for the discussion to settle down. The local leader marched over to Kit and the two pilots. "Thou wilt come with me. Thy weapons will be confiscated until thy disposition is settled."

Kit held up the leather totem. "Doesn't this protect us from all this?"

"Thy totem belongs to Choatan. He has fallen into disfavor since the clan war broke out again after his capture. Perhaps it will protect thee and thine. Perhaps not." He pointed at the guards surrounding them. "Bring them!"

A rifle barrel poked Charli in the small of the back, propelling her after the departing officer. She resisted whipping around and teaching the guard some manners. Now was definitely not the time. She could probably take the guards who were here, but then what would they do?

There was a battle going on in space, and they needed to find out what the situation here was. The marshal would want to know, and this was a great chance to learn more about the Beorlok clans and how they operated. Until now, that had been a mystery.

The guards escorted the trio off the spaceport. The two warriors who'd traveled with them had vanished. After they finished arguing with the officer, they'd stayed behind to find their own way to wherever home was. It was best for Charlie and Lindy to do what Kit was doing and follow obediently.

They walked through a bustling city filled with Beorloks, young and old. Many pointed in their direction as they passed, and a buzz of conversation followed them through the streets. She understood. They were the first humans many had ever seen. Some probably hadn't even seen holograms of other beings from the larger galaxy.

After walking for over an hour, they reached a long, winding flight of steps that led up a mountain. Charli tilted her head back and saw tall buildings atop the plateau above. That was probably where the bigwigs lived. Time to see if Kit had the juice she thought she did with the Cloud-Bringer clan.

The climb left Kit and Lindy winded. Charli's

nanocytes kept her muscles oxygenated and moving on the way up. The officer approached a pair of ornately carved doors, drew a dagger from his belt, and used the pommel to pound on one heavy door.

A few seconds later, the doors parted, and the officer waved them through to the open courtyard beyond. A group awaited them at the foot of a tall stone structure—a pre-space-age fortress.

The bent and aged Beorlok at the center of the group leaned on a tall wooden staff with carvings and gold and silver inlays decorating its length. The officer stopped them five meters from the Beorlok dignitaries.

"Great Chieftain, I bring thee the interlopers who landed without permission. They bear the totem of Choatan and request an audience based on that."

"Who bears the totem of my son?"

"I do, Majesty." Kit took a step forward to stand beside the officer. "I have heard many great things about thee from Choatan. He speaks of brave battles and victories for the Cloud-Bringer Clan."

The old chief coughed several times. It took Charli a second to realize that he was laughing. "Thou hath a way with compliments. My son told me about one such as thou who saved him. Were thy companions also part of the rescue?" The chief used the butt of the staff to indicate Charli and Lindy.

"No, but they are my companions. I request their protection under the shield of the totem as well."

"That is unusual, but I suppose thou hast earned a boon of some sort from me. To remain with us, they wilt have to prove themselves worthy."

Kit nodded. "I understand. We appreciate thy generosity, Wise and Merciful One."

Charli thought she was laying it on pretty thick, but it appeared to be working. Kit knew these aliens and Charli did not. She was concerned about the comment about proving themselves, but Kit didn't seem to be bothered by it, so Charli let it pass.

"If it isn't an imposition, Great One, where is thy son? I had hoped to see him here. I have news to share with both him and thee."

"My son took my flagship and left us to investigate a rumor of an attack by our ancient enemies. We are sorely in need of the ship's might now since the cursed Wind Riders have attacked without warning."

"That is what I came to tell thy son and thee."

"Thou knew of this attack before it happened?"

"I may have, Honored One, though only in part. Wind Rider and Star-Current parties attacked us in the Kolo System."

"They have no business in that area. That is our sovereign territory, as settled in a war long ago." The old chief leaned on his staff while he stared into the distance over their heads.

Charli wondered if he was having an episode after more than a minute passed in silence. No one else moved, however, so perhaps this was normal behavior.

When the chief spoke again, it was in a powerful voice that carried through the courtyard. "The war against the Star-Current and Wind Rider clans is renewed. This is not an ordinary raid by dissidents. We must prepare for a greater fight to come. Bring the newcomers to my council chamber. We will discuss this there. I must sit and think about what we are to do."

The chief used his staff to help him walk through the collection of advisors and entered the stone fortress, followed by his retinue. The officer beckoned to the three humans, and they followed the chieftain's group into the fortress.

The ancient structure had high, vaulted ceilings. The central hall inside had several hallways branching off from it. They followed the group through the great hall past a raised carved bench that might have been a throne. Behind the bench was a door that led into a room with a long polished metal table with benches surrounding it.

The chief walked to the far end, handed his staff to one of the followers, and sat on a narrow bench. His long scorpion tail swayed from side to side as the others took their seats on the benches at the sides of the table. Charli, Kit, and Lindy remained standing at the foot of the table with the officer who'd escorted them from the spaceport.

"We must rally our forces." The chieftain's frailty was subsumed by the urgency of the moment. His voice was clear and strong. "My son sought to head off this war but was unsuccessful, and he has left us without a means to retrieve him and his ship. He must have been captured by our enemies."

"If we fight off the attack here," one advisor suggested, "we might have enough forces to mount the rescue of thy son."

"That would leave our home undefended. No, we must find another way to bring him home."

Kit cleared her throat. "What if thy son was rescued by a third party, Great One?"

"Who didst thou have in mind, female?"

"My friends represent a great force of warriors. Perhaps thou hast heard of the marshals?"

A gasp rippled down the table, and all faces swung to stare at Charli and Lindy.

The chief held up a hand to quiet the group. "Thou art the ones who defeated the trap set by the Black Tail clan. Many bards have written great sagas about that fight. There are those who call you our greatest enemy."

Charli stood. She had to say this the right way. "We are deputies with the Tardex marshals. That is true. We are no one's enemies, though, except those who attack innocent settlers seeking to live peacefully beside their neighbors in the Cluster."

"Lies!" A Beorlok wearing ornate robes stood and pointed at Charli. "Surely, Thy Majesty sees through the subterfuge this one perpetrates to cover the taking of systems sacred to all the clans. We should hand them over to the Black Tail clan leader."

Charli didn't like the sound of that. It would be hard to fight free here and get back to the starport. She had to find a way around this.

Lindy must've seen Charli's dilemma. She stood. "Great One, wouldst thou or one of thy advisors explain what makes these systems sacred to your people?"

The one who had accused them of desecration laughed with that coughing sound. "Every child knows of the gas spheres that harken back to the creation of all things. We model our lives around their shape and power."

Charli didn't know what that meant. Luckily, Lindy understood what the translator had missed. The accuser must be the high priest.

"Gas giants? Dost thou refer to the large gas planets that are part of some systems?"

"It matters not what thou callest them, interloper," the priest shot back. "They are sacred to us. Any who inhabit those systems understand what sacrifices must be made to them to remain, or they are infidels."

Charli asked, "What kind of sacrifices are we talking about? Thou dost not sacrifice people to the gas giant planets."

The chief's tail bobbed, silencing the priest before he could speak. "We are not savages, Deputy. We send first fruits of the harvest, and when we enter those systems, we jettison items of great meaning to show that we understand their place in the formation of all we see in the Cluster."

Lindy seemed to get it. "And since the colonists don't observe that practice, they're attacked."

"When the first of thy colonists arrived, they were observed not just failing in their sacrificial duties, but also siphoning gases from the coronas of the sacred planets."

Lindy looked at Charli. "Replenishing fuel for their fusion generators."

Charli nodded and addressed the group. "That was done in ignorance of thy practices. Perhaps we could remedy the oversight and improve their understanding in the future."

The priest's tail jerked in Charli's direction. "It is too late for that. Thy people's failure is evidence of their unworthiness to occupy those holy systems, and all must be eradicated. Great One, this transcends clan politics. It is fundamental to all our beliefs."

All eyes fell on the chieftain. His frailty showed in the droop of his tail. "If only my son were here to advise me at this moment."

Charli saw a chance to win, not just for herself and Lindy but for all the marshals fought for. "What if we rescue thy son so his wise counsel would once again be available to Thy Majesty?"

"Thou canst not promise that. He hath surely been taken to the prison planet of the Star-Current clan."

"Prison breaks are one of our specialties. Let us come up with a plan. I'm confident we can get him out."

"Such a rescue would receive a great reward from my clan and me."

Charli grinned. "Good. Then all we need is a safe way back up past the battle in orbit."

"Sadly, while the attack above is on and the blockade is in place, we are cut off from leaving the system."

Kit stood. "After I complete repairs, I can slip back through in my ship if I have an escort to break through. Then we could rescue thy son."

The chief considered Kit's request. "We have enough firepower in our large spheres to help you get away from the planet. However, we have no pilots to fly the escort ships that would accompany thee. Without them, thy escape attempt would be short-lived."

Charli laughed, and all eyes turned to her. "Well, if all you need are pilots…"

CHAPTER TWENTY-TWO

<u>Dervas Cluster, Thursten Two</u>

Charli helped Lindy pull out the long bench they'd just unbolted from the Beorlok fighter's cockpit. The younger pilot held up a hand to signal a break and wiped her sweaty brow.

"Gears, I know you're a great engineer, but converting these fighters to a configuration we can use to effectively pilot them is a huge task. We don't have the time."

"Don't sweat it, Dancer. I've figured a way around having to fly these using Beorlok controls." She pointed at the datapad plugged into the cockpit's forward console. "That's going to be our secret weapon."

"What is? Your datapad?"

"Yes. It's connected to the *Argos'* EI. The ship has one of the latest models. It has extensive computational ability, and I have it working to create an interface we can use to fly these things."

"If you say so." Lindy took a swig from her water bottle. "We still need a place to sit after we remove these seats."

"That's the easy part. We'll install the extra two acceleration couches from *Argos'* cockpit. They can be reconfigured into seats with enough strength to withstand the G-forces in a fighter's cockpit."

Lindy smiled. "Have you told Kit that you're dismantling her ship yet?"

"I'll save that for last. First, we have to make room for the couches. That means getting these benches out of the fighters."

Lindy clipped the water bottle to her belt and bent down to help wrestle the detached bench out so they could pull it through the open cockpit hatch in the side of the spherical fighter. That took most of the day.

Beorlok ground crews watched the two human females work. Charli had tried to get a few of them to help when they started but was told in no uncertain terms that this was their problem and they would get no assistance. They had been given the fighters, and that was enough.

Charli liked a challenge, but it would have been a huge help to have a Beorlok ship's engineer assist her with the systems integration. When she and Lindy finished, it was time for a meal. They had to return to *Argos* to eat, and that was the next part of their conversion process.

Kit caught them in the middle of removing the second acceleration couch from *Argos*. That immediately set her off.

"What the hell are you doing to my ship?"

"We're making some necessary adjustments," Charli replied. She waved for Lindy to leave with the first section of the chair. "I told you we had to convert the fighters for our use. I even said we'd need *Argos'* help."

"Help from the EI is one thing. This is cannibalizing my ship's galley."

"Don't worry. I'll put it back better than before. Besides, you barely used these seats. You usually travel alone."

Kit's face turned bright red. "That's beside the point. I don't own this ship. It's on loan. How do I explain this to them the next time I check in?"

Charli shrugged and picked up the rear section of the chair she'd just removed. "I can change the angle on the bridge pickups so they don't see the missing seats in the background."

Kit's jaw dropped, and Charli walked out with the last part of the acceleration couch held in front of her. The conversation was over anyway.

She and Lindy worked through the night. The small fighters had cramped cockpits, especially when she considered the size of the Beorlok warriors who piloted them. When they finished bolting the couch into Lindy's ship, Charli checked on the datapad's progress bar to see where the upload stood. It was a major software patch to convert the ships into craft they could fly without much trouble.

Lindy slid to the end of the seat to watch Charli working on the datapad. "So, how is that going to make flying this thing easier?" She pointed at the trigger bar mounted above the forward screen. "I don't have a tail to activate the weapons the way they do."

"That's what the conversion patch is for. I'm setting it up so the entire ship can be controlled using the datapad. No need to use our shorter arms to reach the main controls."

"That'll work?" Lindy asked.

"It should. We're going to do a low-level test flight in atmosphere as soon as I'm finished." Charli made a few adjustments. Lindy watched from the side, asking occasional questions about the process. An hour later, Charli finished and swiped to close the screen. "That should do it. Ready to take one of these babies up?"

Lindy rubbed her hands together. "You bet. Let's get the preflight done."

They worked together to do the standard pre-flight they used for their fighters. Most of the items universally applied. They modified those that didn't.

When they were done, Charli walked over to the Beorlok ground crew that had watched them all day and night. "Who do we need to ask for clearance to take these birds up and test our flight upgrades?"

"Thou must ask the tower controllers for permission." The crew chief's tail pointed across the spaceport at a squat, round tower that looked like a mushroom at the outer edge of the main landing area.

"Thank you." Charli lifted her datapad and tapped into the flight control network. "This is Deputy Marshal Charli Price. I'd like permission to perform a test flight with two of the grounded fighters. Wouldst thou giveth me leave for takeoff?"

"We have been apprised of thy work on the fighters. Thou hast permission to take off and fly south to conduct thy tests over the uninhabited mountains there."

Charli grinned at Lindy and muted the mic. "They don't have much faith in my engineering skills, do they?" She toggled the mic back on. "Very well. We'll lift off in the next ten minutes."

She and Lindy grabbed their helmets and climbed into the converted fighters. The pirated acceleration couches worked well in the oddly configured cockpits. Charli strapped in and settled the helmet on her head. She'd created a secure channel for the two of them so the Beorlok couldn't listen to their conversations.

"Dancer. How do you read?"

"Loud and clear, Gears. You ready for this?"

"Take it slow to start until you get the hang—" She didn't get the rest of the sentence out. Lindy's fighter rocketed up, then whipped south. A sonic boom thumped Charli through the shielding and armor. It must have been deafening outside.

Charli grinned and used her fingertips to manipulate the datapad she'd mounted in front of her. The response was immediate. She created a sonic boom of her own to announce her passage to the mountain range on the southern horizon.

Two hours later, she and Lindy returned to the spaceport. They'd worked out most of the kinks, including lowering the sensitivity of the flight controls using the datapads. Their landing was much more sedate than their departure had been.

She had just set down when Flight Control contacted them on the main channel. "Deputies, flight alert. Three fighters have broken through our defenses above and are entering the atmosphere. Thou must immediately intercept them."

Charli didn't like taking orders from the snooty tower crew, but this was their chance to show off their skills in the new ships. Plus, she knew the Cloud-Bringers didn't have any pilots to defend their city.

"Deputy Price to Capital Control. Can do. Send their position to our screens. We'll take care of the cleanup for you."

Three orange dots appeared on the forward plot. Charli tagged them as Bogeys One through Three. "Dancer, I'm sending you the attack plot. Dial it in and prepare for takeoff."

"This should be fun. Good thing we used the mountain peaks to hone our targeting."

"I told you we couldn't leave any of this to chance. Take off and follow me."

Charli lifted off the landing pad and zoomed across the city at a low altitude. If she and Lindy played this right, the enemy wouldn't pick them up from the ground clutter until it was too late.

"Stick to me and hug the terrain tight, Dancer. These little birds are almost invisible against the mineral-rich rock that makes up most of this area. We'll use that to sneak up on them."

"Can't wait. I've got your six. Dancer out."

The two flitted down an extended ridge that ran east, following the dips and curves of the hills outside the city. The three inbound bogeys looked different on the plot, and Charli queried the sensor interpretation using her datapad's EI.

"Dancer, those birds look different than I've seen before. Is that just the Beorloks' screen and sensor technology?"

"No, Gears. They are a larger class of spherical fighters."

"How much larger?"

"Fifty percent."

Charli considered the implications and made an educated guess. "Dancer, those aren't regular fighters."

"I wondered why they looked different on the viewer."

"I think they're a class of bomber we haven't seen before. That means we have to pop up and engage them early. We can't let them get into range to launch the payload they're carrying."

"What's the plan? We're too far out to launch our missiles if we reveal ourselves now."

"I know," Charli replied. "Can't be helped. We need them to react to us and launch earlier than they'd planned or peel off and make for space and the safety of their ships in the blockade. Follow my lead."

Charli pulled up, again surprised at the responsiveness of the controls on these fighters. No wonder they were so nimble in combat against the squadron in the past. It gave her ideas about how to improve their fighters when she got back.

The inbound bombers reacted to her and Lindy's sudden appearance on the sensors. However, their response was not what Charli expected. They picked up speed and dropped to a lower altitude to meet the incoming fighters.

"Okay, you want to tangle with us? Let's go, bitches." Charli lit up the lead bomber with active sensors and let fly with the three missiles in her racks.

The trio of missiles was followed quickly by three from Lindy's ship, and all six locked onto the lead bogey. It didn't peel off as expected but continued on its nearly linear descent toward the city.

The six missiles got within a klick of the inbound bombers. Then all three bogeys fired counter-missiles and laser clusters. In seconds, all six missiles were destroyed.

"Well, that didn't work," Charli muttered. "We'll have to do this the old-fashioned way. Tuck in tight, Dancer. Remember, you don't have your usual fighter. These things are fragile, and there's no tendelium sheeting to absorb damage."

"Got it, Gears. Let's go get 'em."

Charli used the Beorlok fighters' increased maneuverability to start a corkscrew approach that brought them in at the trio from a forward off-axis angle. The bombers would have to change course to engage with their nose weapons.

She had been sure the new attack would pull them off course, but the three bombers stayed on their track.

"So be it," she grumbled. "Light 'em up, Dancer."

Charlie used a thumb to mash the icon on the datapad's screen. The orb's blaster cannons opened up on the lead bomber, but, to her surprise, the rounds splashed on an energy shield that extended out from the bombers.

"They've got shields!" Lindy shouted when her rounds failed to penetrate.

"I see that, Dancer. Focus your fire on a single point and see if you can overwhelm the local generators. I'll do the same. You gotta applaud them for using the bombers' increased mass to add extra defenses. These fighters are way too fragile for my taste."

"That's not going to help us get to them faster."

Charli shook her head. "Nope, so we'll do what we can with what we have."

She drilled her cannons into a single point on the shields surrounding all three bombers. They must have a harmonic that allowed them to create a contiguous shield around the entire group, which was ingenious.

"Whoop! I'm in!" Lindy shouted. Her fighter's shots had finally broken through. The right forward quadrant of the shields had gone down, and her rounds now pocked the lead bomber's armor.

It maintained course, however. Lindy pulled up as she flew past, then looped around to come back at the same angle. As she went by, a small turret popped up on top of the lead bomber and fired cannon blasts at her.

She didn't have shields, and her ship rocked until she began evasive maneuvers.

Charli saw the rear two bombers deploy their automated turrets and swing them around to aim at her as she flew past. She jerked the controls to the side and dove below them at the last second, avoiding the inbound fire.

"Dancer, damage report."

"I'm okay, Gears. I've lost a little lateral flight control, but I can compensate. Those turrets were a surprise."

"Yeah, it's time we downed these fuckers. They're pissing me off."

They made a broad loop and headed back toward the determined bombers.

"What's the plan?" Lindy asked.

"I show there's still a gap in the shields where you broke through. We'll hit that same area and try to take out the lead bogey."

"We'd better hurry up. They're almost in range of the city."

Charli didn't need the reminder. She dove in, her targeting reticle marking the hole in the shields. She opened up as soon as it was green, drilling her cannons through the gap and ignoring the return fire from the turret guns.

Lindy's guns blazed beside her.

When the lead bomber broke in half and blew up, it caught them both by surprise. The explosion overwhelmed the shields around the inbound trio and washed over the two trailing bombers.

"They're too close," Charli whispered to herself.

Seconds later, the second and then the last of the bombers created spectacular fireballs.

"We must've hit the payload on the leader," Lindy mused.

"Based on the damage it caused and the radius of the blast, we're lucky they didn't drop that on the city." Charli toggled the comm to contact Flight Control. "Starport Control, we're on our way back. We've dealt with the problem."

"We see that. Thou art cleared to land right away. There will be a vehicle waiting for thee. The chief has something to say."

"Received. Gears and Dancer out."

CHAPTER TWENTY-THREE

<u>Uuru System, outside Uuru City</u>

"We're not leaving empty-handed," Remi growled. "We'll stay and get what we came for." He paced to the window and stared at the buildings around them. The rebels' safe house was in a tenement in the roughest section of Uuru City.

Thendara let out an exasperated gasp. "But they know we're here. We're not going to be able to break in anywhere without them knowing. Your ship is gone, so you can't rely on the EI to do your dirty work anymore."

"All the more reason to press forward with our investigation. They'll never see it coming." Remi turned his attention to Jock. "How's the comms hack going, Growler?"

"We haven't given up on it yet." Jock was working in the corner of the tiny apartment with Shin, the Marine pilot. They had partially dismantled a desktop comm unit and were attempting to modify it for secure intersystem communications.

Shin grumbled, "I don't suppose our hosts could've

come up with a model manufactured this century. This one's so old that I'm not sure it can even do what you want it to."

"Have a little faith, Shin," Jock replied. "It's old enough that we can hardwire it the way we need. That's a pro, not a con."

"If you say so." Shin went back to work on the circuit board using a microviewer linked to his datapad.

Thendara shifted in her seat at the small round table in the center of the room. "See? Shin doesn't believe you, either."

The camera hovering over the reporter's shoulder captured everything they did. Remi was confident that the footage would vindicate them after they uncovered the depths of the corruption in Uuru. He saw himself as the rough-and-tumble hero in the holodrama they'd make about his life. This all played into it.

He walked over and leaned on the table opposite Thendara. "After we get that comm unit working, we can get hold of Jex. She'll have a contact here we can trust to get us the information we need."

"What about the resistance folks who freed us? I noticed you didn't ask them for more than a safe place to hide for the time being."

"Makary has her own motives for helping us. They might be in line with what we want to do, but they might not. Jex should have a handle on whether the Noel-ni can be trusted."

"Hey, I think the new jumper worked," Shin snapped a short cable to a circuit board in the main section of the disassembled comm unit. "Try it now with the scrambler you made."

Jock plugged the thumb-sized tube in next to the cable Shin had attached. He pressed the power button and waited for the system to power up and run through its checks.

He gave Remi a thumbs-up and leaned forward to speak into the on-board mic. "Create a secure connection to Outpost Station orbiting in the Tardex system."

The toaster-sized comm unit hummed for a few seconds. Then a voice came from the small speaker in the side. "June speaking. May I ask who is calling?"

Jock gave two thumbs-up. "Mrs. Cleaver, it's Eddie."

"Eddie Haskel, what kind of trouble have you gotten my Wally into now?"

Remi walked over. "I'm fine, Mom. We ran into a problem down here on Uuru that we need some help with."

"What kind of help? When *Warren's Chance* returned without you, we were very worried. Ward is beside himself. He's organizing a rescue mission as we speak."

"Well, stop him. We're safe. We got away from Planetary Security and are in a location where they can't find us."

"I'm not sure, Wally. I know you think you can solve everything on your own, but you and Eddie have gotten in too deep before."

"I promise that we'll call for help if we need a rescue."

June let out a long sigh. "Very well. Is there anything else you need?"

"We need to talk to Jex. Is she available?"

June said, "She's in her lair, trying to connect to everything at once as usual. I'll ping her."

The signal played music in the background.

"The girl from Ipanema goes walking, and…"

Thendara chuckled. "I can't believe your AI has hold music."

"She's very considerate," Remi explained.

The music stopped. June spoke. "Jex, Wally and Eddie are on the line."

"I hope it's important. I'm working on something urgent."

Remi said, "Don't worry, Jex. This is important and also right up your alley. We need a reliable contact here on Uuru to help us get access to Consortium's secure databases."

"Whatever for?" the Ixtali information broker asked. "Those aren't all that easy to get to."

"We have Thendara with us, and she's promised to help us expose the Consortium's corruption of the Uuru government."

Jex chittered in agitation. "She cannot be trusted. Turn her over to Uuru security forces and return home. The marshal is still trying to fix the mess her report on you two caused."

Remi caught Thendara's eye. "She's really sorry and promises to make it right. We can fix this. We just need to turn the tables on the ones who framed her and us."

"I don't have that many people I trust on Uuru anymore. Most have been compromised. There is a human hacker, but she's working for the Consortium on the side, so she might have mixed loyalties."

"Is there anyone else?" Remi asked.

"Not really. As I said, the Consortium knows I'm

working for you full-time now. They've compromised most of my connections."

"Then we'll just have to engage with this lady in 'trust but verify' mode."

The comm unit buzzed, and a string of text scrolled across the small screen on top. Jex said, "I just sent you the last location I have for her. If she's still there, she'll answer this code sequence. Be careful. I don't know how reliable she is."

"Don't worry," Remi replied. "We've got this. Oh, and can you run a check on a Noel-ni named Makary? She's the one who broke us out. She says she's part of an underground movement working to undermine the Consortium's control over the planetary government."

"I know her. She's shifty, but she has no love for the Skaines. If she's on your side, use her as an asset. Just watch your back. She'll have her own agenda."

Remi nodded. "Good to know. Okay, we'll be in touch."

The connection cut off, and the comm unit powered down.

"I told you we could make this work." Remi puffed up his chest for the cameras and struck a pose with his hands on his hips. "Now we get hold of this person Jex knows and start working our way into the Consortium's systems."

"It can't be that easy," Thendara shot back. "If I've learned anything since I opened up this can of worms, something always goes wrong. I thought I had a safe way in too, and look where I ended up."

"You've never worked with the marshals." Jock grinned. "We always find a way, and our favorite thing is messing up the Consortium's plans."

Remi pulled his jacket on. "I've got the address. Let's hit the road. We'll figure out how we approach this lady when we get there."

Thendara muttered something about getting herself killed under her breath but pulled on a hoodie and followed them out. Her hovering camera followed, recording everything.

CHAPTER TWENTY-FOUR

<u>Uuru System, Downtown Uuru City</u>

"This might be harder than I expected." Remi lowered his binocs and handed them to Jock, who was sitting beside him in the beat-up hovervan. "I didn't expect guards on this person. Jex didn't mention that."

Jock stared through binocs and let out a low whistle. "I count three hefty goons on this side of the building. There are probably more inside."

Makary crouched between the two seats. "We can't get into a gunfight with them in the open. The security forces would be on top of us in under a minute down here."

Remi considered the problem and agreed with Makary's assessment, which didn't mean he would give up. "If we can't walk in and talk to her while she's guarded, we'll have to come up with another solution."

Thendara studied the feed from one of the tiny remote surveillance cameras Makary had recovered from their shuttle when she picked up Shin. Its holosignal hovered above the datapad in her lap. "If only we could find a way to make them leave of their own accord."

Remi's held up his index finger. "Thendara, that's a great idea. Makary, can you lay your hands on gear and uniforms for four public works employees?"

"I think so. We have some supporters who work for the city government. Why?"

"I'll tell you while we drive to fetch the gear. We're going to snatch that hacker right out from under those goons' noses."

Six hours later, they parked down the street from the apartment complex where their target lived and worked. All wore uniforms for Uuru City Public Works. The coveralls Remi, Jock, and Makary wore included a hood that could be converted to a modified atmosuit when needed for safety. That was integral to the plan when Remi described what they were going to do to get in and out past the Consortium's guards.

Remi zipped up his coveralls. "Thendara, you need to play up your end of this. Can you do that?"

She frowned as she looked down at the bulky and ill-fitting uniform. "This doesn't even fit." She tugged at the blue shirt, which had bunched up around the waist of the khaki pants.

"It's better if it makes you look frumpy," Jock soothed. "They won't know what you really look like. Just be ready to react after we all go inside."

"I can do what you want me to. I don't think they're going to believe my remote camera is a sensor drone, though."

"Why?" Jock asked. "What does a public works sensor drone look like?"

"How should I know?" the reporter replied.

"That's the point." Remi grinned. "Neither will they. Just go inside, talking out loud to your datapad. It's important that they hear what you're saying as you go past them. Then wait a few minutes inside and out of sight, pull the alarm, and set off the smoke grenade in your bag. We'll take care of the rest."

Makary asked, "What if this hacker doesn't want to leave?"

Remi explained, "I'm betting the presence of guards around her building means she is a prisoner, not a collaborator. If we give her a way out, she'll take it."

"There are a lot of 'ifs' and wagering in that supposition."

Remi nodded. "That's why we're cheating and sneaking in. We're tilting the odds in our favor. At the very least, she'll want to get out of the building during the alarm. We'll assess her reliability after we're safe again."

Jock popped open the rear doors so Thendara could exit the van out of view of the guards in case they were looking this way. She took a deep breath and hopped out, holding her datapad in one hand and the remote camera in another. Once outside, she adjusted the diagonal shoulder strap of the bag that dangled at her waist.

Remi flashed her a smile. "You've got this. Just do it the way we discussed. We'll be right behind you." He pulled the door closed. Thendara crossed the street and hurried down the sidewalk on the opposite side.

The three in the van had moved so they could monitor

her progress. She held up her datapad and started a running conversation with the fake call on the other side.

"Here goes," Remi muttered. They listened via the comm link as she carried on the fake conversation with her dispatcher.

"I'm checking on the gas pressure drop now. There has to be a leak somewhere in this block. Let me go into this building and check the gauges." She walked past the guards standing out front. Their heads turned as she passed, and they followed her with their eyes as she strode into the building. When she was out of sight, one of them shrugged, and they returned their attention to the street outside. She stopped talking after she was inside the building.

They waited to see what she found inside.

A few minutes later, Thendara contacted them on the comm. "I found the apartment. There are two more guards outside the door. I walked by to make sure. I'm calling you from the stairwell on the eighth floor."

"Pull the alarm, then run through the hallway, calling for an evacuation. Direct them all to the north stairwell. We'll meet you on the way up."

A klaxon blared over the comm a few seconds later. Thendara yelled, "It's done. Get in here and bail me out."

"On our way," Jock assured her.

They jumped out of the van and jogged across the street. People were filing through the front doors by the time they arrived.

Remi had flipped up his hood and sealed it closed to obscure his face. The vocal assist built into the suit amplified his voice when he ran up the front steps to the crowd milling outside the building.

"Everyone, please leave the area. There is a gendalazine gas leak inside this building. It's highly explosive. This whole block could go up."

When the milling crowd didn't do anything, Jock yelled, "It's gonna blow! Get outta here!"

That did it. The crowd in the courtyard and on the sidewalk outside ran for cover in both directions, sweeping the Consortium's goons with them.

Remi, Jock, and Makary forced their way in through a side door and headed for the north stairwell. They waited in their suits at the bottom as a steady flow of people came down and ran past them.

Jock continued to urge the evacuees to keep moving.

"Thendara?" Remi commed. "How far away are you?"

"I'm just behind the guards and the hacker, about half a flight up. We just passed the third floor. They have her in tow. You'll see her hugging her datapad to her chest as she comes down."

"Got it. Still just the two guards?"

"That's all I see."

Jock and Makary stood at the bottom of the stairs on either side, hurrying folks along. Remi spotted two Leath thugs bracketing a thin woman with bright blue hair and moved forward, ready to make his move. When the two guards reached the bottom, Makary and Jock stepped behind them. Each held a hand stunner, and they slapped the exposed necks of the two goons with the devices.

The Leaths went rigid when the powerful electrical charges zapped them. A second later, they toppled to the floor inside the door of the stairwell.

Remi moved behind the woman hugging the datapad

and hooked his hand under her arm. "Keep moving. We're here to rescue you."

"What? Who are you?" She struggled to pull her arm free of Remi's grasp.

Jock appeared on her other side. He grabbed her other arm and kept moving with the flow of people making their way outside.

Remi said, "We'll answer your questions when we get away from here. The guards are only out of the way for a short time."

She whipped her head back and forth to look at Remi and Jock. She kept moving, though, and they soon reached the courtyard and then the sidewalk.

Remi and Jock steered their charge down the street to their van. The crowd had thinned, so they were able to move fairly quickly.

Makary ran up next to them and pulled a remote from her pocket. The side door of the hovervan slid open before they arrived.

Remi pointed inside. "Get in. We don't have much time before the authorities arrive."

"Who are you?" the blue-haired woman asked.

"Jex sent us to get you out." Remi pointed into the van again. "Hurry up."

Makary was in the driver's seat and had the van ready to move. Thendara ran up and jumped in. The woman shot one last look up the street at the apartment building, then climbed inside.

Jock jumped in the back, and Remi got in the front passenger seat. "Go. I hear sirens."

They made it through the next intersection just before a

line of security vehicles and emergency response trucks turned the corner and blocked the street.

"Okay, Jex sent you." The blue-haired woman looked around. "That doesn't tell me who you are."

"I'm Deputy Marshal Remi Canaleta. This is my wing-mate, Deputy Jock Batten. That's Thendara, and our driver is Makary."

"I'm Gamal Hancock." She stopped. "Wait, you're Tardex marshals? What the hell are you doing on Uuru?"

"It's a long story," Remi replied. "However, we're here to counter a Consortium plan, and we're hoping you can help us out."

"I'm not sure what I can do, but if it will fuck up the Consortium and that asshole Zarek, I'm in. They've kept me cooped up in that apartment for almost a year, working for them."

Jock grinned. "That's just what we're after."

Makary slowed and pulled into the traffic on a broad thoroughfare.

The van lurched to the right as the vehicle next to them slammed into their side, and Remi looked out the window to see what happened. He pulled back when he saw the blaster pistol aimed at his head from the speeding car beside them.

The round sizzled against the metal frame a few centimeters from Remi's face.

"Shit, they must've seen us drive away. It's the Consortium goons from out front." Remi drew his pistol. "Get us out of this traffic and go somewhere we can lose them." He leaned out the window and fired at the windshield of the other vehicle.

The driver swerved to the side, sideswiping two vehicles to avoid Remi's shots. That allowed Makary to speed up and veer to the left.

"Hold on," the Noel-ni said as she wrenched the van into a narrow alley between two buildings.

Remi looked back. The car that had been following them was caught in the flow of traffic and sped past the alley's entrance.

"They missed the turn. Get us out of here."

"On it." Makary accelerated down the alley. The van plowed through some trash cans and crates before emerging onto a larger street at the other end. She turned left again, then right. They had to get away from the alley and find a place to hide.

"There." Remi pointed at a parking garage. "Go inside. We need to get off the street. This van is too easy to spot. We need another vehicle."

Makary turned into the garage and drove to the second level so they couldn't be seen from the street. She turned off the van after pulling into a corner slot. "I'll call for one of my resistance friends to pick us up. For now, we hunker down and wait."

Jock frowned. "I need to get out of this monkey suit. It's hot as hell in here."

Remi agreed. The uniform coveralls were very uncomfortable. It would be good to get them off while they waited for the ride back to the safe house.

CHAPTER TWENTY-FIVE

Tardex System, Outpost Station

Beau tugged on his flight suit, making sure it looked presentable. Addy had pressed it to get the worst of the wrinkles out, but he wanted to look his best when Jack Sommers arrived. It was the first time he'd hosted his old friend here, and he was nervous about it. Jack had announced the trip without much explanation, which worried Beau. Jack had always been a planner, so it wasn't like him to make a spontaneous trip for no reason.

Beside him, Addy brushed his hand away. "Stop fussing with it, Beau. You look fine."

"Jack's never been out here. I want to make sure everything is up to standards."

"We're not Fleet, Jack. You tell us that all the time. We're marshals, and we have our own way of doing things."

"That's what's gotten us into trouble back in the core. I can't help but wonder if that's why Jack made the trip out here. Maybe he has bad news."

"We're about to find out."

The indicator light on the docking tube connected to the Fleet corvette switched from red to green. The inner doors opened on the station's landing bay.

Admiral Jack Sommers was the first person out of the tube. He wore his uniform, signaling that this was an official trip and not a vacation. He searched the open bay until he spotted Beau and Addy. He nodded at Beau but didn't smile, which the marshal took as an ominous sign.

A tall Yollin stepped through behind Jack. The Yollin wore civilian attire, but the way Jack gestured at him to accompany him showed deference, which bothered Beau. Who was this?

Beau took the initiative and stepped forward. "Jack, it's good to see you again. You remember Addy Hale."

"Yes. Addy, it's good to see you. How are you and your daughter doing?"

"Lindy is a deputy marshal now, and I've taken over as the station's administrator to free Beau up to handle his marshal's duties."

Before he could be introduced, the Yollin stepped up beside Jack. "Those duties are exactly the reason for our visit, Marshal. I'm Ondine Tes from the Federation Inspector General's Office. There have been reports of illegal activity by your deputies in the commission of their duties, and I've been sent to look into those allegations."

The abrasive intrusion irked Beau. "I assure you, my deputies understand their roles and duties very clearly. They don't break the law."

Jack cleared his throat. "What the marshal is trying to say is things are different out here on the frontier. They have to use innovation and creativity to administer justice."

Ondine clacked his mandibles. "You told me that on several occasions during our trip here." The inspector looked around the landing bay. "I assume you have a suitable location for me to begin my questioning. I'm not accustomed to conducting business in exposed public locations."

Beau squeezed his clenched fists at his sides.

Addy must have noticed his anger welling up. "We have nothing to hide, Inspector. If you'll follow me, we can go up to the station's control room, which has a conference table. Up there, we can move forward to help you understand our operations."

Beau nodded in agreement and wordlessly gestured for Addy to lead the way. The inspector followed her. Beau fell in beside his old friend.

He whispered, "A heads-up would've been nice, Jack."

"I was ordered not to warn you. Don't worry; I'll run interference for you as best I can. That's why I insisted on coming along."

The two fell silent. They had reached the bank of elevators that led to the rest of the station. They took one of the cars up to the next level and the control room.

Addy led them inside and pointed at the conference table. "Please, take a seat there. Would you like me to have our cook bring up some food?"

"If you have something better than the standard Fleet fare I suffered through on the way here, that would be appreciated. We will be here a while, and refreshments would be welcome during the questioning."

"I'll get right on it." Addy excused herself with a nod

and left Beau, Jack, and Inspector Tes to take their seats at one end of the table.

The inspector produced a datapad from his briefcase and laid it on the table. He tapped an icon on the device and stated, "I'm recording our proceedings and my interviews as is standard procedure. We'll start with you, Marshal Ward."

"Of course," Beau replied. "I have nothing to hide."

"Everyone has something to hide, Marshal. Making blatantly false statements only serves to make you appear more deceptive to me."

Jack interpreted, "I think what the marshal meant was in regard to your investigation. He wants to assist you in every way. Right, Beau?"

"Of course. Thank you, Admiral Sommers. Please ask your questions. I assume this is about the news story about my deputies. I want to get all this out in the open."

"We'll get to that. However, I'd like to go back a bit before that. Were you aware, Marshal, that the Barrett Corporation is still missing its CEO? They have used the increased publicity surrounding your activities out here on the frontier to ask very pointed questions about your role in Barkley Barrett's disappearance."

The shift in topic surprised Beau, but he quickly recovered. "To the best of my knowledge, Barkley Barrett was alive the last time I saw him or his ship."

"You say that as if you expected him to be dead."

"I only know that he Gated away from a space battle he orchestrated, probably to hide his involvement in illegal human cloning and trafficking. I put all the information I had in my report to the admiral."

"So, you deny the Barrett board of directors' accusation that you murdered Mr. Barrett in a vigilante justice killing?"

"Yes, I do." Beau looked at Jack Sommers. "A little help, Jack?"

"All of the marshal's Fleet reports have been turned over to you, Inspector. His sworn statement is there for you to read regarding the charges leveled against Barkley Barrett and what transpired in the battle during which he disappeared."

The inspector tapped a file on his datapad, and it opened in holographic form over the conference table. "I have it here. It says you appropriated defense forces from other systems to engage in a pitched space battle outside their individual system jurisdictions."

"Out here on the frontier, there is no Fleet to protect us. We all must assist each other when trouble arises. We file mutual aid agreements as part of the official records in each system. I called upon one of those agreements to supplement my squadron of deputies."

"These are the same deputies who engaged in a running gun battle in the capital city on Uuru Prime. We have social media holovids of them commandeering a tour bus and creating a danger to the public during their fight with rogue elements on the planet."

Beau bit back an angry response. This guy was pissing him off. "The key word there is 'rogue.' One of my deputies was captured and held against her will by a local underworld syndicate. We could not rely on local security forces to assist us since they were compromised by the same underworld organization, so we took the initiative and effected a rescue ourselves."

The inspector flipped his fingers through the air, shuffling through the holodocuments. He stopped on one of them and clacked his mandibles twice. "This underworld syndicate you refer to. Would that be the Skaine Consortium you frequently refer to in your reports to Admiral Sommers?"

"It is." Beau waited to see where the inspector was going with this. Surely, he wouldn't support the Consortium's illegal efforts to control the sector.

He did.

"The Consortium is a registered business entity based on Uuru Prime. They have consolidated and diverse associated businesses all over the sector. They also have ties to the Federation's government. I find it hard to believe the organization would stoop to illegal activity when they're so profitable without it."

"You don't know them the way I do, Inspector."

"Indeed." He flipped open another group of holodocuments. "They've lodged no fewer than twenty-seven formal complaints about your interference in their legitimate business practices. The latest has to do with their majority interest in a place called Cloitas Station. Are you familiar with that place?"

Beau nodded. "That is their latest scam."

The inspector glowered at Beau. "What is this scam you allege?"

"They lure unsuspecting people from the crowded core worlds out here to the frontier. They promise them a stake on a new world and sell them the tools to begin anew at exorbitant prices."

"That is not against the law. Are you telling me they've committed fraud against these people? I see no such accusations from you or any of their customers."

"Many of their customers are unfortunately dead or have been captured and cannot complain. The locations they send these people to are deep within an unclaimed sector adjacent to the Federation frontier that is inhabited by a race called the Beorloks. They are extremely aggressive and don't like the colonies springing up in their midst."

"Are the worlds where these colonies," Tes made air quotes, "spring up, as you say it, inhabited?"

"No, but—"

"Then the Consortium is not committing fraud. I reviewed their contracts with colonists before I came out here. The core legal representative from the business concern in question was most helpful when I asked. The agreements are most thorough in their details regarding the dangers of homesteading and colony building outside the borders of the Federation."

"That's all in the small print. Most of the people involved don't even read it. They just want a better life and the opportunities that come with it."

"Ignorance of the law and a legally executed contract is no excuse, Marshal."

Beau had heard enough. He stood. "No, it is not."

"Where are you going?" Tes asked. "I'm not finished with you yet."

"I'm finished with you. You've made up your mind

about what you expect to find out here. Nothing I'm going to say is going to change it. Since that's the case, I have people out there in real trouble, dealing with actual criminals. I don't have time for your legal nitpicking."

Inspector Tes stood, full of bluster. "That legal nitpicking—your words, not mine—is the basis of the law."

"Not out here, it's not. Out here, the marshals represent law and justice. Stay as long as you like. June, our AI, will be happy to get you set up with a room. You're welcome to interview my people, but only when they can make time in their busy schedules."

Tes slammed his balled-up fist on the conference table. "Marshal, if you walk out that door, the report I submit will not be favorable to your operations."

"I'm counting on it. Good day, Inspector."

Beau stopped halfway to the door and nodded at Jack, who'd leaned back and covered his grin with a fake cough. "Addy and I would like to invite you to a private dinner with the two of us. She'll be in touch with the time. It's her idea. See you then."

He left the control room, made a beeline for the elevator bank, and rode down to the landing bay.

Elspeth saw him enter. "Marshal, you look like you're in a hurry. Can I help you?"

"I'm taking one of the ready five fighters out for a quick recon around the system."

"Is there something I need to know about? Should I prep the other fighters?"

"No. I need to clear my head and remind myself who I am and why I came out here. The best place for me to do that is in the cockpit of a fighter."

She nodded. "Take the first in line. I'll alert Keeril that you've taken it out. He'll join you shortly."

"I don't need company," Beau grumbled.

"Your regs state that all pilots will fly with wingmates at all times."

Beau sighed. "Very well. Tell him I'm headed out to circle around Tardex Six. He can catch up if he wants."

"I'll pass that along."

She'd followed him to the side of the fighter. Beau climbed into the cockpit. One of the ground crew techs ran over with his personal helmet. Lobo was stenciled on the front above the visor. He slipped it on and powered up.

Keeril galloped in, waved at Beau, and veered over to the second ready five fighter. Elspeth must have used her neural chip to contact the Yollin pilot when Beau told her what he was doing.

Beau lifted off to hover a meter off the deck and slowly moved toward the energy barrier leading out to space.

The comm chirped in his helmet. "Lobo, give me a second. I'm right behind you."

"Catch up if you want, Legs. I'm taking off. I've got some things to work out."

He shoved the throttle to full and shot through the energy barrier across the bay's wide entrance. He looped around and set a course for the biggest planet in the system, which was currently on the far side of the Tardex star. Let Keeril catch up. In seconds, the fighter was gone.

CHAPTER TWENTY-SIX

<u>Dervas Cluster, Thursten Two</u>

Charli was prepping her fighter for takeoff when her comm chirped.

Kit's voice came over the headset in the Beorlok orb. "I heard back from the Cloud-Bringer chieftain. They're going to fire a barrage at the blockading attack spheres as soon as we're ready to go. That'll be our cue to escape to the outer system."

Charli tapped the key to start her fighter's drive and disconnect from the charging dock at the starport. "Dancer and I will fly close escort out to the Gate point. Hopefully, we will completely escape notice, but if they launch fighters after us, we'll cover you."

"Are you sure using the tractor beam to hold onto your fighters while I Gate out of the system will work?"

"The engineering and physics of it compute fine," Charli replied. "In the practical sense, we won't know until we try. Worst case scenario, you leave the fighters here when you head out to rescue Choatan."

"That would be bad. I can't do this on my own. I'm not even sure we can pull it off with just our group."

"Relax. You have our two Beorlok warrior friends on board. They volunteered to come along."

"It won't be the same as having you two with me. You bring your own brand of luck to the party."

Charli laughed. "I'm so glad you noticed. Don't worry. It'll work. We'll be in our fighters, providing cover in space and on the ground for the rescue. The spies assure us Choatan is being held on a prison asteroid deep in Wind Rider territory. They'll never expect us to rescue him."

Lindy added, "Don't forget. As soon as we get free of the blockade's jammers, you have to send that recorded message to the marshal in Tardex."

"I know. Do you really think he'll agree to come and help break the blockade around Thursten Two?"

"I think so," Charli replied. "We won't know for sure until we ask him. Either way, first things first. We have to rescue the chief's son. Then we'll come back with the cavalry."

There was a long pause before Kit replied. "I just heard from the high command. They're ready for the diversion."

"So are we. Right, Dancer?"

"I've got your six, Gears. Let's break outta here."

Charli lifted the spherical fighter off the tarmac. On the opposite side of *Argos*, Lindy did the same with her fighter. Between them, the research vessel powered up its drive and rose. The nose angled upward, and the ship ascended into the sky. Charli and Lindy took up positions just behind and to either side of the larger ship as they rose through the atmosphere.

"Tell the chief to start the attack. We're ready to break through."

The orbital station and the two Cloud-Bringer battle spheres fired at the ships blockading the system. The light show of the powered weapons and missile explosions would have been fun to watch if it didn't represent so much destruction.

Charli pulled her attention from the display. "Go into stealth mode now, *Argos*. We'll tuck in close and try to slip past their sensor net with you."

Their plan to escape the system was simple. The *Argos* could move through space in a mode that was almost undetectable, but it could not hide in atmosphere. Thus, they hoped the attack would camouflage their departure until they reached space.

The first part of the plan worked according to their expectations. None of the nearby enemy vessels turned their guns on the small ship or the accompanying fighters. The weapons stayed trained on the station and the two big battle spheres.

Charli checked the plot as they slipped past the nearest of the enemy ships without a reaction. "Tuck in a little tighter, Dancer. Let's present as small a profile as possible."

The other fighter moved closer to *Argos*. They were almost past the second layer of the blockade, and there was still no reaction. Charli was about to let out a long breath to release her tension when six red icons separated from one of the enemy attack spheres.

"Bogeys inbound," Lindy reported.

"I see them. There are six, so we need to be careful. Kit, go to full speed. No sense hiding at half-power anymore.

They see us. Head for the Gate point. We'll be there as soon as we can."

"You two can't take on six fighters," Kit protested.

"I have a plan. Now, get going. I can't be worrying about you, too. We'll be there when you're ready to Gate out."

Argos accelerated away.

"Plan B, Dancer. Just like we talked about."

Lindy laughed. "It's so crazy it's gotta work, Gears."

Charli chuckled. The kid had repeated her words to her. She just hoped it wasn't an empty attempt at a justification for insanity.

The two spherical fighters flew at ninety-degree angles from their previous location. After Lindy and Charli split up, the inbound six Beorlok fighters split into two groups of three.

Charli ticked off that step. Part one of their plan was going fine. The next part was the tricky one. She'd had some time to tinker with the Beorlok fighters, and specifically, the targeting and missile evasion system. She'd discovered that the superior missile evasion systems were not automatic. The pilots had to target individual inbound missiles for the countermeasures to work. It was that part Charli counted on working in their favor.

She looped around and dove at the three fighters, then launched the three missiles in her racks. She didn't target the fighters coming at her but used the comm connection she'd created to Lindy's fighter to target the three fighters coming at her wingmate.

She watched for countermeasures targeting them, and a grin spread across her face when the countermeasures failed to work. The missiles weren't target-locked on the nearest fighters, so the electronic spoofing failed to work.

The three missiles flew past the incoming Beorlok fighters. Step two was complete.

As soon as they passed them, Charli performed a one-eighty turn that would have been impossible in her squadron fighter, then gunned her drive and zoomed away from the approaching fighters at full speed.

This third step was key. She had to engage the instinctive chase drive in the other pilots so they'd focus on her escaping fighter and not the threat zooming up behind them.

She kept her eye on the tactical plot. Lindy's three missiles sped after the three fighters trailing Charli as Charli's three missiles chased the other three spheres.

Just before the missiles reached them, the lead Beorlok fighter realized his mistake and juked up and to the left to lose the missile on his tail. His wingmates didn't recognize the threat in time, and both turned into orange fireballs.

The lead fighter spiraled away from the chasing missile as its proximity fuse detonated. The blast must have damaged the drive since its acceleration was halved, and it turned to limp back toward the attack spheres engaged with the Cloud-Bringer defenses.

Charli turned after it, then pulled up. Her missiles had only taken out one of the fighters chasing Lindy. The other two were still on her tail.

"Hang in there, Dancer. Mama Gears is on the way."

"The plan worked. We whittled them down to two operational fighters."

"True. Just keep juking around until I get there."

Charli increased to full speed and raced to her wing-mate's assistance.

Lindy did a fair job of staying out of the pursuing fighters' firing arcs, but she couldn't loop around and turn the tables on them. Every time she tried to get behind one, the other drilled in on her six to chase her off. It was going to take both Charli and Lindy to finish off the final pair of fighters.

Technically, the four were evenly matched since their craft were essentially the same models. Charli might have been able to change that had she had more time to tinker with the spherical fighters, but it was going to come down to the pilots' skills in the cockpit.

In that arena, Charli was willing to bank on herself and Lindy.

Charli flew into the swirling melee around Lindy's fighter. She waited until the last second, then targeted the nearest fighter and loosed her blaster cannons. At this range, the energy rounds blew through its pitiful shields.

The rear half of the orb disintegrated under the concentrated fire. The forward half spun away in a series of tight loops. Charli couldn't tell if the pilot had survived the destruction.

Lindy took advantage of the respite from enemy fire and flipped her fighter end over end to fly at the enemy behind her. She fired her cannons as she charged the trailing ship.

Charli winced. That maneuver might have worked in their up-shielded and armored Lone Wolf Squadron fighters, but in these fragile Beorlok birds, it was nearly suicidal.

It worked. The attacker's forward canopy blew apart, and the rounds roasted the pilot.

Lindy looped away with a whoop over the comm. "Woohoo! Gears, did you see that!"

Charli resisted the urge to chastise her for taking the chance. "Good shooting, Dancer. Now, form up on me, and let's catch up with Kit and *Argos*."

It took the pair an hour to catch up with the nimble science vessel. Kit had almost reached the location from which she was supposed to Gate out, but she slowed to let the two spheres catch up with her.

Kit contacted them when they got closer. "I saw you take on six of the enemy fighters, and I wouldn't have believed you'd survive if I hadn't seen it for myself. How did you do it?"

"Trade secret, I'm afraid," Charli replied. "Right, Dancer?"

"A hundred percent. Don't worry. We're on your side, Kit."

"I'm glad you are after seeing that display of skill and tactics. You two ready to get out of this system for a while?"

"Let us get close enough for the tractor beam to latch on. Then we'll finish up and be on our way."

Argos stopped, which made the close-in maneuver Charli and Lindy had to perform easier. They lined up with the airlock one at a time, and the universal umbilical connected with each fighter in turn, allowing the two women to transfer to the larger ship. After the pilots exited, the tractor beam snugged the fighters against the hull. Automated clamps on the spheres locked to brackets Charli had welded to *Argos* for that purpose.

When she and Lindy were aboard, Kit opened a Gate, and they slid through to a neutral system to plan the next parts of their raid to recover the Cloud-Bringer chief's son.

CHAPTER TWENTY-SEVEN

<u>Dervas Cluster, Approaching the Mahavir System</u>

Charli studied the image on the forward screen. Lindy sat at the console behind her, piloting the drone they'd appropriated from the Beorloks' armory on Thursten Two. Charli had worked her magic and given it stealth capabilities beyond what the Beorloks possessed.

Lindy floated the drone around a large asteroid and steered deeper into the field of orbiting rubble. "I don't see anything in here. We've been looking for four hours."

"Keep looking," Charli directed. "If the intel is accurate, then the facility is out there."

Kit stood behind Charli, hand on the back of the co-pilot's seat. "It has to be there. The old chief's spy network said his son was being held in a prison facility hidden in a former nickel mine in the asteroid field of a Star-Current system. The chief's economic advisors only knew about three. This one has been abandoned for almost a hundred years. It makes the most sense that they'd use this one."

"Pardon my opinion of your Beorlok friends," Charli

sniped. "But I'm not sure I'd call them the most logical race of beings at this end of the galaxy."

Kit shot back, "That's where you're wrong. You're making assumptions based on human nature. The Beorloks do things on behalf of their clans first and themselves second. They don't have our sense of individuality. They find me traveling around the Cluster alone very strange."

Charli laughed. "That makes two of us. I think you're nuts to fly around out here all alone with your prospecting gear."

"It's not that bad." Kit smiled. "I've made some friends and only a few enemies. As long as I'm careful, I am safe enough."

Charli turned around, leaving the piloting of the drone to Lindy. "I consider myself pretty daring, but I'm not sure I'd want to wander around out here on the fringes of nowhere alone."

"I'm not alone. I have Trigger."

"Thank you, Kit," the science bot said. It had settled into its charging station on the far side of the tiny bridge. "The feeling is mutual, I assure you. You have enabled me to see things I never would have encountered in a university lab in the Federation's core."

"Aw, thank you, Trigger. I'm glad you came along for the ride. Though, to be truthful, Dr. Herlanger connected me with the Erwina Group. They're the ones who gave me *Argos* and the resources to acquire Trigger. They sent me to go find new pharma components and sources."

"They sent you to this part of the frontier on your own without any guidance?" Charli found that hard to believe.

"Not at first. Early on, they sent me to settled systems.

When I rebelled against the enviro rules I had to follow while working in the field, they gave me more latitude. When I uncovered a potential cure for Wakemee Fever, they let me go where my nose took me."

The Wakemee Fever outbreak had covered three systems before they controlled it, and that was only through strict quarantine rules. There weren't enough Pod-docs to be everywhere at once, so people had to tough it out. Charli asked, "I read about an experimental drug discovered by a promising Ph.D. student. That was you?"

Kit nodded. "That was me. In the beginning, I discovered a potential material for a gene splice. Others synthesized the drug into a therapeutic state."

"I suppose I need to call you Dr. Bridger."

"Nope. Plain old Kit will do."

"Didn't you get your doctorate after finding the cure? I heard they gave the Federation Science Leadership Award to the team that cured that outbreak."

"I was a little too rough around the edges for the public-facing part of the Erwina Group. They paid me very well and sent me on my way."

"That's horrible!" Lindy protested. "You could be the star of a holodrama with all you must have done to come up with the discovery."

Kit laughed. "I got what I really wanted." She waved a hand around at *Argos'* cockpit. "I got complete autonomy and some of the key upgrades on this ship that enable me to go wherever I want. The stealth systems are military-grade. I have no idea how they got hold of them."

Charli understood. "If there's one thing I've learned from my BFF Katy, it's that everything is available for the right price. You made them enough money to be willing to get you the best."

The board in front of Lindy pinged. She turned away from the conversation to check the notification. "There's an unknown type of transponder signal up ahead. It's coming from a small Beorlok satellite floating in the middle of the asteroid field."

"Let me see it." Kit looked at the main screen, and Lindy put up the newly acquired video.

Kit leaned over the forward console. "Can you zoom in?"

"I'm holding back to make sure no one sees the drone. Usually, a satellite that size has rudimentary sensors."

Charli ordered, "Move closer, Dancer. Slowly."

Lindy edged the surveillance drone closer to the satellite.

Kit smiled. "Stop. That's close enough. We're definitely in the right place. That's a Star-Current warning totem. See the crossed stripes down the length?"

Charli saw them but didn't understand. "And those mean…"

"They don't want people poking around this area. There's only one reason they'd do that at an abandoned mining operation."

Charli saw where she was going. "No need to warn people away unless it's not abandoned."

"Exactly. The prison facility has to be somewhere around here."

"How do we find it?" Lindy asked. "There is a thousand-kilometer field of floating rocks out there. We haven't even covered a quarter yet."

"It has to be close to that totem," Kit mused. "Fly a wide circuit around it to remain undetected. The facility has to be nearby."

Lindy shifted the drone to the right to circle around the totem-decorated satellite. Charli watched the passing space rocks, paying attention to the largest. The mining platform would be situated on a big one.

"Hold." Charli pointed at the left edge of the screen. "There. See it?"

Lindy focused the drone's camera on an oblong hunk of rock. She put a digital measurement scale on the screen to size it.

"One-point-five klicks across," Charli said. "And see that cave on the nearest side? It's way too regular to be natural. That has to be it."

"I'll take the drone in closer and see if I can pick up emissions." Lindy tapped the controls, and the asteroid in the image got larger.

"Careful, Dancer. We don't want them to know we're here. You probably won't pick up any emissions from inside a hollowed-out asteroid. The nickel and iron in the walls will block most transmissions. It's perfect for a secret prison or hideout."

Lindy shrugged. "What do you want me to do?"

Charli narrowed her eyes. "Fly around it at this distance. Let's see if there's another way in on the backside. I wouldn't build something like that without another way out."

Kit nodded. "The Beorloks always have an escape route. There has to be a way to depart besides through the main entrance."

Lindy flew a wide circle around the asteroid's perimeter, but they saw no obvious openings. She took a chance and dipped the drone closer to thoroughly map the surface.

"I see something." Lindy zoomed in on a section of the surface. "See that?"

"What am I looking at?" Charli asked.

"There's a circular crack running around that rocky knob. The diameter is as large as a Beorlok transport sphere. And look next to it. There's a smaller circular depression in the rock that could be a personnel access point."

Charli was impressed. "Good eyes, Dancer."

Lindy beamed at the praise.

Kit studied the area and settled back into the pilot's seat. "There's a long flat spot just south of that area. We can touch down there."

"What if they see us coming?" Lindy asked.

Charli shook her head. "I think they're as blind to the outside as we are to what's inside. They're relying on staying hidden and secret. Besides, the stealth capabilities of this ship are beyond what standard station sensors could pierce. Unless they've got someone on the surface when we set down, we should be fine."

"That's what I'm thinking." Kit took the controls and turned *Argos* in a wide loop to the rear of the prison asteroid. "As long as I have stealth mode on, we should be safe from passive sensors."

Charli was ready to jump in and help if needed. Kit was a good pilot, though. Shortly thereafter, they floated close enough to the surveillance drone to recover it.

"Still no sign they've noticed us," Lindy reported. "No active transmissions or sensor sweeps."

"Good," Kit replied. "Let's land. Then we'll see about opening the back door."

Argos drifted closer. Kit took her time, keeping her thrust to a minimum to ensure they weren't detected. A short time later, they thumped down on the asteroid's surface. The landing gear had to grip the irregular, rocky surface since the asteroid wasn't large enough to produce gravity.

Charli stood and zipped up her flight suit in preparation for converting it to an atmosuit with the helmet. "Let's go check out this back door, shall we?"

Kit slipped into her atmosuit while Charli and Lindy retrieved their helmets. Each also grabbed a blaster rifle to supplement their pistols. Lindy stopped by the airlock with her rifle. Trigger hovered behind her.

Charli nodded at the bot. "He's coming, too?"

"Yes. He'll be handy if we have to hack the security systems to retrieve Choatan."

"Suit yourself. I was going to rely on Lindy and her datapad or me and my pocket tools, but you're right. This is probably better."

Kit smiled. "Of course it is. Let's go."

They stepped into the airlock. After it cycled, they stepped onto the asteroid for the first time. They had to move carefully in the microgravity to avoid bouncing off into space.

Kit pointed them at a knob-like hill about fifty meters from *Argos*. They half-jogged, half-shuffled their way to it across the rugged surface.

Lindy laughed and pointed down. "I told you it didn't look natural." There was a metal hinge attached to the false hill. "I'll bet it's hollow and swings back out of the way when ships fly in or out."

"I think you're right," Charli agreed. "Let's do a circuit and see if we can locate that personnel entrance you spotted earlier."

They found what they were looking for a quarter of the way around the hill—a circular depression about five meters across. Charli crouched to examine it.

"How does it open?" Kit asked. "There should be controls nearby."

Charli bit back a snarl at the obvious question. "I'm looking for them right now. Give me a second. We don't want to bull our way in and alert everyone we're coming." She walked the circular depression as she searched.

Trigger found the controls before she did, hidden on the far side of the depression. The bot extended an appendage and inserted it into a gap in the circle. A one-meter-tall pedestal rose next to the hovering bot. "It's a lift." The bot mechanically interfaced with the pedestal. A thin cover disguised to look like the asteroid's surface slid back and revealed a metal panel beneath. "Step on that circular platform. That is the base. I will activate it to lower you into the complex."

Kit asked, "Can you cover the internal sensors so they don't know it's active inside?"

"Already doing it. This is not my first time helping you break into someplace we didn't belong."

That piqued Charli's interest. There was a story there, but they'd have to wait until later to hear it. Kit had stepped onto the disk. Charli and Lindy joined her, rifles at the ready.

Trigger activated the lift and hovered next to them as the elevator descended into the prison asteroid.

Charli grinned. Now came the fun part.

CHAPTER TWENTY-EIGHT

<u>Dervas Cluster, Mahavir System</u>

After the lift descended into the asteroid, artificial gravity took hold. Charli no longer felt as if she'd accidentally leap too high. After they descended about three meters, a hatch sealed the opening. A hiss of pressurization and the blinking green indicator in her helmet's HUD told her they could unseal their atmosuits.

She left her helmet on her head, but she unsealed the collar of her flight suit and raised the integrated visor. Lindy did the same. Kit had lowered her atmosuit's hood and reached back to free her long ponytail from the back of her suit.

The lift shuddered to a stop, and Charli shouldered her rifle. "Get ready. They could be waiting for us despite Trigger's attempt to cover for us."

"I assure you, Deputy Price, my hack into this prison's system was both complete and secure. Also, I stopped the lift. I am monitoring the internal security cameras throughout the station, and this access point terminates directly across from a guard station. I spoofed the indicator light that would show the lift was descending. We will not, however, be able to exit without being seen. I await your orders, Kit."

Charlie grunted. "It figures. Okay, time for Plan B." She slung the rifle across her shoulders, then scanned the hatch and the overhead above the elevator until she spotted what she needed. "Dancer, give me a boost."

"Why?" Lindy looked up as she moved over next to her wingmate.

"Because engineers are engineers, no matter what species they are." She pointed at the faint outline of a square in a smooth ceiling panel. "That is a maintenance and rescue access hatch. Time to go up and out."

Lindy crouched and cupped her hands into a stirrup. Charli put one foot in and reached up while Lindy lifted.

"Hold me steady." Charli traced the outline with her fingertips until she found one side slightly depressed into the ceiling. She pushed and waited. There was no hiss of escaping atmosphere when it opened. The shaft was pressurized as well. She pushed harder and the panel flipped back, revealing the elevator shaft. She gripped the edge and pulled herself up. When she was on the roof of the car, she reached into the opening.

"Let's go before someone comes along and uses the elevator button down there."

Lindy gripped her wrist, and Charli pulled the other pilot through the opening.

Trigger floated up next. "There is no danger. No one is

aware that the elevator was in motion or has approached the lift console."

"That's good. Move out of the way so I can get your boss." Charli reached down and pulled Kit up. After they were all perched on the roof, she closed the hatch and stood to look around. She spotted what she was looking for five meters up in the side of the shaft—a rectangular gap in the curved side of the shaft.

"That opening is our way out of here." She went over to the wall, where a narrow maintenance ladder ran up and down inside the shaft. It was a reach, but she was able to lean out and grip the rungs as she jumped over.

"What's up there?" Kit asked. "Maybe we should know before we crawl around inside the station."

Trigger floated up to the opening ahead of Charli and illuminated the opening with a blue scanner beam, then trained its light inside. "It is an access tunnel carved into the rock of the asteroid. I do not see where it goes. It's not on the schematics in the main database."

Charli climbed higher to make room for Lindy and Kit on the ladder. "We'll find out. If it's not on the station map, that's even better. They don't know it's here." She reached the opening and entered inside. She had to crawl, but there was enough room for them all after she moved forward.

It got too dark even for her enhanced vision, so she unclipped a headlamp from her belt and clipped it to her helmet. The light played down the tunnel into the distance. That made the going easier. The horizontal tunnel continued for at least a hundred meters. It looked like it ended in a vertical shaft. When she reached the opening, it was only slightly larger than the tunnel, and it only led down.

Charli leaned out and scanned the shaft for a way to descend. "They must have used personal grav lifts to travel up and down this thing. There's no ladder. There is a D-ring bolted next to the tunnel's exit if we had climbing gear."

"I have a coiled safety line in my pack," Kit offered. "How far to the bottom?"

Charli estimated the distance. "About fifty meters."

"I can get us close, but the line's not rated to hold all three of us at once. We'll have to go one at a time." A few seconds later, Lindy tapped Charli's shoulder and passed her a coil of the thin polymer safety line people used to tether an atmosuit to a ship in space. A metal clip terminated both ends. Charli dug into the belt pouch snugged against her back. She had a pair of carabiners she could use to grip the thin line, as well as slow their descent.

She clipped one end of the coil to the D-ring in the wall next to the opening and let the line drop down the shaft. She tried to judge how close to the bottom the end was and figured it was about four meters short.

"There's going to be a drop at the other end. I'll go first." She used the two large carabiners from her belt pouch to create a friction belay system and swung out into the shaft to test it while she kept one hand on the tunnel's lip. It worked.

"When I get down, pull the line back up and slide the line back through the loops in the carabiners to reset it for the next person."

She lowered herself until she reached the clip at the far

end. The drop was more like six meters than the four she'd estimated, but there was no way in except down. She unclipped the bottom carabiner from her belt and hung with her arms outstretched above her for a second before she let go.

Her Wechselbalg muscles helped her withstand the landing, though she tumbled to the side and landed on her shoulder. She stood and rubbed her upper arm while she looked back up the shaft.

"Go ahead and pull the line up, then reset the carabiners. I'll catch you when you reach the bottom."

Lindy went next. It took her a bit to get the hang of the carabiner system to lower herself down, but she soon reached the end.

Lindy let her belt take the weight while she braced her feet against the side of the shaft. "It's a long way down."

"I said I'll catch you, Dancer. Unclip and come down here."

Lindy fiddled with her belt and detached before she could grip the end of the line with her free hand. Her arms flailed, and she fell on Charli.

"Shit," was all Charli got out before Lindy crashed into her outstretched arms. They both tumbled to the floor. This time, Charli landed on her tailbone. She was going to be very sore by the time this mission was over.

Lindy climbed off her and stood. "Sorry, Gears. It was a little tricky to unhook."

Charli got to her feet, ignoring her sore ass. "That's all right. You can help me catch Kit."

The bioprospector came last, with Trigger floating above her as she descended. The experienced adventurer didn't have the problem Lindy had with detaching. She hung down and dropped feet first.

Charli and Lindy caught some of her weight, and her strong legs took the rest. Of the three, Kit's landing was the smoothest.

That done, Charli turned to examine a door in the shaft. It was sealed, which made sense since the tunnel system could open to the vacuum of space at the top of the elevator shaft. A plain metal panel was embedded in the rock wall next to the door.

After studying the rectangular panel for a few seconds, the Were stepped back. "Trigger, there are no controls. Maybe you can figure out how this door opens."

The bot hovered next to the door. After a full minute passed, Trigger extended a mechanical arm and pressed the small panel. With a hiss, the door unsealed and popped open a few centimeters.

"All you had to do was press the button, Deputy Price."

"I see that." Charli flushed, and her face felt hot for a second. Putting aside her embarrassment, she pulled the door open and stepped into a storage space. Several rolling carts and a couple of buckets were scattered around. There was a large sink against one wall and a door centered on another.

"It's a janitor's closet, I think. Come on in." Charli walked across the room to press her ear against the metal door. She didn't hear anything on the far side. She stepped back and waited for the rest of the team.

The others filed into the small room, and Lindy shut the hatch. It sealed with another hiss as the gasket locked back into place.

Kit checked the door. It was unlocked, so she opened it a crack and peered out. After a second, she pressed it closed. "The hallway is empty. Trigger, do you have our location on the schematic of the complex?"

"I do. We are on the detention level, and I have located Choatan's cell."

"What about the cameras outside this room?" Kit asked.

"The corridor is clear of recording devices." Trigger projected a holographic map of the corridors on this level. It showed their position in green and a single red dot at a four-way intersection to the right. "There is a guard patrolling the corridor at the next intersection. He is currently walking away from us. Choatan's cell is marked in yellow." A cell down one of the side corridors glowed yellow.

Kit nodded. "Let's make our move. If we're quiet, we can slip around the guard and turn the corner before he starts back in this direction."

Charli thought they were cutting it close, but it might be their only chance. Besides, a single guard could be dealt with easily enough. She drew her blaster and popped the door open, sliding past Kit to go first. Trigger bobbed along behind her with Kit and Lindy in the rear.

The intersection was only about twenty-five meters away. The guard walked down the corridor on the opposite side of the crossing in the opposite direction at a leisurely pace. Charli raced to the turn and ducked around it just far enough to make room for the others. She peeked around the corner to check on the guard as the bot and her human companions ran down the passage that led away from the intersection.

The guard continued to saunter away from them, his scorpion tail lazily waving left and right. Charli pulled back from the corner. The others had moved toward the holding cell in which they expected to find their target. Hopefully, he was still alive.

CHAPTER TWENTY-NINE

<u>Dervas Cluster, Mahavir Prison Asteroid</u>

Charli checked to make sure the guard was still walking away, then ran after her friends. When she had caught up with the others, Trigger had interfaced with the door controls for the selected cell.

"We have to hurry," the bot stated. "A system notification says an interrogation team is on the way to take him for additional torture and questioning."

Kit slapped her hand on the metal bulkhead. "Then hurry up and get us in. We don't want to have to fight our way out of here."

"Almost there. This encryption is different from the complex's core infrastructure."

Charli raised the rifle barrel to her shoulder, pointed at the overhead. She looked for a place to take cover if anyone came. There wasn't much choice, just narrow alcoves by each cell's entrance. "Dancer, take a position over on the other side. We'll watch the intersection. Shoot first. Don't hesitate."

"Got it." Lindy lifted the rifle to her shoulder and moved to the far side of the corridor. She braced the gun on a vertical post and sighted down the barrel at the intersection.

Anyone who came around that corner was as good as dead. Lindy was a crack shot with that rifle.

The door to the cell finally hissed open. Kit ducked inside while Charli backed up to cover the opening.

"Kit Bridger!" the battered Beorlok prince inside exclaimed. "What art thou doing here?"

"Thy father said thou needed rescuing again. This is getting to be a habit, Choatan."

"I am glad of thy rescue once again, my friend. The clans arrayed against my people have planned a great assault on my system soon. They sought to find out the defense codes to our orbital fortress."

"Then we'd better get you out of here."

Trigger interrupted Kit. "The interrogation team is almost here."

Kit bent and helped the injured prisoner to his feet. "We'll deal with the invasion force after we're out of here." She pulled one of Choatan's arms over her shoulder with one hand and pointed to the exit with the other. "Let's go. Charli, lead the way."

Charli didn't need to be told twice. "Trigger, is there a back way out of here that will avoid the guards and the torture squad?"

"There is, but I didn't mention it because it is dangerous."

Charli checked the intersection, which was still clear. "It can't be more dangerous than running into whoever is coming to retrieve our friend. Lead the way. We can figure out how to protect ourselves when we get there."

"Very well, then follow me." The hovering bot floated away from the intersection at top speed.

The others had to jog to keep up. Charli ducked under the prince's other arm and helped lift him so Kit and Choatan could keep up. Lindy brought up the rear and watched their backs.

Trigger stopped at a blank part of the wall at the end of the corridor, extended an arm, and removed two screws that secured an access panel in place. "Quick, get inside. The interrogators are almost at the cell block."

Charli helped Kit slide Choatan through the gap in the wall, then waited while Kit and Lindy went through. "Go, Trigger. I'll go last."

"I must replace the panel. Go."

Charli nodded and dove into the opening. A crawl space led away from the cell block. Lindy had moved down the passage to a turn about ten meters away. Kit helped Choatan crawl forward. One of his legs was broken, so the going was slow.

Trigger picked up the panel from outside the opening with two mechanical arms, then backed into the crawl space. A third extension came out of Trigger's side, and the bright sparks of arc welding quickly tacked the panel in place. Anyone who tried to follow would need a plasma torch to cut through.

"Good work, Trigger," Charli said.

"I fear we are cut off should we change our mind about this route. I have reservations."

Charli gritted her teeth in frustration. "Yes, yes, it's

dangerous. We heard you the first time. Where do we go from here?"

"Down the passage. It leads to the central reactor system for the complex."

Charli stopped. "Wait, the fusion reactor is down this passage?"

"Yes. That is the danger I spoke of. We must pass hot plasma conduits and open conductors to reach the safest exit point."

Charli resisted the urge to scream at the bot. She looked at the welded panel that would have been their way out if it wasn't closed forever now.

"What's the problem, Gears?" Lindy asked. "It's a maintenance tunnel. There must be a way past all that stuff."

"If we could shut down the reactor, maybe. Without that, this is nearly suicidal."

Lindy cocked her head and grinned at her wingmate. "Only *nearly* suicidal? That doesn't sound too bad."

Charli chuckled. That kid was crazy-reckless sometimes. "I guess we've been through worse. Let's go. We'll figure it out when we get there. I'll take the lead. It is going to take some work to bypass the power systems, if I even can."

Lindy smiled and turned to Kit and Choatan. "Don't worry. My friend has an awesome set of tools on that belt of hers. She'll get us out of here if anyone can."

Charli wasn't as confident, but they didn't have a choice. She led them through the passage as it wound and twisted. Five minutes passed before a distant klaxon blared.

"What's that?" Charli asked.

Trigger responded, "That is the escape alarm. They've discovered that Choatan is missing."

Charli shook her head. "Took them long enough."

"Based on the chatter on the network, there was some confusion about who had custody of him. It seems that there are two competing interrogation teams." Trigger bobbed in place. "They have been taking turns, and one team thought the other had jumped the queue for the prisoner."

"Whatever." Kit waved a hand. "They'll be watching for us now. We need to keep moving."

Charli stared down the long tunnel. In the distance shone the nearly blinding light of open plasma lines. It was about to get very hot in here.

"Let me go and see if there's a shut-off valve. Trigger, you join me."

"Why?" the bot asked.

"You're my thermal shield." Charli crouched and stepped behind the hovering meter-square bot. "Lead the way. I'll crab-walk behind you. That heat is going to build up quickly."

Trigger floated forward, and Charli bent over to keep the bulk of the bot in front of her. The ambient temperature rose as they approached the small, contained sun that was the fusion reactor.

She risked a glance around Trigger to see if she could spot a valve to control the flow. It wouldn't be so bad if she had a thermal suit on. Her atmosuit helped, but not nearly enough.

It took a few seconds of searching the walls before she found what she was looking for. "There. Trigger, see that handle on the left side? That's got to be the flow regulator."

"I read the temperature there at a hundred degrees Celsius, Deputy. Your blood will boil."

"My blood has nanocytes. They'll cool me long enough for the two of us to pull that lever down and shut off the flow."

"My systems will fail if I go much farther." Trigger's complaint fell on deaf ears. They were both in trouble if they didn't shut off the regulator.

"It'll only be hot for a few seconds. Let's get this over with. I promise I'll personally replace any scorched parts when we get out of here."

"You mean, *if* we get out of here, Deputy Price."

Charli ignored the negativity and nudged the bot forward, gritting her teeth against the searing heat. Even through her gloves and the thermal insulation of her suit, the pain from the heat was intense.

Resisting the scream she wanted to loose, along with the urge to change form, Charli ratcheted the lever up and down several times. Down the tunnel, the flow of naked plasma lessened. Her skin was blistering inside her charring suit's arms, but she pumped the lever until the plasma stopped flowing.

It had taken too long, so she had to pry her burned fingers off the lever. She cradled her injured hands to her chest and crouched as she ran back to join the others.

"Good God, Gears. Are you okay?" Lindy stared at the charred remains of her flight suit's forearms and gloves.

"I'll live. My nanocytes cut the pain receptors off from my brain." Charli looked at where the plasma had flowed across the corridor. "We'll give that a minute or two to cool down. Then we have to hurry across before anyone notices we've cut the feed."

Kit asked, "Trigger, after we get through here, how far is it to the elevator back up to our ship?"

"The elevator is guarded, remember? You meant, how far to the janitor's closet, right?"

"No. We'll never get Charli or Choatan up that safety line to the crossing tunnel. We'll have to surprise the guards at the elevator's entrance before they can call for help."

Lindy patted the stock of her rifle. "There are only two. If you two can distract them, I can take them out before they know what hit them."

"What do you think, Trigger?" Kit asked. "Can you manufacture a disturbance on their comm system that would keep them busy for a few seconds?"

"I believe that can be arranged. First, we have to get to them unnoticed."

"One thing at a time." Kit frowned. "Lindy, you help Charli. I'll support Choatan. Let's move."

Charli shrugged off Lindy's hands. "I'm fine." She held up her blackened gloves and flexed her charred fingers. Pink skin showed underneath. "I'm already healing."

"You're lucky." Lindy went after Kit and Choatan. "Stay close."

"Yes, ma'am." Charli snapped a salute and strode after Lindy.

The tunnel skirted the fusion chamber without leading them into any other plasma flows. They soon reached another access panel.

Trigger hovered by the way out. "The passage on the other side is around the corner from the bottom of the elevator shaft."

"We'll have to be quiet while we go through," Kit suggested. "We can't cut our way out."

Charli ambled forward and looked at the inside of the panel where it intersected the wall. The ends of the screws that secured it barely poked through their side of the metal frame. "We can drill these out from this side if Trigger can magnetically secure the panel from falling out into the corridor."

Kit shook her head. "Won't the drill make too much noise?"

"No, Grasshopper. This isn't my first stealth mission. The drill's driver is dampened. It's slower than a regular power drill, too." She fumbled with the tool pouch on her belt, struggling to unzip it with burned fingers.

"Here, let me." Lindy gently pushed her hands away. She opened the pouch and dug inside for a second before she found the tubular driver and the packet of bits. She inserted one and held it up for Charli's approval.

The engineer nodded. "You just need to drill through the thickness of the outer frame. Leave the screw heads in place on the outside so they don't fall out and clatter on the deck."

"I've got this." Lindy moved to the panel and waited until Trigger applied magnetic appendages to the inside of the plate. Then she started on the first of the four screws. It didn't take long to drill all four. She returned the tool to Charli's belt pouch and gripped her rifle.

Trigger floated through the opening, holding the panel

out in front of it. Outside, the bot lowered the panel to the deck. Kit leaned it against the bulkhead and hopped through, followed by Lindy.

The women in the hall helped Charli and Choatan through the hole. The klaxon still blared in the distance, signaling that the jailbreak was still in progress.

"Let's get out of here," Charli growled.

Trigger floated to the right. "This way. I will prepare the distraction."

Lindy followed, and the bot stopped them before an intersection. An appendage pointed to the left and held up two finger-like stubs.

She nodded and brought her rifle up to her shoulder. A second later, a loud squeal of feedback filled the left-hand side of the intersection.

Lindy moved to the corner and took a knee, then fired a pair of silenced double taps.

Charli moved up behind her. Both guards were down with headshots. Damn, that girl was good with a rifle. Her dad would have been proud.

"Let's get on that elevator."

Trigger surged ahead. "It's waiting for us."

The group quickly moved inside the waiting lift. As the doors closed, Charli frowned and looked down at her hands. Her suit's gloves had burned away.

"Uh, we've got a problem."

"What?" Lindy asked.

"Choatan doesn't have an atmosuit, and mine is compromised." She held up her hands.

Kit cursed. "Shit. We'll have to risk moving *Argos* and

connecting a docking tube to the top of the shaft. They might notice it when it gets that close to the entrance."

Charli suggested, "We wait until we're at the top before we move it. Then we'll all pile in and get out of here. If we move fast, we should be able to get away far enough to use your stealth gear to avoid anyone chasing us."

Kit nodded and pulled out her datapad to connect to her ship. The elevator rose until it was just below the hatch at the top of the shaft, and Kit moved *Argos* into place. The maneuver took less than two minutes. The docking tube locked around the top of the shaft, and when the tell-tales on the datapad blinked green, Kit nodded.

Trigger opened the hatch, and the elevator rose into the docking collar.

"Lindy, get to the ship and get ready to fly us out of here," Charli ordered.

Kit snapped back, "That's my ship."

"You need a fighter pilot for what's coming up. I can't fly, and she's damned good. You and I have to help Choatan up into *Argos*."

Kit frowned but finally nodded. "Let's get out of here."

In less than five minutes, they were zooming through the asteroid field. They were well away from the prison asteroid before anyone thought to launch armed shuttles to pursue them. By that time, *Argos* had become a sensor ghost, then disappeared.

They'd made it. Now to contact the marshal. They were going to need help for what came next.

CHAPTER THIRTY

<u>Tardex System, Outpost Station</u>

The incoming call chime woke Beau from a dead sleep. He groaned and rolled over while he reached out to flip on the bedside lamp. "Who in the hell could that be?"

Addy pulled the covers over her shoulder. "It must be important, or June wouldn't have passed it through while you were sleeping."

Beau squinted at the ceiling through the dim light cast by the bedside lamp. "June, who's calling? And can it wait? I'm exhausted from the inspector's week of questions."

"It's Charlene, dear. I told her you were sleeping, but she said it was urgent."

"Fine." Beau flipped the covers back and sat up. He rubbed his eyes. "I'm never getting back to sleep at this point. Might as well get up. Tell Gears I'll take her call in a few minutes in the control room."

"Of course, dear. I'll let her know."

Addy, half-asleep again, muttered, "Don't forget to turn off the light, honey."

Beau pulled on his flight suit and zipped the front. He leaned over and kissed the top of Addy's head, then turned off the light as requested. *This had better be important. It had been a long week.*

As he approached the control room, the door was open, and women's voices came from inside. Beau entered and stopped. June's holographic image hovered over the conference table. She laughed at something Charli had said, then spotted Beau. "Hello, dear. I've been catching up with Charlene and young Lindy. It's good to hear from those ladies. They've been on a jailbreak."

Beau rolled his eyes. *That didn't sound good.* He hoped it was somewhere the inspector wouldn't care about. He didn't think he had any more explanations in him.

"Put them on the main screen at my desk."

Beau sat in his chair, and Charli's image popped up. Lindy was in the pilot's seat behind her on the small bridge of an unfamiliar ship.

"Hello, Lobo. Sorry for the wake-up, but we've got a situation here in the Cluster that needs our intervention. By 'our,' I mean the marshals. A clan war is about to start between key Beorlok tribes, and it could spread like wildfire across the entire sector."

He didn't like the sound of that, but he wasn't sure he could afford to worry about the situation. "Why's that our problem, Gears? Don't we *want* the clans to kill each other off?"

Two new individuals knelt on either side of Charli. One was a human woman. The other was a Beorlok warrior.

Charli said, "Lobo, this is Kit. She's a bioprospector and

was responsible for getting us away from *Drifter's* wreck when the Beorloks were closing in. Her companion is with the Cloud-Bringer Clan."

Beau stated, "I thought all the Beorloks were the same."

Kit jumped in. "There are clans who are not hostile to all settlers, Marshal. I have met some of them, and they don't deserve to die in the coming attack. With the right help, these clans could prove friendly to your Federation's settlements."

The Beorlok spoke next. "I am Choatan, the son of the Cloud-Bringer clan chief. I have heard of thy prowess in battle, Marshal. I most humbly request thy intervention to save my people."

"It's not that simple, Choatan." Beau struggled to adapt to the formal speech of the clans. "Uh, thy people are outside the Federation's boundaries, and we do not have a treaty with any of the Beorlok clans."

Charli interjected, "That's only because we haven't had an in with them. Now we do. Kit knows this clan. This could go a long way to helping us settle the colonists and homesteaders in safe areas away from the aggressive tribal areas."

"I'm not sure we can offer help to anyone in the Dervas Cluster right now. I've got a Federation inspector here performing the investigative version of a colonoscopy. He's looking into everything, thanks to that stupid news article the brewmasters walked into."

"Can't you fix that?" Charli asked, confused. "A news article should be easy to refute."

"You'd think so, but I have discovered otherwise. I have

Six-shooter and Growler working on it, but it's not certain that they'll be successful."

"I hope they resolve it soon, boss. We're going to need the whole squadron for this one. There's a big multi-clan task force gathering to attack Choatan's homeworld as we speak. We don't have much time to save them."

Beau sat back and raked his fingers through his hair. He wished Jack Sommers was awake and listening to this. The admiral would have a better idea of what the inspector would do if Beau gathered his forces and flew off to intervene in a clan war outside the Federation's borders in the middle of an investigation.

"June, rouse Admiral Sommers. Tell him I need to speak to him alone in the control room as soon as he's awake enough to listen." Beau shifted his attention back to the holoscreen. "Charli, I need details on what's coming to attack this potentially friendly clan. I won't commit the marshals to a fight we can't win."

"We can do that, boss." Charli looked at her companions. The warrior's long tail briskly swung back and forth behind him.

Kit Bridger nodded. "I'll get the intelligence from the chief and go over what Choatan learned while he was in captivity. We'll put all of it together and get back to you, Marshal."

"The sooner, the better," Beau replied. "I'll recall the squadron and see if Nort and *Tortu* are available. By the time you find out what we can expect from the invasion fleet, we'll have the team ready to fly."

"Perfect, sir. Thank you." Charli smiled. "I think this is

going to be important for us and the colonists settling here."

The screen went blank, and Beau gathered his thoughts. "June, time to wake everyone up. Tell all the department heads to prepare for a trip to the Dervas Cluster with everything we can muster. Full loadouts for every ship."

"I heard, dear. I thought you were going to wait to talk to Jack."

"It's going to take time to mobilize everyone. Better to have the team ready to go if I decide to pull the trigger. I'll call Nort and find out when his assault ship can be available, too."

"You do that," June replied. "I'll wake the others and tell them to prep for emergency deployment."

Jack Sommers strode into the room, and Beau nodded and smiled. His friend must've already been awake.

"June, wake Aaron and see if he can send up breakfast and anything with caffeine."

"I already woke him, dear. He's on his way with food for both of you." She smiled and nodded a hello to Jack before her holographic image winked out.

Jack laughed. "That AI is among the strangest I've ever met, Beau, and I've met more than a few."

"She gets things done. We couldn't run this place without her."

Jack sat down across from Beau and leaned forward to rest his forearms on the desk. "So, what's important enough to wake an admiral from a sound sleep?"

Beau chuckled. "Admirals get too much sleep. Besides, you got here fast enough that I know you were up."

"True," Jack agreed. "I *was* considering getting back in bed. What's so important it couldn't wait until breakfast?"

"It's got to do with a pending operation and how we deal with the inspector here on the station. It'll be impossible to hide that we're gearing up for something."

"And you want to divert Inspector Tes' attention from what you're planning. That smacks of hiding things, and that's exactly why the guy is here."

Beau sat back. "That's just it, Jack. We can't do our jobs if we're worried about what some bean counter thinks of our choices and methods. We're in the thick of bad things out here, and sometimes, that necessitates cutting corners."

"What kind of corners, Beau? This guy is good at his job. He'll notice if you break the law or play fast and loose with the rules while he's here."

The situation set Beau's mind whirling with different options. Most of the answers were non-starters. However, one popped up that he hadn't considered. "Maybe I've been going about this the wrong way. This inspector has never been in combat, right?"

"Not that I know of." Jack frowned. "What are you up to, Lobo? I don't like that look in your eyes."

"I think it's time we give our inspector friend a look at the kind of action that is required out here on the frontier."

Aaron arrived with their breakfast, and Beau and Jack moved over to the conference table. The station's cook set up the food and drinks from the rolling cart he'd brought.

"I brought a broad selection for you, Marshal. This should hold you while you plan our next mission to save the galaxy."

"Thank you, Aaron. It's not all as dramatic as that."

"It is, sir. Every time you achieve a victory, it passes along a message to the little folks like me out here who are just trying to get along. It tells us to stick it out and stand a little taller, so don't stop now. Get out there and do what you and the others do best."

The young cook nodded to Beau and Jack and left.

Jack loaded a plate with pastries. "I can't get over the devotion your people have for you, Beau. It's inspiring. If I'd known you had that kind of leadership ability, I'd have promoted you higher than lieutenant commander in the Fleet before I ever thought to send you out here."

"Good thing you didn't. If you had, I might not have met all these fine people. I'm as devoted to them as they are to me. We're a team, Jack. No, I take that back. We're a family, and everyone in it knows they're part of a whole that makes this corner of the universe a safer place. I'd forgotten about that in the face of that investigator's questions. He made me forget what I love most about being out here."

Jack spoke around a mouthful of masticated dough. "You're committed to bringing the investigator along for this next excursion?"

"Yep. You wanna come too?"

"The Fleet doesn't have an official presence out here, Beau. You know that."

"Then join me as an observer. Come on. It'll be fun being in the thick of the action again. You've been flying a desk for far too long."

Jack barely paused. "What the hell. I'll do it. I'd love to see what you're doing firsthand, and maybe together, we can convince Tes to go back to the core and leave you alone to do all the good you do out here."

Beau smiled and started on his breakfast. While the two ate, they came up with a plan to demonstrate to the inspector what life was like out here on the fringe, far from the relative safety of the core worlds.

CHAPTER THIRTY-ONE

<u>Uuru System, Outside Uuru City</u>

Remi turned off the comm unit and turned around in the cramped apartment. "That was the marshal. He'll call us back immediately. We have one day to do what we can here and find a way to off-planet to a rendezvous point."

Jock shook his head. "One day? We haven't found our way in yet, let alone how to get into the key systems for the evidence we need."

"You're assuming the information exists," Gamal countered. She sat in a plain plastic chair at the square table by the kitchenette.

"It exists," Remi asserted.

"How do you know?" Gamal asked.

"Because we need it to," Remi stated. "Besides, organizations like the Consortium are both cocky and paranoid. They don't think they'll get caught, and they don't trust each other. In my book, that adds up to keeping records on their activities."

Thendara had been leaning back in her chair on two

legs opposite Gamal. She set the front two legs down and sat up straight. "That's just speculation. I went looking for the same thing, and not only didn't I find what I was looking for, but I also got caught."

Gamal frowned. "I don't get caught. If there's something there, I'll find it, but I need access to the physical servers to do it. A remote link won't work."

"That's what Makary is working on," Remi told her.

As if she'd heard her name, the Noel-ni entered the apartment. She checked the hallway, then closed the door. "I found a way in. It'll be dirty as hell, but I think it'll work."

Jock shook his head. "How dirty are we talking about?"

Remi shrugged. "Who cares, as long as it gets us what we need?"

"I'm glad you feel that way. The access point I found for the Consortium records vault is only accessible through the city's sewer system."

Jock barked a laugh. "Aw, come on. You're kidding, right?"

Makary shook her head.

Jock's nose wrinkled. "Shit."

"Exactly. The good news is the whole monitoring system for that part of the city's underground infrastructure has been down for weeks. We can just walk in...well, crawl through parts of it. It should be easy to get in and back out."

Remi saw everyone frowning and realized he needed to put a positive spin on this. "Hey, this is the break we needed. What's the target once we get into the sewers?"

Makary took a seat at the table and broke off a piece of bread. She spoke as she chewed. "Everything I found out says the server room beneath the downtown Consortium tower is located in the lowest sub-basement." Makary showed her teeth. "If we're careful, they'll never know we were there. We'll cut through the room's outer wall and access the backs of the server racks. We'll be gone before they can blink."

Gamal nodded. "That'll work. If you can get me in there with that kind of access, I'll find out what size underwear Factor Zarek wears."

"Great." Remi nodded at the Noel-ni. "Good work, Makary. Now, I have another task for you."

"What?"

"You need to arrange transport off Uuru for all of us. We'll need a shuttle to orbit and a freighter willing to take on five passengers with no questions."

"Where are you bound? That might matter."

"We'll tell them after we leave orbit." Remi smiled. "Don't worry. We'll make it worth their while. Tell them we will pay them in cases of Marshal's Reserve."

"I'll get on it after I drop you off at the sewer drains on this side of the city. I can do it while I wait for you to get back from your little excursion."

Thendara grimaced. "Oh, joy. I can't wait. Maybe I will stay in the van with you."

"No way," Jock stated. "You have to document the whole thing. We want to demonstrate where and how we got the information. We don't want the Consortium or their paid-for politicians here on Uuru to say it was all faked."

"I was afraid you were going to say that. Jeez, I'll be glad when I can go back to covering simple corporate espionage in the core. It was a mistake to come out here."

Jock grinned. "Aw, how can you say that? Then you never would have met all of us."

It took several hours to gather everything they needed and load it into the new van they'd acquired. Makary drove them to the edge of the city and pulled up next to a drainage canal. It was mostly dry, but it was broad enough to carry a significant flow when the area's rainy season came around.

"There's stairs over there by the hole in the fence that leads down to the outflow area." Makary pointed at the edge of the canal. "You'll have to carry everything with you or drag it on that grav sled I got you. There was only one available that would fit through the access tunnels, and it won't hold everything."

"We'll make do," Remi assured her. "Thanks, Makary. Get our transportation off-planet arranged and be here when we come out. We'll do the rest. If everything goes as planned, we should be able to upset the current government with the information we uncover. That will force their parliament to hold a new election and install a new prime minister."

"I hope so. Things are pretty dark for us in the resistance. I'm glad you came when you did."

Remi hopped out of the back with Jock and set up the grav sled at the back of the van. It was only a meter wide and a meter and a half long, but they loaded as much gear as they could and strapped everything down. Its repellers whined, but it supported the load.

The rest of the gear went in everyone's backpacks, and they were soon on the move. It took a little creativity to get the sled down the steps without upsetting it. They worked it out and finally reached the canal's concrete floor.

The broken metal grate over the sewer outlet was where Makary had said it would be. It was easy to pull it aside and slip everyone through to the other side. They didn't have to crawl, but it was tight as they waded in a crouch through the knee-deep water inside. The headlamps mounted on the straps around their foreheads lit the tunnel. Remi and Jock led the way and Thendara and Gamal followed, managing the grav sled hovering behind them. Their pilot Shin had stayed back with Makary to provide security while their host worked on getting them transit off the planet.

It took them almost two hours to get through the warren of tunnels to the location marked on Remi's datapad. He pointed at the roof. "This says we're directly beneath the Skaine Consortium's tower. How do we locate the server room from here?"

Gamal sloshed over to the grav sled and rummaged through the gear strapped on it. She came up with a handheld device with a pistol grip and a small screen. "This detects electromagnetic shielding through meters of concrete. When we find the shielded area, that's the server room."

She aimed the device at the ceiling and moved up and down the tunnel, watching the screen. She kept coming back to a location ten meters from where the rest stood.

She finally waved them over. "It's above us and slightly to the north." She pointed at a spot in the corner where the tunnel wall met the ceiling.

Remi rubbed his hands together. "Okay, let's get to

work. We're going to have to cut and clear a lot of debris, and we've only got a few hours."

Growler pulled the sled over since it carried the bulk of their tools. "Good thing Makary got everything on our list. The nano-plasma cutter should make quick work of the concrete and steel, but we'll have to be careful when we get to the shielding. That has to be bypassed so it doesn't trigger an alarm."

Remi frowned. "Gamal, can you get around that?"

"No problem."

"Then let's get started."

Thendara stood back and operated her remote camera drones to pick up the work from several angles. She annotated the recordings with her voice as they progressed.

Remi didn't pay attention. He couldn't hear her all that well, and what he did hear sounded harmless. He hoped she didn't screw them again with the coverage of this caper.

He and Jock were covered in concrete dust and rust when they reached the outer wall of the shielded room. The meter-wide circular opening was nearly three and a half meters deep and sharply angled up into the room. They had to cut hand and toe holds in the short tunnel to help them climb inside.

Remi slid his goggles up to his dusty forehead. "Okay, Gamal, you're up. We've reached the outer shielding."

"You didn't breach it, did you?"

"Nope. There's a lattice of electrical conduits around the outer walls of the room. It's definitely powered."

"Yeah," Jock added. "It hums."

Gamal hooked her arm into one strap of her backpack

and climbed into the tunnel until she disappeared from view. One of Thendara's remote camera drones followed her. Remi stepped back and took a swig from a water bottle. He swished it around and spat it into the sewer water flowing around their feet. The dust from the tunnel walls had caked the inside of his mouth. The taste was awful.

Jock chuckled. "We sure do stink, Six-shooter. I can't wait to take a shower."

"Focus on the job at hand. A shower waits for all of us. First, we have to get this done and meet up with the squadron. They're going to need all of us in the cockpit for the coming fight."

"Did I hear you right? Lobo said we're going to defend one of the Beorlok clans."

"Yup. Gears and Dancer made some friends, it seems. That's a good thing. It could help us a lot with future ops in the Cluster."

Gamal slid out of the tunnel and interrupted them. "It's done. I've outlined the area that's safe to cut with white chalk."

Remi hefted the nano cutter and grinned. "Good. We'll be inside the server room in a few minutes. Get your gear ready. I don't know how much time we'll have."

"I'm good at what I do," Gamal muttered. "They won't know I was even there."

"They will eventually," Jock countered. "We can't cover up the hole in the wall when we leave."

Remi climbed into the hole and set the cutter up on the square line marked on the wall. He slowly engaged the blade, and a low whine indicated that the cutting edge had contacted the reinforced concrete wall. He took his time and cut around until only a few centimeters remained connected.

He passed the cutter to Jock. "Hand me a crowbar. I should be able to break this last chunk free with that. Be ready to roll this block down into the sewer."

Remi wedged the steel bar into the gap opposite the connected part and pulled with all his might. With a mighty crack, the square block fell away and slid down the tunnel into the sewer.

"Watch out below," Jock called to Thendara and Gamal.

The splash was followed by a string of curses from Thendara and Gamal. Remi smiled and pulled himself into the Consortium's server room. They were behind the server racks, just as they'd planned, and it was up to Gamal to do her thing.

He hoped there was something to find. If not, they would have to leave without completing the mission. That thought left a sour taste in his already foul mouth.

CHAPTER THIRTY-TWO

<u>Uuru System, Consortium Server Room</u>

Remi caught himself pacing again and stopped. There wasn't much room, and he didn't need to show his impatience with Gamal's progress in cracking into the Consortium's files. The room was set up like a vault, with banks of servers lining all four walls like rows of safe deposit boxes. The door in the wall had a wheel on the inside to unlock it, and there were indications on the interior screen that it had a timed locking system. Based on the readout on the small panel mounted on the vault's door, the regular access time was just under an hour.

Jock leaned over to Remi's ear. "It's been three hours. How much longer will this take?"

"I don't know," Remi whispered back. "And I don't want to ask."

"I can hear you, you know," Gamal grumbled. She didn't look up from her datapad as she spoke, and her hands never stopped moving on the holographic keyboard. "They've got tighter security than I've ever seen on this stuff. I've located their most sensitive records, but it's hard to get in."

Remi checked his watch and compared it to the readout on the vault's door. "We don't have much more time, Gamal. We have to bug out in forty-five minutes."

"Then leave me alone. I can do this."

Remi looked at Jock, who shrugged and leaned against the wall beside the door. Nearby, Thendara murmured into the mic pickup clipped to her collar as the hovering cameras continued to document their work. He hoped he was right to trust her not to screw them over again.

It took forty-three more minutes to break through the encryption and access the files. Gamal called Remi over as she booted up video file after file with recordings of politician payoffs and legislative agreements. There was even evidence of them blackmailing the chief of planetary security. It was all there, and they had it.

"Thendara, you getting this?"

"Yes, but I'll need copies of the actual files for independent verification by my editorial staff."

"You'll get it," Gamal told her. "I've downloaded everything."

Behind them, the door clicked and whirred as the wheel spun as someone opened the lock from outside.

Jock exclaimed, "Fuck! They found us, and they're early." He drew his pistol and backed away.

"Quick," Remi ordered. "Everyone down the hole."

Thendara jumped in first and slid down the steep slope to splash into the muck below. Her floating cameras automatically followed her. Gamal went next, with her datapad and the spare drives hugged to her chest.

The door was pushed ajar, and the helmeted head of a guard peeked around it.

Remi snapped off a shot, drilling the hapless guard through the forehead. "Growler, go! I've got this."

Jock only hesitated for a second. There wasn't room for both to go at the same time. He snapped a pair of shots through the narrow opening and jumped into the hole.

Remi backed up as the door swung wide.

A quartet of black-uniformed guards in tactical gear pointed their weapons at him.

He fired a steady stream of shots from the hip and jumped back, hoping he'd hit the opening and slide through. He dropped out of sight as dozens of blaster rounds blew apart the server racks behind which he'd been standing a second before.

Remi slid and flailed his arms as he landed on his back in the flowing sewer water. He coughed up a mouthful of the foul brew. "Let's. Get. Outta. Here," he said between gasps.

Jock hauled him to his feet. "The women are gone. Come on." He tugged Remi's elbow, and they ran past the grav sled. They didn't need the gear anymore.

A pair of splashes followed by disgusted grunts told them the guards were on their tail. Thendara and Gamal ran ahead of them about fifty meters down the gently curving tunnel. Remi wanted to catch up so they didn't get separated down here. They needed what both of them carried to clear the marshals and expose the corruption in Uuru's planetary government.

Blaster rounds blew divots out of the concrete wall

beside Remi's head, and he fired at the pursuers. There were at least five racing down the tunnel after them.

"We need to lose these jerks," Remi growled.

"Way ahead of you." Jock pulled a palm-sized disk from his belt and slapped it on the wall as they ran past. A few paces down, he placed another one. Both disks stuck to the walls, and their grayish-black color helped them blend in.

"When I say 'duck,' dive for cover."

Remi didn't have time to ask his partner where to dive.

"Dive!"

"I thought it was 'duck?'"

Jock held up a hand clutching a small tube with a red button on top.

Remi didn't need a second warning. He dove to the tunnel floor, submerging in the muck again.

Jock landed beside him and plunged his thumb down on the button.

A pair of explosions rocked the tunnel behind them.

Remi stood and coughed to clear his throat, then stumbled to the side. His ears rang.

Jock pulled on his shoulder. His friend's mouth moved, but he couldn't hear his words.

Jock tried again, then shook his head. He pointed down the tunnel away from the explosion, then ran after the women. Remi forced his unsteady legs to move and barreled after his best friend.

Thendara and Gamal were waiting for them at the first intersection. Remi stopped. Thendara said something, and when he shrugged and pointed at his ear, she pointed at his ears, too.

He reached up with two fingers and felt the sticky

wetness from his blown eardrums. He looked down with his headlamp to light his hand. The blood smearing his fingers confirmed his suspicions. He was headed for a round in the Pod-doc unless it wasn't as bad as it seemed.

"Keep going." Remi pointed to the right, the direction that would take them back to the outflow. They still had a ways to go before they were out. He hoped Makary and Shin had their escape route planned. He had a feeling the Consortium goons weren't going to let a collapsed sewer tunnel stop their pursuit.

Jock tugged his elbow and gave him a gentle shove to lead the way. Thendara and Gamal were next, with Jock bringing up the rear. Remi had his datapad out and followed the route back to the exit. Amazingly, his hearing was returning. He heard distant echoes of voices as he exited.

Makary and Shin stood on top of the canal's concrete wall and waved for them to hurry. Remi could barely make out their words as he ran for the metal stairs.

"All hell's breaking loose up here. Hurry." Makary waved for them to speed up.

Remi climbed into the van. He shouted so he could hear his voice when he spoke. "What's up?"

Shin said, "There are news reports of a terrorist attack in the center of the city. Police units are scrambling to find those responsible." His voice sounded like it came from inside a metal drum, but Remi could hear it.

"What about a way off the planet? If the heat's on that fast, we need to be somewhere else."

Makary answered. "I've found a freighter that'll take

you, but you have to find your own way up to his ship. He's leaving in five hours whether you're there or not."

"Looks like we're stealing a shuttle then. Where's the nearest private airfield?"

Makary paused, then pointed west. "There's a small landing field adjacent to an industrial park about three kilometers that way."

"Let's go, then. Drive slowly. We don't want to draw attention to ourselves."

Makary nodded and hopped into the driver's seat. She pulled away from the canal and drove west. Remi had hoped they'd get in and out of the vault without drawing attention to themselves, but that had been wishful thinking. Now he had to deal with the repercussions.

He'd bribe a shuttle pilot to ferry them up or, if needed, steal one and fly it. Either way, they would get off Uuru with their evidence and the news story to back it up. He couldn't wait to comm Marshal Ward about their success.

CHAPTER THIRTY-THREE

<u>Edge of the Dervas Cluster, Kitredge System</u>

Beau checked the plot for the fiftieth time in the last hour. There was nothing there except the five barren rocks circling the tiny star in the heart of this uninhabited system. He was waiting for Charli and Lindy to arrive, as well as Remi and Jock. He needed all of them for the fight to come. Charli had sent him word about the number of ships they were about to face. The Cloud-Bringers had two ships defending their homeworld, but even with the marshals' help, it would be a close fight.

Nort and *Tortu* had arrived yesterday and floated next to *Warren's Chance*, which was beside *Dregs*. The three big ships were ready to fight. He'd also picked up fighter support from the Barrett System and other planets they'd helped along the way.

All told, they'd have about twenty total fighters to deploy in two flights. It was nice to have votes of confidence from other systems about what they were doing out here. The core might not like the marshals' tactics, but the frontier folks knew how things really worked on the fringes of the Federation.

"Incoming ship, Lobo," Grady called from the sensor console. He'd parked himself there so he would be the first to see Lindy back safe, even if it was to go into battle. He'd been pining for the girl for weeks.

"Who is it, Beaver?"

"Transponder info coming in now. It's not large, more like a fast pinnace or a yacht than a free trader. It has a Gate drive, though."

Beau said, "My guess is that's the *Argos*, with Gears and Dancer aboard."

As if in answer, the comm chirped. Beau depressed the stud to open a channel. "Go for Marshal Ward and *Dregs*."

"*Argos* here, sir," Charli replied over the comm. Her face popped up on the forward screen. Lindy waved from the background, and the Beaver waved back. Kit Bridger was in the frame, too, along with the Cloud-Bringer chieftain's son Choatan.

"Good to see you, Gears. You, too, Dancer. We're glad you're back safe and sound."

"Safe and sound for now, sir. Things are going to get dicey before we're truly out of trouble."

"More bad news?" Beau asked.

Kit Bridger jumped in to answer. "Choatan received a coded message from his father. The blockade of his planet is complete. The message only got out through a spy in the Wind Rider force surrounding the planet."

"How many ships are in the attacking fleet?"

"Three large attack spheres," Kit replied. "There are reports of three more inbound from the Star-Current

Clan. When they arrive, they will overwhelm the single surviving Cloud-Bringer sphere, as well as the orbital defense station."

Choatan's tail twitched rapidly. "Thou canst not let this happen, Marshal Ward. My people sorely need thy assistance."

Six attack spheres with the accompanying fighters would be tough nuts to crack with only the ships they had. Even with the help he'd brought along, only *Tortu* and *Dregs* could slug it out in a stand-up fight. *Warren's Chance* was a converted freighter with offensive and defensive systems added. It would act as their backup carrier for the additional fighter support they'd brought along.

"Choatan, what happened to thy people's fleet? There must be more than one attack sphere."

The warrior's tail drooped over his shoulder. "They were picked off piecemeal in a series of sneak attacks on our bases and business ventures. My attack sphere, *Privileged Son*, barely got away when I was taken prisoner on one of our remote settlements. I have called for its assistance and await a reply. It was destroyed or taken, for all I know."

"The addition of even one large ship would help even the odds, Choatan. Thy ship would be welcome." Beau had reservations about letting the Beorloks into their comm network, but if that attack sphere arrived, they'd make it work.

"I sent them a coded message with thy rendezvous coordinates. If they can be here, they will come. I am sure of it."

Beau nodded. "Good. Then we should get thee, Ms.

Bridger, Gears, and Dancer aboard to continue planning. We will extend a docking tube to *Argos*. Come aboard, and we'll get our ducks in a row."

"What is this duck thou refers to?"

"Never mind. We'll make our plans. See thee soon."

The signal cut out. Beau noticed Grady staring at the blank screen. "She's back, Beav. You can relax. Why don't you head down and supervise the docking procedures? That way, you can be the first to see her. I'll join you shortly."

"Yes, sir!" Grady hopped up and ran off the bridge. One of the techs took his seat and continued to monitor the sensors for other ships arriving.

Beau was about to rise and meet everyone coming over from *Argos* when the sensor tech said, "Incoming ships. Two different vectors."

"Identify." Beau scanned the system plot on the forward screen. Two ships had appeared on the plot almost directly opposite each other compared to *Dreg's* position.

"One is positively identified as a Beorlok attack sphere. We registered one of their dark Gates opening. The other appears to be a junk trader outbound from Uuru—the *Belvedere*.

"That'll be Six-shooter and Growler. Give them the rendezvous coordinates." Beau called, "Tactical, give me an attack plan for that inbound sphere."

"They're hailing us, sir," the tactical rating countered.

"The *Belvedere*?"

"No, sir. It's the sphere. They've identified themselves as *Privileged Son*. They're looking for their captain?"

Beau understood. "They're with Choatan. This must be

the ship he expected to meet us here. Open the channel. I'll take it here."

He waited until the comm lit up on the arm of his chair. "Thou art speaking with Marshal Ward, commander of the carrier *Dregs*. To whom am I speaking?" He tried to keep his speech formal in the mode the Beorloks used.

"Marshal, I am Kilchet, captain of *Privileged Son*. We received word to meet thee here. It is my hope thou hast news of the missing son of our chief?"

"I am happy to tell thee that he hast just boarded our ship. If thou wilt take up position near us, I will put him in touch with thee directly." Speaking all the fancy words felt awkward, but the Beorlok on the screen seemed to take it in stride.

The captain's tail bobbed once over each shoulder. "That is excellent news. I thank thee for his rescue."

"Thank my two deputies. They performed the rescue."

"Then I shall convey our clan's thanks to them upon my arrival aboard thy vessel. Expect my shuttle shortly."

The channel closed, and Beau got up. Everything was coming together, which was good, given the urgency of what they had to do. He left the bridge and headed to the captain's ready room, which was an area in the cavernous launch bay, sectioned off by cubicle walls with a big conference table in the center. He'd hold the meeting there. There was room for the whole squadron, the Marine captain, and their visitors. It was time to plan their attack to free the Thursten system from the blockade.

It took several hours for everyone to arrive and get the greetings and other necessities out of the way. Grady used the time to catch up with Lindy about her adventures in the Dervas Cluster with Charli. The interval gave Beau a chance to meet Choatan and Kit Bridger and assess them as allies.

The bioprospector intrigued him. He wasn't sure he'd have the nerve to travel into the unknown by himself as she did. He was happy to have a squadron at his side when he did something like that.

The clan chief's heir was a different story. Their experiences with Beorloks to date had been adversarial, but he got a different impression from the young warrior. He was fierce when he had to be, but he had a lighter side. Beau was fascinated to learn that Choatan was considered an accomplished artist and scholar by his people.

When Kilchet arrived with his attack sphere, he shuttled over to *Dregs* to join the planning conference. Beau welcomed the captain and his first mate when the shuttle docked. The two soldiers appraised each other with questions about past actions and exploits. Within fifteen minutes, Beau found he liked the Beorlok and agreed with his belief in order and justice for his people.

Beau smiled as Jack walked in, with Ondine Tes silently striding behind him. He and Jack had made the situation clear to the investigator. He wanted to know what they did? Well, this was his chance to find out firsthand. His only requirement was that the inspector remain silent during the operation. He was welcome to take notes and ask questions later, but he wasn't to interfere with their work.

With the final two in attendance, Beau brought the meeting to order with a rap of his metal tumbler on the tabletop. "Let's get down to business, people. We are under some pretty tough time constraints right now."

Everyone sat down and directed their attention to him. With all eyes aimed his way, Beau went around the table, having everyone report on their recent activities.

Off to one side, Thendara watched while her camera drones hovered around the table. Inspector Tes stood beside her, taking notes on his datapad. Beau cast sideways glances at them. He didn't trust either of them, no matter what Remi said about the reporter's remorse. She and the Federation inspector represented a problem he had yet to solve in the current subset of challenges facing the squadron.

The most interesting report came from Kilchet. He relayed that they'd been shadowing a battle group from the Star-Current clan. They had been traveling in a circuitous route around the territories of other clans to join the attack on Thursten. Beau pounced on that detail.

"Canst show me on a star map of the Cluster in which this battle group is located?"

"What art thou thinking?" Kilchet asked.

"If they're close enough, we could ambush them before they get to the larger battle. That would cut the final odds significantly."

Kilchet's tail waved twice. "Hmm. Thy plan is ambitious. We would have to hurry to catch them. They are close to their destination."

Remi cleared his throat, and Beau nodded in his direction. "What do you have, Six-shooter?"

"What if the Beorlok captain here offered to defect?"

"I would never go over to the other side." Kilchet's tail quivered over his head, ready to strike.

Remi shot him a sly smile. "I know that, and you know that, but they don't. We just need them to slow down long enough to get our forces in place and ambush them. If they think they'll gain another attack sphere for their battle group, they might go for it."

Kilchet considered what Remi had said. "Thou art clever for one so young. If you were under my command, you'd be ripe for either promotion or culling for being too clever."

Beau jumped in before Remi figured out what the captain had said. "We would choose promotion. Thy plan is good, Six-shooter. Kilchet, is that possible? Canst contact them?"

"I can, but the play is not without its risks. They know my family has long been tied to the chief's line. It will be hard to convince them of my willingness to commit treachery."

Kit raised her hand. "Thou wouldst only have to tell them about your shame for losing the chief's son. Tell them that convinced thee to defect. Tell them thou canst not return to thy homeworld now."

"Good idea," Beau agreed. "If they think thou art humiliated, they might buy it. Canst thou act in a way that would convince the enemy commander?"

"Bah! The Star-Current leaders are all fools. I can play the part of a traitor if it will help us free my homeworld."

"Then that is what we'll do." Beau pulled up a holographic star chart of the Dervas Cluster and had Kilchet display the last location of the battle group he'd followed.

They selected a system between their prospective path and the Thursten system. After that, it was a matter of planning the ambush, using the four ships and two squadron wings at their disposal.

Beau leaned back and smiled as the group worked together to come up with a battle plan that left him sure they'd be successful. If they pulled this off, they'd have a much better chance to break the blockade of the Thursten System. All they had to do was make it work.

CHAPTER THIRTY-FOUR

<u>Dervas Cluster, Ambush System</u>

Beau leaned back in the captain's chair, stared at the forward screen on *Dregs'* bridge, and smiled. The words "Ambush System" ran across the top above the system plot. The name had stuck when they chose the place to spring their trap. It only had a star number designation and no name, so Jock had named it.

Beau wondered if the history books would get the reason for the name correct a hundred years from now. They'd probably make up something innocuous and forget about the battle that would happen today. People would be injured, and others would die in the coming battle, and none of that would matter to anyone but those who fought here.

The trap was simple. *Dregs* and *Warren's Chance* would hide at the outer limits on one side of the system. *Tortu* would lurk on the opposite side. All would make a short Gate hop to the center of the system when *Argos* messaged them. The smaller ship's stealth systems and size made it perfect to hide close to *Privileged Son* and pass along the coded signal when the trap was set.

They had to wait until all three of the Star-Current attack spheres entered the system. It was imperative to catch them inside the system's closest planetary orbits so they couldn't leave quickly. The Beorloks' dark Gate drives were affected by the proximity of a star's gravity well, and that would keep them from getting away quickly.

The Star-Current battle group's leader had replied to Kilchet's request to defect with contempt, but after a period of gloating, he'd agreed to meet the traitorous Cloud-Bringers in the Ambush System. That notification had come to Kilchet several days before, and they had all settled down to wait for the enemy battle group's arrival.

The sensor tech broke the silence. "Surveillance Drone Thirty-one reports dark Gate opening. No, check that. Make that three opening on the far side of the system. It's them. I have three attack spheres inbound to the central part of the system, sir."

"Notify *Argos* with the planned coded burst transmission," Beau responded. They'd set up short, simple code groups for the most likely possibilities. The small ship would pass the message to Kilchet and *Privileged Son*.

"Message sent, sir," the comms rating reported. "I've received the affirmative code."

"Good work. Record this for coded transmission to *Tortu* via Etheric tight beam." Beau keyed the ship-wide channel. "They've taken the bait. Six-shooter, Growler, Beaver, and Legs will lead the first wave after we Gate in. Gears, Junkyard, Dancer, and I will launch with the follow-up wave."

The plan would have two groups of Lone Wolf fighters leading ten of the volunteer pilots against the smaller Beorlok fighters they expected from the inbound attack spheres. The first group would engage the fighters, and the second group would prevent the enemy orbs from backing away and escaping. They couldn't let any of the ships get away since they could warn the ships blockading the Thursten system that help was on the way.

Beau stood. He smiled at Jack and Addy, who were standing nearby. "Addy, you have the conn. Let Bud do the heavy lifting. The bridge crew will take care of the rest. Jack's here in an advisory role only, but he will help, too. Right?"

"I won't leave her side, Lobo. Count on it."

Inspector Tes clacked his mandibles. "I reiterate my protest at being brought along on this insane venture."

Beau glared at the Yollin. "You came out here to learn what was going on. This is what we do, Inspector. We go where the trouble is and try to save lives. It's plain and simple work. We don't have time for bureaucratic niceties and red tape. Lives are on the line, and we save as many as we can. The people in the Thursten system are counting on us."

"That's nonsense. They don't even know you exist."

"That's beside the point. We're the marshals of Tardex. We don't do things for the accolades. We do them because they're the right things to do. Now, go sit in the corner and watch us work."

Beau returned his attention to Addy. She laid a hand on his arm and sat in the captain's chair.

"I've got this. You go out there and fly your little fighter."

"'Little fighter?'" Beau laughed. "We need to talk about how to pump up a guy before battle."

"I thought that was what I did last night." A sly grin turned up the corners of her mouth. "Just come back in one piece."

"Always." Beau left Jack at her side and headed for the launch bay in the rear of the carrier. *Dregs* had plenty of space in her cavernous main bay, but as Beau entered, it felt cramped. The usual Lone Wolf fighters were sharing space with the small attack craft on loan to them for this campaign. The other ten loaners were launching from the *Chance*.

Charli stood near the entrance, talking to one of the ground crew chiefs tasked with keeping the ships ready to fly. Beau angled her way.

"Gears, how's it looking?"

"Good. We were able to equip the fighters who joined us with upgraded missiles and targeting suites. That should counter most of the ability of the orbs to shake off our birds."

"I hope so. We could use an easy win. Maybe they'll see what they're up against and surrender."

Charli shook her head. "Not in their DNA, Lobo. I've gotten to know them a bit, and they're driven by honor. It's everything to them. Surrendering after they're attacked is counter to their beliefs."

"I hate just killing them. I was hoping we could strand them on a habitable planet with rations until this fight is over. Choatan's father could decide what to do with them afterwards."

"I could be wrong." She shrugged. "It's happened once or twice."

Beau laughed along with her. They walked over to their fighters on the racks, which were ready to launch when it was their turn. Charli peeled off, and Beau went over to Lindy.

Dancer crouched next to her ship, looking at the undercarriage. She pored over the pre-flight checklist on her datapad.

"Problems?"

"I don't think so. There's residual carbon scoring on the landing gear that I'd hoped would be looked at before I went into combat. It's not essential until I land again, though. Chief D'Arnold assures me it's up to specs."

"We have to trust our ground team, Dancer. It's the way of fighter pilots before a fight. They have our backs, and we count on that. If the chief says it's fine, I'm sure he's run it by Gears or Elspeth."

"You're right. I'll move on to the rest of the list and make a note to replace the forward landing gear the next time we're home."

Beau nodded and slipped his datapad from his pocket. He had his own preflight to do. He ran through the items in record time. His ship was in top condition. Of course, he didn't see the action that others did nowadays. He planned on making up for that deficit over the next week.

Addy's voice came from the overhead speaker. "The attack spheres have entered the inner system. Prepare for Gate drive activation and fighter launch."

Beau raised his voice so everyone in the launch bay could hear him. "This is our opportunity to make the fight to come after this one go our way. No one escapes this trap. Let them surrender if they want to, but the ships must be disabled. Got it?"

A chorus of "Ayes" came from the assembled pilots of a half-dozen planets the marshals had helped while they'd been out on the frontier.

Beau reached for the ladder to climb into his cockpit. There was no hurry. His group would go out second, and they had to rendezvous with the ten fighters launching from *Warren's Chance* in the second wave. That was all the converted freighter's launch bay had room for.

Charli had the first part of this fight. She and Katy were in their ships. The pair was back together after Charli's forced hiatus in the Dervas Cluster. Beau caught Grady waving at Lindy from his cockpit, and her brief smile and return wave before he lowered his canopy warmed Beau's heart. Beaver and Legs would launch after the Gears and Junkyard. Their ten support fighters would follow.

The plan was complex enough that they had drilled together in the simulators on the way to the selected system. The new additions were as ready as they could be. They didn't have the experience the Lone Wolf pilots did, but most had been trained by one of the key pairs of marshals. They all wanted to prove they were worth being invited along for this fight.

The carrier lurched. The Gate drive had opened, and they'd just slipped over the event horizon to the center of the system. It was time to kick ass.

Beau keyed the private comm channel to the Lone Wolf

pilots. "Go get 'em, team. And make sure everyone comes back in one piece."

"We're going to overwhelm them with inbound missiles, boss," Charli replied. "They won't be able to target all of them plus fight off the larger weapons from *Dregs*, *Tortu*, *Chance*, and *Privileged Son*."

"Let's hope our calculations are correct. Launch now."

Charli whooped in joy as her fighter shot through *Dregs'* shielded opening. Katy followed her, along with five of the ten newcomers. Then came Grady, Legs, and the final five volunteers.

Beau watched the main plot on his forward screen as the rack mount moved his ship into the launch position for the second half of this fight. He hoped everything held together so he and his team would have something to do.

Jock echoed Beau's thoughts on the comm. "I sure wish that was us going out first. I could use some action in my cockpit. All this planetary intrigue is too much for a simple country pilot like me."

Beau laughed, but his chuckle had an edge. His eyes shifted to Thendara, who was recording the operation with her remote cameras and feeds from the tactical net about the fight outside. Beau hoped Remi and Jock weren't wrong about her. She could really screw them again if she wanted to.

CHAPTER THIRTY-FIVE

<u>Dervas Cluster, Ambush System</u>

Charli adjusted the dial to angle her shields forward. Then she banked to wait for Katy and the five newbies to join her. She checked the plot as everyone assembled and nodded in approval. At least they knew how to form their wedge now.

"Good work, Flight One," she told them. "Bailey, tighten up there on the edge. You want your shields to cover your wingmate and for his to cover you, too. Stay close for safety, people."

"Roger, Gears," the new pilot from Barrett replied. She was from the second group to go through their new flight academy there. The leadership said she was one of their best.

The last fighter in the line shifted a little, and the formation tightened into a proper flying wedge with Charli at the lead. She entered a flight plan on her system plot and sent it to her wing. As expected, they followed her when she rolled right and flew toward the trio of attack spheres.

Those Beorlok bastards were probably shitting themselves. They'd stepped in it but good, having come deep into the central system before the trap was sprung.

Privileged Son opened fire on the nearest. *Tortu* engaged the second orb, and *Dregs* used their massive spinal laser to blast a divot out of their assigned attack sphere.

"Hey," Bailey called. "I hope they leave some for us."

"Cut the chatter, kids," Charli snapped. "We're here to tangle with their fighters, not keep score."

Katy interrupted. "Speaking of which. Gears, I have eighteen bogeys, six from each of the attack spheres. They must've emptied their hangars. They usually only have three fighters in a launch group. Looks like they loaded up to take the Thursten system."

"We'll deal with it. We might have to ask Lobo and his group to come out and play early." Charli checked the tactical plot. "Beaver, bring your wedge around from the left. Let's see if we can divide and conquer."

"Roger, Gears." He and Keeril led the other wedge formation into a loop to the left. If the enemy fighters stayed on their current path, they'd expose their flanks to the second inbound Lone Wolf fighter wing.

The Beorlok fighters immediately reacted to the divided threat. Nine split off toward Grady's fighter wing. The remaining nine stayed the course toward the first fighter wing.

"Okay, we planned for this," Charli continued. "We stay in a tight formation for the first pass. They'll have to break away in a head-on fight, given their lesser shielding. We can take more punishment in that kind of engagement. Trust the tendelium."

Bailey grumbled, "I still don't see how those thin sheets will do that much to protect us."

"Trust Gears," Katy advised. "Stay in formation and follow the plan. Also, you talk too much. We're calling you Chatter from now on."

"Woo!" Bailey cheered. "I'm official now. Chatter in formation and shutting up."

Charli smiled. Getting a pilot's handle was a big deal, and they'd trained these new pilots in other systems to trust the program and earn their pilot names in combat as the Lone Wolf pilots did.

The approaching Beorlok fighters closed quickly. Charli was watching the wing's missiles on her ship's tactical plot. They'd launch at the last possible instant, but they weren't targeting the fighters. They would surprise the incoming fighters by targeting the propulsion systems on the three spheres. Then they'd trust their gunnery skills to finish off the quick little Beorlok fighters. Maybe they'd surrender after their mother ships got hammered.

"Ready for missile launch," Grady called on the private comm channel. "Firing on your mark, Gears."

"Okay." She watched the closing plot. Several of the inbound fighters opened up early with their blaster cannons. She ignored the random rounds streaking past her and stared at the targeting plot. As soon as it turned green, she shouted, "*Mark! Go, go, go.*"

She mashed the button, and her seven fighters fired their missiles in unison. A second later, she spotted missile separation from Grady's second wing, too. Dozens of missiles streaked away from the two fighter groups and zoomed past the Beorlok fighters, who scattered in the face of what they thought was an attack on them.

Charli stopped watching the missiles on the plot. "Break into your fighter groups. Chatter, you're with Junkyard and me. You other four have your wingmate assignments. Watch each other's backs."

She juked right and dove, following the lead trio of Beorlok fighters. It wouldn't take long for them to realize that they weren't in danger when the missiles streaked past toward their actual targets.

Charli opened up with her rail cannons. Katy and Bailey followed suit as the fleeing fighters turned green in their HUDs. Charli's rounds blew the leading fighter apart before it even knew it was under attack. One of the others wildly spun away as its propulsion system failed on one side and sent it into a death spiral. That was Bailey's target.

"Good shooting, Chatter."

The one Katy had targeted somehow evaded her incoming fire. It twisted on its central axis in a move a Lone Wolf fighter could not manage and flew away at a tangent. It was clear that they were trying to leave the fight.

"Let them be." Charli checked the plot. "Let's go help our friends."

The other two pairs in Wing One were in a wild melee with the other Beorlok ships. They'd splashed two of the remaining six fighter orbs, but the other four were giving them trouble.

"Hansen," Charli commed the lead of one of the pairs.

"Take on the group I'm tagging as Beta with your four fighters. We'll take the Alpha group. Let's finish this."

The battle lasted only a little longer. Charli's wing easily finished off the final four Beorlok fighters since they outnumbered them. Grady's second wing only took a little longer. Out of commission, one of the loaner fighters drifted nearby, though the pilot appeared to be okay. *Dregs* would send a rescue shuttle to pick them up and tow their ship in.

Charli looked up from her display to see one of the large attack spheres blow up in a spectacular fireball. *Dregs'* spinal laser must have pierced it and ruptured its reactor's containment.

The other two Beorlok spheres turned to run for the edge of the system. They had to get far enough from the central star to Gate out.

Marshal Ward spoke over the comm. "I just launched. Under no circumstances are they to get away. Disable their engines however you can. I'll be there shortly with Wings Three and Four."

"On it, Lobo." Charli lit up the closest sphere. It was limping along at half-power on its run for safety. "Looks like our missile attack slowed them down. We'll leave you the trailing orb."

She switched to the squadron channel. "Wings One and Two. We're going after the faster one. Target their main drive. We do not want them to Gate out of here. They *cannot* get away to warn their clans about our trap."

She looked at the display and came up with a plan of attack. "We'll line up like a conveyor belt aimed at their drives. I'll go first. Form up behind me in the order I'm sending you. Let's get them to stop or surrender."

Charli lined up and waited for her targeting reticle to light up with positive range lock. When it went green, she let fly with all four of her rail cannons, and the hypervelocity slugs tore through the rear shields. She ignored the outbound fire, which was less than she'd expected. She realized that was because she was directly behind the fleeing sphere.

She sent the attack course and opened a channel to her wings. "They can't depress their upper and lower turrets enough to cover our approach vector. Stay on the track I took going in, then go evasive on your way out."

"It's almost too easy, Gears," Grady replied.

"We haven't stopped them yet. Just keep pouring on the fire."

The fourteen fighters in the two wings flew their initial attack runs, and the sphere was moving much slower when they finished.

"Keep going until we break through their shields, Gears," Katy directed.

"I think you're right, Junkyard. Line up on me, team. We'll do it again and again until they're done."

The fighters lined up behind her, and Charli began her next firing run.

CHAPTER THIRTY-SIX

<u>Dervas Cluster, Ambush System</u>

The launch rack shot him into space, and Beau's body tensed as the g-forces pressed him back in his seat. He looped around so he could watch his group follow. Lindy was next, then Remi and Jock. After they joined him, they flew toward the growing flight of fighters launching from *Warren's Chance*. The ten dots formed into two groups of five as he and the other Lone Wolf pilots arrived to take command.

"Six-shooter, you and Growler have Wing Four. Dancer and I have Wing Three. We'll concentrate on nailing the nearest of the final two attack spheres. *Dregs* finished off the first one, and Wings One and Two took down the fighters they had flying cover."

Remi remarked, "Nice of them to leave us something to shoot at. What's the plan, Lobo?"

"They're trying to break for a point where their Gate drives can cycle up. *Privileged Son* and *Tortu* are giving chase, but we can use our guns to slow them down. We need to stop them before they get to the transit point. Gears set her wings on the farther of the two, trying to take out their drives. We'll concentrate on that nearer one." Beau tagged the proper attack sphere with a glowing red ring. "We'll take out their conventional drives so they can't navigate. Maybe they'll give up."

"We'll have to break through their shields first," Dancer responded. "Those things aren't like the light fighters. They have some protection."

"Let's come in from above and below, targeting their aft thrusters," Beau offered. "We can interlace as we pass them and loop around to come in from the opposite direction on the next pass."

"Dibs on going high first," Jock bellowed and swooped up to get above the fleeing orb. Remi followed along, tailed by their escort fighters.

"Well, Dancer, I guess we go low. Wing Three, on me."

Beau dove as they approached the big sphere. The close defense turrets targeted the fighters as soon as they got close enough. Beau took the lead, angling his energy shields forward to ward off lucky shots at his juking ship. He couldn't miss the sphere at this range, but he had to zero in on the engines. When his target reticle turned green in the HUD, he opened up with his rail cannons.

His group didn't have missiles. They'd put all their allotment for this fight on Wings One and Two to overwhelm the fighters and take down the one big sphere's drive. That plan had worked well, but it left his team using cannons alone to disable their sphere, along with the incoming fire from *Tortu* and *Privileged Son*. Nort's ship slugged it out with their big guns.

Most of Beau's rounds splashed on the extended shields. Only every tenth slug broke through to hit the sphere's hull plating. Then he zoomed past, twisting to watch Remi zip by in the opposite direction. Beau passed all five of the Wing Four fighters, then came back to begin his second attack run.

It was hard and dangerous work, and by the end of the third pass, all had taken hits from the defensive systems protecting the attack sphere.

Charli commed on a private channel. "We're attacking from astern. The guns can't get the right angle to target us, and the outgoing fire is way less."

Beau immediately saw what she meant. "Thanks, Gears. Good to know. I owe you a drink when we're back aboard *Dregs*."

"I'll take you up on that."

He opened a channel to his wings. "We're changing our tactics. Everyone loop around to the attack sphere's rear. We'll attack from a different direction. Line up and come at them from the back."

"Butt shots! Awesome, Lobo," Jock cheered.

Beau shook his head and led the way. He kicked himself for not coming up with that plan himself. The incoming fire from the sphere decreased by fifty percent as he flew on that vector. He banked and flew back in the way he'd come, angling his shields to the fore for the inbound trip. He still juked around to avoid target lock from the few guns that could reach him, but the new approach got him back out without taking more hits.

Between *Tortu* hammering at them from one side, *Privileged Son* from the other, and his two wings blowing chunks out of the engine nodes, their Beorlok sphere slowed to a near-stop. After the third attack from the rear, it drifted forward on residual acceleration, drives down. The Beorlok vessel only had its attitude thrusters left to hold position, and they used them to rotate damaged areas away from *Tortu's* and *Privileged Son's* guns.

The assault ship and the friendly sphere had taken damage, too. Beau saw the red and orange flags that marked damaged or destroyed areas on the forward screen. It was nothing compared to the wrecked Beorlok sphere. Captains Nort and Kilchet had given as good as they'd gotten in this fight.

A quick check of the main tactical plot showed the other attack sphere crawling away from *Dregs'* and the other fighters' attacks.

Addy commed. "Beau, I have an incoming call from the junior captain in charge of the two remaining attack spheres."

"Put him through. Conference in Nort, Kilchet, and *Argos*, too."

"Done. Here they are."

Static crackled, and then a garbled video signal filled the forward screen. It took Beau a second to realize the distortion was from smoke wafting in and out of the pickups on the Beorlok ship. A warrior with a bloody bandage around his head watched him.

"I'm Marshal Ward, commander of the Tardex flotilla. Who art thee?"

"I am Junior Captain Ngatu. Thy weapons hath destroyed most of both remaining ships. We request thy mercy and time to collect our dead and tend to our wounded before we resume combat. Then we shall all die as warriors."

"There's no need for that, Captain," Beau replied. "Surrender, and we will assist thee with thy injured."

The warrior's eyes widened, and his tail whipped from side to side. "What is this trickery? Why wouldst thou lend aid to thine enemies?"

"Because thou art not my enemy if thou surrenders." He winced as he tried to stick to the archaic formal wording. "It is our way. Wilt thou stand down?"

Choatan's face filled the screen. "Warrior Ngatu, I am Sub-chief Choatan of the Cloud-Bringer clan. Listen to the marshal. He will spare thee and thine."

The junior captain's eyes narrowed beneath the bloody bandage. "Thou are not supposed to be alive, Chief Choatan."

"Sub-chief," Choatan corrected.

"Dost thou not know of thy father's demise? We assumed that was the reason for thy vessel surrendering to us here."

"My father is..." Choatan stopped, his words trailing away as if he couldn't bring himself to say it. His tail dipped to cover his face in the holopickup.

Beau knew grief when he saw it, and he took over. "Tell us what is going on, Captain Ngatu. Is that a trick? Is the Cloud-Bringer clan chief really dead?"

"I speak the truth. I am a warrior of honor. Our armada broke through in the Thursten System several days ago. I was not there, but I understand it was a glorious battle. The old chief fought to the death, surrounded by his clan warriors in the palace hall as befit a leader of his renown."

Beau cursed. This wasn't going well. If the Thursten system had already fallen, their rescue mission was for naught. On top of that, that would affect things in the Dervas Cluster in a bad way.

In his short time with Choatan, he'd learned that the Star-Current and Wind Rider clans were among the primary aggressors against the incoming settlers. He had hoped to defeat them and push them away from this part of the sector to provide a safety buffer for the colony ships until they could establish their defenses.

That was apparently off the table. If those clans controlled this part of the cluster, it would be harder for his team to protect inbound colony ships. They needed to regroup.

"Sub-captain Ngatu, do you agree to stand down and surrender? I swear to treat thy people well in accordance with our traditions of war. No one who comes peacefully and swears their parole of non-aggression will be harmed."

The Beorlok sub-captain leaned toward the pickups. "Thy concept of parole is intriguing. Is thy oath binding forever?"

Beau considered the question. It had gone many ways historically. It was up to him to choose. "We will ask for thy parole and that of your warriors for one standard Federation year. Before that time is up, we will deposit thee and thy people on a safe world with the means to contact thy clan for pickup after we leave."

The Beorlok warrior stared into the screen as if he were searching Beau's face for signs of deception. After a few seconds, Ngatu's tail swayed again. "I accept thy terms.

I will impress upon my people to comply with thy commands and to take the oath of parole."

Beau let out the breath he'd held slowly so no one noticed. He had no desire to slaughter all these people, and neither would he leave them in derelict ships to die in the hard vacuum of space. There had been enough killing to go around.

"Very well. I will put thee in contact with one of my deputies to take thy parole and see to the disposition of thy people, especially the wounded."

Beau cut the channel to the sub-captain, keeping the others on the call. "Nort, keep an eye on them in case they try anything shifty. I'll leave it to you to handle the parole, along with the crew of *Warren's Chance*."

"I can do that? Do you have the facilities to handle the injured?"

"I do. Doc Maundy came, along with a full team of trained medics and nurses. They can supplement the Beorloks' medical teams from the two spheres with help from the medics on *Privileged Son*."

Nort tagged a series of orange beacons on the plot. "Who will pick up the pilots of the destroyed fighters that are still alive? We can't leave them out there."

"No, of course not. I'll have the shuttle crews from *Dregs* handle the pickup. We have a few of our own to retrieve, too. We can have Marines on hand to take custody of the prisoners until they get word from Ngatu on the parole oath."

"That works," Nort agreed. "I'll take care of it."

"Good. Now we need to bring the fighters back in to reload in case more trouble comes along. Team leader meeting aboard *Dregs* in ten hours after mop-up ops are finished. That should give us all a chance to get the bulk of the work done here. Choatan, I know thou art grieving, but it would be helpful if thou wert there to help us understand our next moves."

"Of course. I am at thy beck and call. It seems I am clanless now."

Beau let that drop. They'd figure it out. For now, there was a lot of work to get done.

CHAPTER THIRTY-SEVEN

<u>Dervas Cluster, Ambush System, aboard *Dregs*</u>

Remi climbed out from his cockpit and twisted to stretch his back. Welcome cracks down his spine followed the maneuver. They'd stayed out covering the rescue ops with the shuttles and *Tortu* for the last nine hours. He wanted to get a sonic shower and freshen up before the meeting in the ship's ready room.

He took off his helmet and tucked it under one arm. He ran his free hand through his matted hair as he walked through the corridor to the crew quarters.

"Remi!"

He twisted to see who was calling him. It was Thendara. She ran over to join him, but he kept walking toward the exit. Nothing was going to keep him from his shower. The reporter could talk as he walked.

"What's up, Thendara? You finish up the latest story with word of our glorious victory here? That should top things off very well, I should think."

"That's the problem. I don't think I can post it."

That stopped him. "What do you mean? That was the deal. We saved your ass and gave you a chance to redeem yourself. In exchange, you would post a retraction story, along with a new story about the work we're really doing out here."

"That's what I'm trying to tell you. I went to upload the story after the battle ended. I included everything, including that the marshal showed mercy after the fighting ended."

"Okay. Sounds good so far."

"They wouldn't take the story. My account with CFNN is closed, and I have no access. I reached out to my editor, but she didn't answer my questions. She wouldn't even accept the call. She just sent me this." Thendara held up her datapad.

Remi took it and tapped the screen to open the message. A hologram of a poster with a picture of Thendara floated above the pad.

Wanted: Dead or Alive
100,000 CR

Thendara Doyle, formerly a reporter for Central Federation News Network, is wanted in connection with the crimes of espionage and murder on the planet of Uuru. She is considered armed and dangerous. Take precautions and handle with extreme caution.

Contact Uuru Planetary Security for details and warrants.

"Well, well. The Consortium is playing hardball."

"Is that all you have to say?" Thendara spluttered.

"There will be bounty hunters after me. With this in hand, they have clearance to shoot me first and ask questions later. What am I going to do?"

Remi sighed and rested a reassuring hand on her shoulder. "First, take a deep breath. I've been wanted, too. It's no big deal."

"No. Big. Deal." She threw her hands in the air. "That's yours and Jock's stock answer to everything. Go with the flow. It's no big deal." She grabbed the datapad and held it up. "Well, this is a *huge* fucking deal. I'm a criminal, I've lost the only job I ever wanted, and I'm stuck in the middle of nowhere with no way out of the situation."

Remi let her pace in the narrow corridor while she let everything out in an angry stream-of-consciousness rant. When it looked like she'd run out of steam, he said. "We'll fix this, Thendara. The marshal has connections. Plus, we have all that dirt we retrieved from the Consortium's servers. That's what this is about. They're trying to stop you from releasing it and making it public."

"That's just it," Thendara said. "It doesn't matter. I have no way to release the news. They got to CFNN and tainted my reporting. No one will take the story from me now, and if they did, the public won't believe it. At the very least, I'm blacklisted until these charges go away."

"Then we'll find a way. The marshal has called a meeting. You should come and be part of it. Afterwards, I'll bring it up with him. There has to be a way to deal with all this."

"When is the meeting?"

Remi checked his chrono. "In a half-hour. I need to freshen up first. Meet you in the launch bay. The meeting is at the ready room table in there. Bring all your notes on the Consortium and that wanted alert, too. The marshal will want to know."

Remi left the distraught reporter in the corridor and headed to the small stateroom he shared with Jock. He needed to get there first. Jock took too much time in the refresher and sonic shower. With everything going on, it wouldn't look good to be late for the meeting.

CHAPTER THIRTY-EIGHT

<u>Dervas Cluster, Ambush System, aboard *Dregs*</u>

"Be seated, everyone," Beau began. "We have a lot to go through."

The collection of pilots, deputies, and visitors moved around the large oval table until everyone had a seat. He wanted everyone to be in on this since the decisions they made here would affect their operations in the Dervas Cluster and at home in Tardex for an extended period.

The only people not present were Jack Sommers and Inspector Tes. Jack had taken the investigator to his quarters and would stay there with him. Ondine Tes had been visibly shaken by the carnage and damage from the space battle. Beau and Jack thought it best that he rest and think long and hard about what he had witnessed.

Once everyone had settled, Beau walked to the head of the table. He remained standing. "I hope you all are ready to get creative since we have a myriad of problems and not a lot of easy solutions."

Jock said, "Creative problem-solving is our middle name, Lobo."

"We'll see if you feel that way at the end of our meeting, Growler." Addy was sitting beside him. Beau met her eyes, and she nodded. With that vote of confidence, he continued. "It comes down to two different problems. First, forces within the Federation want to shut our operation down, based on Thendara's initial negative news story."

Grady raised a hand. "I thought Remi and Jock worked that out with her." He looked at the brewmasters, who sat with the reporter. "What were you doing on Uuru if you weren't fixing it?"

"Things got more complicated, not less." Remi shrugged. "The Consortium is more resourceful than we gave them credit for. They made our information-gathering raid into a major crime. They've put out a felony warrant for Thendara and have Growler and me listed as persons of interest."

Thendara scowled. "You forgot the 'Wanted: dead or alive' part."

"That *is* a problem," Remi admitted.

Katy nodded. "That's going to set every bounty hunter after her and probably the two of you for good measure."

Beau interrupted the discussion and addressed Remi and Jock. "The question Beaver posed is valid. We need a solution to this problem. What are you going to do?"

Remi smiled. "We found what we were looking for on the Consortium. I can't help but think we're missing a direct connection to our colonist attacks."

"You think the Consortium is selling the colonists out to the clans in the Dervas Cluster?" Charli asked.

Remi nodded. "That, or someone at Cloitas Station is involved without their knowledge. That means getting someone on at Cloitas Station to take a look at the operation there from the inside."

Katy shook her head. "You two can't go. You're wanted, and you are going to have to protect Thendara until we can clear her name."

"I know," Remi replied. "I have others in mind for this mission." He smiled at Grady and Lindy, who were seated shoulder to shoulder.

Grady's eyes widened, and he exchanged glances with Lindy. "You think we're a good choice? I don't know the first thing about working an undercover operation. Neither does Dancer."

"The rest of us are too well known," Remi countered. "As mentioned, Growler and I are definitely unavailable. The Skaines know Junkyard and Legs will stand out, no pun intended. I think the boss has plans for Gears, so that leaves the two of you." Remi winked. "Do you feel up to an undercover mission?"

Beau said, "It's up to you and Dancer, Beav. This will put you out in the deep end without local support for an extended time. Are you two game?"

Grady and Dancer gave each other sideways glances and answered in unison. "We're in."

Lindy added, "If there's evidence on that station to use against the Consortium, we'll find it."

Beau nodded. "Good. After we get back to Tardex, get with Junkyard and Jex. They'll work out a cover story for you. Now, on to part two. Choatan will lead that discussion."

He sat back down, and the Beorlok stood up from his seat next to Kit. His scorpion tail hovered over his head, quivering as if ready to strike.

"Greetings to thee and thine. I offer the thanks of my entire clan for thy assistance with my rescue and the battle here. With a heavy heart, I must ask for further help. My father is dead. However, the Star-Current sub-captain told me that my mother and younger siblings were taken to a work colony as hostages to ensure my clan's subservience following the defeat."

He looked at Kit and said something the translator didn't pick up.

Kit stood. "It is difficult for Choatan to ask for help with what comes next, a mission so dangerous that he is reluctant to ask us for assistance. I have assured him that we *will* help him, and I have pledged my aid. I ask for one other to assist me."

Beau knew what was coming next, and he joined Kit in staring at Charli.

"What?" the engineer asked. "You don't need to pussyfoot around, Lobo. If you want me to do something, just ask."

"This one will put you in more danger than Beaver and Dancer."

"Shit, what's a little danger among friends?" She smiled at Kit. "What did you have in mind?"

Kit grinned. "*Argos* and its stealth tech might be able to penetrate Star-Current territory. If we can find and land on the work colony, we can try to rescue Choatan's family, but I'll need someone to tune the shields in real-time so we can get through and back out."

"That's the easy part. We did it once, and we can do it again. I assume you and I will lead the rescue of Choatan's mother and family?"

"No," Choatan interjected. "I will lead that part of the mission. I have hand-picked a team from among my warriors. Kit and thou has only to get us there."

"I'm in either way, though I would like to kick more Star-Current butts if you have room in the rescue party."

Choatan's tail bobbed twice, and he resumed his seat.

Remi looked around. "That's the rest of the team accounted for. What about you, Lobo?"

"I'm going to handle the trickiest part of this whole thing. I have to navigate the Federation bureaucracy and clear all our names. Jack and I are taking the inspector back to the core to clean up the mess from that side."

"Better you than me," Charli sniped. "Me and mindless functionaries don't get along."

Beau smiled. "I know, Gears. Stick to your part of the mission." He clapped. "Okay, people. We have our assignments. Nort will keep protecting the colony ships outbound from Cloitas Station. Thendara will stay on the run with Six-shooter and Growler in *Warren's Chance* until we're ready to clear her name and ours. Beaver and Dancer have to work on their cover identities. Everyone, stay safe until the family is back together again."

Most assembled around the table stood and filtered out. Beau and Addy stayed, and he finally sat down. Addy stood and slid between Beau and the table to sit on his lap. "Don't worry, my dear. They'll get the job done. Those people would do anything you asked."

"That's what worries me. Did I ask them for too much

this time?" Beau stared at the now-empty table and hoped it would be full again someday.

AUTHOR NOTES: JAMIE DAVIS

FEBRUARY 16, 2024

First off, as always, thank you for reading this book. There are a lot of other books out there, and you chose to read this one. I'm glad you did and don't take that time spent lightly.

Before I get to my personal update, I want to thank the LMBPN beta readers who always help keep my Lone Wolf Squadron stories on track. Kelly, Rachel, and Malyssa, you're all awesome and read so fast. Thank you for reading through the draft so quickly and for catching my errors and story slip-ups. Without you all, this book wouldn't be nearly as good.

I'm currently in the middle of writing *Star Deputies*, book 9 in this series. I'm also preparing for a trip to Scotland with my wife. We need a break together so this is our Valentine's Day gift to each other. I'm also going to sneak in some story research for my Extreme Medical Services urban fantasy series while I'm there. I feel book 10 in that series coming on in the distance and I think it takes place in Scotland.

Other than that break to go on vacation, I'm head-down and focused on writing for the next few months, with a lot of projects scheduled to come out later this year. That includes a whole new series to release. More to come on that, so stay tuned.

I'll be back at the end of Star Deputies, book 9 in the Lone Wolf Squadron series. We'll see how my muse strikes me after that. I might have three more books in me for this series to take it to 12 total. If you want to stay up to date on what I'm writing and more updates, visit my site. Get a free book and a lot of fun in my email newsletter at Jamie-DavisBooks.com/list.

Peace and stay safe out there,
Jamie Davis

AUTHOR NOTES: MICHAEL ANDERLE

WRITTEN FEBRUARY 20, 2024

Thank you, as always, for journeying with me through the twists and turns of my latest narrative adventure. It's a privilege to be able to share these tales with you, and equally so, these author notes that allow me a moment of your time to reflect on the broader implications of our rapidly changing world.

As I delve into the closet of my office—a sanctuary lined with tomes of D&D and the remnants of fantasy role-playing games—it strikes me how these books are not just relics of a passion but catalysts for reflection on the future. I extend my gratitude for your companionship on these narrative expeditions and for the opportunity to share more than just stories, but the musings they inspire.

Navigating the Wardrobe of Tomorrow

While I'm typically an ardent cheerleader for the future's potential, today's musings come from a rather domestic origin. You see, my clothes reside in a large closet that's become a bastion for my basic outfits and more important many of my books.

This isn't due to some territorial dispute with my wife over closet space—though let's be honest, her domain is the main closet in the bedroom we share. Instead, my closet lies 'out in the back 40,' metaphorically speaking, nestled comfortably next to my office on a completely other floor.

So, when I get up in the morning, 'heading to the shower' is the same thing as saying 'I'm heading to my office.'

It works for me.

Spellcasting in the Silicon Age!

For the longest time, the notion of wielding magic has been confined to the realms of fantasy and fiction. We've dreamt of incantations and arcane rituals, of wizards and sorceresses who bend reality to their will with a flick of the wrist and a well-placed word. Today, however, we stand on the cusp of what could be the closest reality has ever come to this fantastical power—the age of artificial intelligence.

AI is the New Magic?

As we integrate AI more deeply into our lives, we're beginning to see the outlines of what it means to be a magic user in our modern age. The AI prompts we share, the data we feed into these systems, the models we interact with—they're becoming the new spells, the new grimoires of knowledge.

Consider the unique recipes we're creating: a blend of interface, language models, personal databases, and the all-important prompts. These are our modern incantations, and they're becoming increasingly valuable. The right combination can transform industries, revolutionize productivity, and give rise to personal assistants that know us better than we know ourselves.

Corporate Espionage and Personal Enchantments

As an author who's written about the future, it's both exhilarating and concerning to see predictions come to life. We've imagined worlds where corporate espionage and data theft are commonplace. Now, it seems we're entering an era where these narratives are not so far-fetched. If you have an AI that elevates your capabilities beyond your peers, that's a form of power—and power is something that has always been coveted.

It's worth pondering what might be at stake. Your personal AI, tailored to your thought patterns and behaviors, could be as desirable as any secret spell once was in the stories of old. What measures will we take to protect our digital grimoires? How will society adapt to the inequalities that access to such powerful tools might exacerbate?

These are more than idle musings; they're the very questions that will shape our future as the lines between humanity and technology blur.

In Closing

I want to thank you for reading not just my stories but also for indulging these reflections. As we navigate this brave new world together, it's important to consider the implications of our creations, to remain vigilant and thoughtful about the magic we're bringing to life.

And, of course, to continue dreaming up new worlds and possibilities—because that's what we do best.

Ad Aeternitatem,
Michael Anderle

PS: For ongoing musings, story previews, and the occasional philosophical ramble, don't forget to subscribe to the MORE STORIES with Michael newsletter HERE: https://michael.beehiiv.com/

CONNECT WITH THE AUTHORS

Connect with Jamie Davis

Author site is: https://jamiedavisbooks.com

Facebook group is: https://facebook.com/groups/funfantasyreaders

Twitter — https://twitter.com/podmedic

Instagram — https://instagram.com/podmedic

Connect with Michael Anderle

Website: http://lmbpn.com

Email List: https://michael.beehiiv.com/

https://www.facebook.com/LMBPNPublishing

https://twitter.com/MichaelAnderle

https://www.instagram.com/lmbpn_publishing/

https://www.bookbub.com/authors/michael-anderle

OTHER SERIES BY JAMIE DAVIS

The Huntress Clan Saga

(with Michael Anderle)

Read book 1 - Huntress Initiate

Extreme Medical Services Series (8 Urban Fantasy books)

Read book 1 - Extreme Medical Services

The Delivery Mage (5 Urban Fantasy books)

Book 1 - *Deliver or Die*

The Broken Throne Series (5 Urban Fantasy books)

Read book 1 - *The Charm Runner*

The Accidental Traveler LitRPG Trilogy

(with C.J. Davis)

Read book 1 - *The Accidental Thief*

Accidental Champion LitRPG Trilogy 2

(with C.J. Davis)

Read book 1 - *Accidental Duelist*

Sapiens Run (3 Dystopian Sci-fi books)

Book 1 - *Cyber's Change*

Eldara Sister Series (2 Historical Fantasy books)

Read book 1 - *The Nightingale's Angel*

BOOKS BY MICHAEL ANDERLE

Sign up for the LMBPN email list to be notified of new releases and special deals!

https://lmbpn.com/email/

For a complete list of books by Michael Anderle, please visit:

www.lmbpn.com/ma-books/

www.ingramcontent.com/pod-product-compliance
Lightning Source LLC
Chambersburg PA
CBHW032001150726
47990CB00005B/1803